Praise for *Hope Between the Pages*

"Enchanting from the first page, readers will be swept along on a journey that proves true love isn't just a fairy tale to be found in books. Romance and charm are around every corner as two people find that differences mean nothing when they share the same heart."

–J'nell Ciesielski, author of
The Socialite and *Beauty Among Ruins*

"A hauntingly beautiful dual-time story laced with the elegance of the Vanderbilts and the lure of a cozy bookstore. Pepper Basham entrances readers with a love story that will linger long after they tuck the book gently back onto their shelf. This is a story of love, of challenge, and most of all, legacy."

–Jaime Jo Wright, author of Christy Award–winning
The House on Foster Hill, and Christy Award–
nominated *Echoes Among the Stones*

"An amiable escape into the beloved world of books. Splitting time between the present and the past, Basham creates vivid historical landscapes to transport the reader to the age of the Great War and to the lavish world of the famed Vanderbilts' mansion. Paired with modern-day jaunts from a storied bookshop to the famed Asheville estate and the charm of the English countryside, vintage-loving heroine Clara's uncovering of her own hidden past will leave readers wishing they've walked in the characters' footsteps themselves. *Hope Between the Pages* is a love letter to libraries and literature. . .to books and their quaint little shops. . .and to the timeless stories they tell—a fairy tale of a journey that will invite readers to fall in love with their favorite stories all over again!"

–Kristy Cambron, Christy Award–winning author
of *The Paris Dressmaker* and *The Butterfly and the Violin*

T0027286

HOPE

Between the

PAGES

PEPPER BASHAM

BARBOUR
PUBLISHING

Hope Between the Pages

©2021 by Pepper Basham

Print ISBN 978-1-64352-826-7

eBook Editions:
Adobe Digital Edition (.epub) 978-1-64352-828-1
Kindle and MobiPocket Edition (.prc) 978-1-64352-827-4

All scripture quotations are taken from the King James Version of the Bible.

This book is a work of fiction. Names, characters, places, and incidents are either products of the author's imagination or used fictitiously. Any similarity to actual people, organizations, and/or events is purely coincidental.

See the series lineup and get bonus content at DoorsToThePastSeries.com

Cover Photograph: Mark Owen/Trevillion Images

Published by Barbour Publishing, Inc., 1810 Barbour Drive, Uhrichsville, Ohio 44683, www.barbourbooks.com

Our mission is to inspire the world with the life-changing message of the Bible.

 Member of the
Evangelical Christian
Publishers Association

Printed in the United States of America.

Chapter 1

A *ny story that begins with a library is bound to be an excellent tale.*
I smiled as I weaved my way down the narrow corridors of
Biltmore's servants' halls, careful to keep myself hidden from the newly
arrived guests. My mother's quote ushered my feet into a faster pace.
There were many pleasures in working in the illustrious estate house,
but none rivaled seeing the expressions of guests as they stepped over
the threshold into Biltmore's library for the first time.

Into *my* territory.

The main second-floor sitting room stood vacant as I peered
around the doorway from the servants' corridor. Early morning still-
ness blanketed the room like the sunlight through the tall eastern-
facing windows of the grand stairwell, giving the dim passageway a
sleepy golden hue. Nothing stirred. Not one movement.

Gripping my skirt, I dashed down the hallway and around the
corner, finally disappearing into the darkness of the secret staircase.

I could have used myriad other entrances to the library, of course,
but this one was my favorite. More intimate and special. Every morning I would find my way to the secret staircase behind the massive
marble fireplace and begin taking care of the library. It was mine, so to
speak. Mine to dust and organize and present with as much pride as
each of the ten thousand book spines commanded from the two-story
shelves surrounding the room.

It was due to Mother that I obtained such a coveted position as
the "book maid." Mr. and Mrs. Vanderbilt had been kind enough to
allow me to assume her position when she grew too ill to manage it,

and I would not take the opportunity for granted. How could I? I was entrusted with a page-ridden wonderland. Few people appreciated such an appointment as I did. Books breathed to me.

I emerged from the shadowed staircase into the massive room that woke with morning light like something from a fairy story. My gaze immediately moved to a shelf to my left that held some Brothers Grimm, Andersen, and even MacDonald, though most of the fairy-tale stories were scattered throughout the rest of the house. Also under my care.

The host of characters from Pellegrini's enormous painting stared down from their clouded perch on the ceiling as if watching the movements of the room from heaven itself. Sometimes, I felt like them, wondering how the stories on the shelves might match or impact the stories of the lives stepping into the room. It was a fascinating study—a beloved pastime—and welcome entertainment for a servant who loved books and lived to be invisible.

Stories held power and everyone told one, whether the characters within the story knew it or not.

I'd only served in my position for nine months, gratefully pulled from the kitchens, so I hadn't carved out the time to read every volume; but one day, I'd know each one on these shelves. My gaze took inventory of the enormous space, viewing the rows and rows of wonderfully symmetrical adventures, romances, histories, and dozens of other genres waiting for a new reader's perusal.

Duster in hand, I started for the shelf I'd ended on the day before when footsteps from below paused my feet. There was nowhere to hide except the cornered shadow between the bookshelf and upper part of the two-story window curtain draping with heavy red cloth to the story below. I dashed for the spot and slipped down behind the balcony railing, hoping the shadows and my black dress kept my presence concealed. Of course, the wealthy were raised to ignore servants, which should only help my cause, though the Vanderbilts broke such aristocratic expectations on a regular basis. Mr. Vanderbilt had even stooped to help me retrieve a stack of books I dropped when he accidentally opened a door in my way once.

Luckily, my place in the corner gave me a perfect view of the guests' entrance into the library, and the newest arrivals did not disappoint. With due admiration, the two men grew wide-eyed and open-mouthed, displaying acceptable wonder at the grandness of the two-story library and overarching ceiling painting. They must have been father and son, or some close relation, from the familial resemblance of light hair and facial features. Their impeccable dress highlighted their class, from the starch of their white shirts to the glisten of their shiny shoes.

"Where does one possibly begin?" the younger of the two breathed, his voice echoing through the room, the glint in his eyes a fascinating reward.

"Wherever one wishes, I suppose," responded the elder.

Ah, even better. English aristocracy, I wagered. Mr. and Mrs. Vanderbilt had mentioned the arrival of some of their English friends aboard one of the few passenger liners braving the Atlantic waters during a war. If I didn't know better, I'd guess this particular party was one of Mrs. Vanderbilt's subtle attempts at matchmaking people she held in high esteem. My shoulders relaxed. I would certainly remain invisible from *them*. The English were excellent at not seeing the servants.

"Well." The elder man took a step deeper into the room. "You were interested in locating something a bit lighter in tone than Machiavelli, as I recall?"

"Anything not related to estate business or the current war in Europe would suit me fine," the younger replied. "The latter I read about in spades much too regularly, and the former—" He sent a ruthless grin towards the older man. "You've nearly worked me to the bone."

"Don't you mean bored you to tears, Son?" The older man chuckled. "The hard work commences when we return home, as a matter of fact." His voice lit with untamed merriment. "This may be an opportune moment to begin studying on the very subject. I imagine Mr. Vanderbilt should have a wealth of books on landscape architecture or accounting."

"Now, Father," came the younger's quick reply, his palm rising in ready defense. "You promised a holiday, and that includes a respite from subjects related to our upcoming employment back home. Besides, I shall have plenty to do once the final school term begins in October if I'm not whisked away to the battlefield to join Robert before then."

Their pleasant banter inspired my grin.

The elder released a sigh, meant for nothing more than show from the twitch of his lips. "Ah, well, I did promise that, didn't I? Besides, I should relish your company while I have it. Very well, what will you choose during this. . .respite?"

His son stepped forward, sending another appreciative glance around the room. "I must admit, this room makes me feel nostalgic. Maybe an adventure or childhood favorite? You know, I've never read any of the Tarzan books. Do you think Biltmore would have them?"

Before his father answered, Mr. Noble, the butler, entered the room. "Pardon me, sirs, but breakfast is ready. May I escort you to the Breakfast Room?"

The elder man turned without hesitation, but the younger paused and glanced up in my direction, almost as if he saw my hiding place. His pale eyes sparkled in the morning light and an expression I could only interpret as spellbound gave his soft smile an almost boyish look.

I covered my grin, unable to dampen the connection. . .the awareness.

I stared into the face of a kindred spirit. Another soul who understood the power of story and imagination and of worlds beyond the borders of a binding, and for some reason I couldn't explain, I felt as though I'd uncovered an impossible friendship.

I had just finished setting up the library as I thought best for the guests, when the expected murmur of voices approaching from the Long Hall broke into my humming of some classical piece Mrs. Vanderbilt had been playing on her phonograph. With a grasp for my dust brush and a quick tidying of the sofa-side table, I dashed for the spiral staircase and barely made it behind the secret stairway entrance before the small group entered.

I should have left, I suppose. Disappeared until the guests dispersed for their afternoon activities, but curiosity always overcame my nudge toward invisibility. After all, I'd been the conduit of world introductions, if one wanted to think about it poetically. When I spoke in such bookish fashion aloud, my fellow servants stared at me as if I'd spoken Swahili, so I usually kept those ideas to myself. Mother would have understood. She's the one who taught me how to speak above my station. In private, of course.

I slid my hand into my apron pocket and drew out a small mirror, raising it around the mantel's side enough to catch the light. Then, with a tilt in the right direction, the room below came into view, just as the party entered. Would the guests enjoy my hand-picked selections, now on ready display throughout the room? Would they even notice?

"I shall keep my appreciation of the landscape to my view from the loggia." A woman's bell-like voice bounced off the white-framed ceiling. "I am a fine horsewoman, as you well know, but I have no desire to engage in miles of riding when I can see the display as well from here as there."

"Oh Lorraine, you really are missing out on closer inspection." This in Mrs. Vanderbilt's familiar voice. "And there are so many natural waterfalls and waterways. George simply adored the views."

Her voice trailed into an uncharacteristic quiet at the mention of her dear husband, gone over a year now. Could it be so long? The memory came with a strange mixture of long ago and immediate all at once.

When Mr. Vanderbilt died everything at the house changed, Mother had said. The number of parties and the number of servants decreased. A light, which once glowed from the very core of the house he built, somehow faded with his absence, though Mrs. Vanderbilt and her daughter, Cornelia, endeavored to keep it alight. Remembered.

And it was, in every limestone brick of the grand estate. In every beloved book.

"A capital prospect, Edith," an Englishman responded. Perhaps the same older gentleman I had heard earlier? "I only wish I'd come early enough to tell George what I thought of his magnificent estate. But I shall tell you, for you are part of him."

"Yes, and I feel certain he would smile gently at your compliment and then turn the conversation away from himself," Mrs. Vanderbilt responded, her voice brightening. "Anyone for tea?"

"Mrs. Vanderbilt, I must say I'm a bit perplexed." This from the younger of the two Englishmen. I noticed through my reflected spying that he had picked up a book from the side table.

My heart erupted into a pitter-patter. Had I chosen well?

"What do you mean, Oliver?" his father questioned.

Oliver. Ah, they must be the Camdens. The housekeeper had spoken of their arrival. Oliver Camden. A very pleasant name to the mind.

"Only this." He raised the book for their inspection. "Before breakfast I was speaking to Father about wanting to read an adventure or childhood classic, and here I find on the table one of the very books I mentioned."

I couldn't tame my smile. The beautiful evergreen color marked the cover of *Tarzan*.

"And here, look." He returned to the table and brought another book from its place, one of my particular favorites as far as adventures were concerned. "*King Solomon's Mines*? And. . ." He laughed, a sound so warm and alive it made me think of an azalea-scented breeze in late spring. "*Dracula*?"

"I've never seen anyone become so excited over books." The lady, Lorraine, sat shaking her golden head, her expression disclosing her distaste of Mr. Oliver's passionate reaction.

I actually appreciated his response. Some of the upstairs group, excepting the Vanderbilts, kept their opinions and emotions so dulled, one would wonder if the house wasn't filled with magnificently costumed mannequins.

"Then I've not surrounded you with the right people, Lorraine." Mrs. Vanderbilt had regained her humor, a smile in her words, though the direction of my mirror did not afford me a view of her face. "A happy remedy with Oliver around, I'd say."

"If that isn't the understatement of the week," came the elder Mr. Camden's response. "I think without books the poor boy would shrivel up and die under constant estate work and gardening."

"Though, Father, I do enjoy gardening."

How could I ever fail to appreciate a mutual book lover? Even if I'd never speak to him.

"Sadie Blackwell, what on earth are you doing?" A forced whisper erupted from behind me.

My smile fell from my face and heat shot up my neck. I turned to meet the pinched face of the new housekeeper, Mrs. Potter, her beady eyes taking in my position, my undeniably red face, and my extended mirror.

"Spying? You are spying on the guests?" Her harsh tones lifted into a squeak before she released a very unBritish-like groan. "This shall not be borne. Just you wait until Mrs. Vanderbilt hears of it."

Chapter 2

I*f one possessed a wizard's hat, it seemed almost criminal not to wear it now and again.*

Clara Blackwell adjusted the tall, pointy gray hat on her head as she balanced a stack of books against her chest and weaved through the rows of bookshelves toward the back of the shop. An eager collection of children had already started gathering on the carpet by Clara's usual reading nook, many sporting their own wizardly apparel. She caught her smile with her teeth. Story time had to be one of her favorite parts of owning a bookshop. Of course, there was a long list of other wonderful elements, such as the smell of fresh-brewed coffee mixed with "book," the breath-halting excitement of unwrapping a new shipment, and the pride each morning in opening the doors of a one-hundred-year-old family dream come true. Yes, those were all wonderful. . .but story time? Well, inspiring children's imaginations to come alive through the wonder of books certainly fit within the top five best parts of Blackwell's Books & Things.

From what she knew about her dad and had heard about her great-grandmother, the story-delight ran in her blood.

"You wore your hat, Miss Clara," called six-year-old Amy Ferguson, the first to catch sight of Clara.

The rest of the children turned in her direction, and she unveiled her grin. "If we're reading about wizards and dragons, I thought I ought to come prepared too."

"You said this book has a princess in it." Five-year-old Sophia's eyes squinted with a hint of suspicion beneath her towering princess hat.

"It does."

Her cherub grin inflated.

Blake groaned, his brow wrinkling all the way up to his erratic red curls.

"And a sword-fighting knight," Clara reassured the eight-year-old. She took her seat, lowering her voice to a whisper. "And a surprise at the end."

The comment brought the little group to alert, and Clara settled in to reading *The Dragon's Secret Fire*, her favorite book her father had written.

As usual, the crowd remained spellbound until the very end, with a few giggles about the surprise, an expectation of which Clara never grew tired. After dismissing the kids to plunder the children's books and merchandise, Clara joined her mom behind the counter. That book always garnered a few purchases from the crowd.

"He would have loved it, you know." Eleanor Blackwell opened up a new shipment of books, the careworn wrinkles of her face softening into a smile. "Reading one of his books to the children every year during his birthday week."

Clara smoothed a hand over the brightly illustrated cover that boasted her father's name before placing the book on the special shelf behind the register counter, the one reserved for the full collection of her father's children's books. "My favorite of his."

Her mother paused her movements, her soft gray hair framing her face. "His favorite too."

Clara swallowed through the gathering emotion that accompanied such tender talk of her dad. Did it ever get easier? Even after almost a year? "But. . .I would rather have him back here with us than all the books in the world."

"Ah, yes." Mother said before returning to unpacking the box. "But at least we have his books. He's still with us in those."

Somehow holding the story in her hands always made him feel closer, nudging a little voice inside her to relocate whatever magic she'd once believed in as a child. Those faraway dreams, impossible ones, beyond the books and the walls of the shop.

Adventure. Travel. Mystery. True love.

She sounded like a voiceover from *The Princess Bride*.

With a sigh, she shook away the thoughts. This wasn't the time to dream about adventures, unless it was ensuring the bookshop's stability, especially since the newest chain bookstore moved in nearby. Sales reflected a slight shift Clara wasn't quite sure how to counteract, but she hoped it was only a glitch. If she could just find the time to increase the shop's online presence and put a few marketing ideas in place, maybe the slump from the competition wouldn't last long.

"And, we sold three of his books during your brilliant performance as the Wizard Larison." Her mother's gaze rose to take in the massive hat still atop Clara's head.

Clara chuckled and slid the hat off, gently smoothing some of her erratic hair back into the twist at the nape of her neck. "It's always more magical with the hat."

Sending a wink to her mother, she gathered a handful of newly delivered children's classics and started toward the colorful kids' section. Just as she rounded the counter, the front door burst open, revealing the massive presence of Uncle Julian.

Her shoulders dipped. And she'd had such a lovely morning.

Julian's silhouette matched the boxlike shape of the entry but somehow did nothing to keep the chilly December breeze from unpinning a few local flyers attached to the announcements board by the door. Clara slammed the books on the counter and made a mad dash for the dizzying flaps of paper twirling in all directions.

Without so much as a glance at the confusion, Julian Claflin stomped into the shop, adding his muddy footprint to the Young Storytellers contest flyer Clara had created to encourage her middle-school readers to try out their writing skills during winter break.

"Why on earth do you have papers on the floor?"

Clara stifled a groan and stared hard at her uncle, hoping to encourage his self-awareness, but he blinked blankly back at her. She doused her annoyance with a smile. "What a surprise. You're not usually this far south of downtown."

Mama's brows shot northward in warning, but Julian didn't seem to notice the tiny jab.

"Do I need a reason to visit my favorite sister-in-law and niece?"

"We're your *only* sister-in-law and niece."

He sniffed enough to shake his overly fuzzy mustache and cast another appraising look around the busy shop before settling his attention on Clara as she rose from collecting the final papers from the floor.

With an awkward tilt in her direction, he lowered his voice, his overly indulgent cologne nearly making Clara's eyes water. "Just because your parents had you when they were nearly fifty doesn't mean you have to. . ." He waved toward her clothes. "Why do you dress like an old woman? Is business so bad you have to wear your mama's hand-me-downs?"

Clara blinked a few times, trying to comprehend Julian's insult, and then followed his gesture to her pale blue belted swing dress, complete with white collar and matching cuffs on the full-length sleeves. *Mama's hand-me-downs? Mom hates wearing dresses.*

"It's called 'vintage,' and I just bought this dress from—"

"Don't you ever want to get married, girl?"

He made the dastardly comment in passing, continuing his forward momentum toward the counter. Clara's eyes drifted closed and she pivoted to follow him, enjoying the spin of her *vintage* skirt as she did. Of course she should expect poor manners from her uncle. He'd shown little else since Dad's death, but why go insulting perfectly stylish vintage apparel? Even if he was still bitter about her father leaving the bookshop to Clara instead of him.

"What brings you by on this blustery December day, Julian?" Clara caught the glint of steel in her mama's caramel-colored eyes. One of the many physical features they didn't share. She had her mother's smile, but her eyes were all Blackwell. A ghostly pale kind of blue.

"Looks a little slow today," he murmured as he stroked his mustache. "No surprise with the new bookstore down the street, eh?"

Clara scanned the busy room and pinched her lips together to catch an entire diatribe of defense. Yes, Clara was in her midtwenties. And yes, she could speak her mind all on her own, but the idea of bringing any more trouble into her mama's life curbed Clara's tongue better than anything else.

"To tell you the truth, Julian, we ended November just fine." Mama may have exaggerated just a teensy bit, but Duncan's opening hadn't impacted their sales as much as expected, thankfully.

"That's good, isn't it?" His dark brows rose and he nodded, taking another extended look around. "I suppose the real hit won't happen until after the holidays."

What a swell guy.

"Clara, Mr. Lawson called during your story time." Mom gestured toward her phone, her interruption perfectly planned to save Clara from further conversation with Julian, but a little too late to protect her from another onslaught of his cologne. "He said he needed to speak to you right away, if you have the time to drive to his office this morning?"

Clara turned back to her uncle. "I'm sorry, Uncle Julian, duty calls."

He grumbled some unintelligible response and rubbed at the corner of his mustache, a habit which always seemed to inspire thoughts of gangsters and '80s police shows. "Well, no matter. Have you seen my son today?"

As if summoned, Robbie Claflin came into view at the top of the stairs, the stack of books in his arms reaching almost to his chin. His countenance took a downward shift at the sight of Julian. "Father, what are you doing here?"

Since Julian and Clara's father had been half-brothers, Robbie was her half-cousin, though they'd bonded more like siblings or even best friends. Both only children. Both book enthusiasts. Both on the odd side of normal. So when Robbie showed interest in working at Blackwell's to get away from his overbearing dad, Clara's father took the young teen without hesitation. He'd worked alongside Clara ever since. "Weren't you here last week?"

"Can't a father come see if his son wants to join him for lunch?"

Robbie's brow crinkled beneath his fiery red curls and he shared a knowing look with Clara.

Julian Claflin was up to something. "Well, that's a first." Robbie attempted to shift the books as he finished his descent down the narrow stairs, his signature lopsided grin crooking as Clara rushed to assist him. "I'm free right after I shelve these fairy tales in the right place."

"I had them in the proper place upstairs, Robbie."

"Proper place, my eye." He winked, his grin spreading in elf-like mischief. "How many times do I have to tell you that the fairy tales should be downstairs in the children's section not upstairs in the adult section?"

She plucked four of the books from his arms and narrowed her gaze at him. "Only because you keep moving them."

"To the *right* place."

Their continual banter about fairy tales being for adults versus children had been ongoing for years. Robbie's presence, his constant teasing, brushed away some of the chill his father's presence brought into the charming bookshop. She hadn't realized how much she'd come to rely on him, until her father's death rocked her world. But he'd been a rock, guide, or clown as Clara learned to navigate the painful transition that included taking care of her aging mother alone. Well, not completely alone with Robbie nearby.

"Come now, Robbie, I haven't got all day," came Julian's retort as he buttoned up his coat and took a few steps back toward the doorway. "What does it matter where the books go? Though, in my opinion, fairy tales have always been for children. Not that I recall reading any of them. They didn't make any sense."

"Well then, Father, you just solved our dilemma." Robbie's brows rose to his hairline before he shot another wink to Clara. "Once I place the books *upstairs*, I'll be ready for lunch."

Clara's grin slipped wide and she placed the books back in his arms, leaning close as she lowered her voice. "I should have your father visit more often. See how well he helps us solve our disputes?"

Robbie chuckled and disappeared up the stairs.

"I hope the shop is doing well with all the new. . .er. . .businesses in the vicinity."

Clara spun around. Hadn't Uncle Julian already voiced his pessimism about Duncan's? His attention was on Mother, who donned her brightest smile. "As I said before, Blackwell's is doing just fine." She waved a graceful hand to the busy storefront. "Can't you tell?"

"Well, you know how these things go though. Smaller shops can only compete so long with discount prices." His forehead wrinkled into dozens of frowns to match the one under his mustache. "Have you considered what you could do if you sold the place? Retire? Give Clara a dream wedding, assuming she could ever find a husband."

He said the latter under his breath, but Clara made out the grumblings. *How did Robbie come from such a man!*

"Blackwell's isn't for sale, Julian. Christopher loved this place, and Clara and I promised to keep it in our family for as long as possible." Mother sighed as her gaze trailed the room, from the unique Celtic carvings framing the front room to the colorful stuffed creatures lining the rows of bookshelves. "Granny Sadie once told me that Blackwell's was built out of love and will continue to thrive from love. Love for story and community. And since there are so many wonderful books in the world, I don't see why a new chain bookstore should threaten us."

"Fairy tales, indeed. My half-brother and his grandmother didn't foresee the competition." He sniffed the air and gave his head a slow, consolatory shake. "Times are changing, my dear Eleanor, and we must change with them. Brick-and-mortar independent stores are as old as some of those dusty books on the shelves that no one ever buys but everyone admires."

"And that, my friends, is why you should shop at Blackwell's," Robbie announced as he reached the bottom of the stairs and waved toward the onlooking patrons. "Stories matter, and Blackwell's has been a part of the story of Biltmore Village for years. Keep us celebrating books by doing more than admiring the dusty shelves. Take some of those lonesome stories home with you."

Robbie's pitch loosened the tension in the room, and with one sweeping gesture, he and his father disappeared into the cool December afternoon, leaving a jingling of bells and a hesitation of disquiet before the room resumed its happy book murmurs.

"That was odd." Clara leaned forward with her elbows on the counter, watching through the large front window as Uncle Julian and Robbie disappeared down the street.

"Your uncle has been odd for ages."

"True." Clara released a sigh. "But he twirled his mustache more than usual, which made him particularly odd."

Mother chuckled and returned to her chair behind the register, a resting spot Clara made sure to keep at the ready in case her mother grew tired, which happened more often than it used to.

"I can't believe he doesn't like books," Clara said. "That feels almost unnatural." And his spiel about Duncan's and Blackwell's? The cold wind of the afternoon seemed to permeate the room again.

"He's never been the reading sort, my dear." Mother followed Clara's gaze to the door, her expression softening into a compassionate frown. "Can you imagine how dark it must be inside his mind? It's a good thing Robbie has us in his life or else the poor boy would have been cast into the pitch of numbers and nonfiction without a spark of fiction to light his way."

Clara laughed and slid her arm around her mother's thin shoulders. "Between you and Father, I had no choice but to fall in love with thousands of worlds and characters and creatures before the age of ten."

"Ah, but we were determined to prepare you." Mother patted Clara's hand against her shoulder, the glimmer resurrecting in her eyes.

"Prepare me?"

"For life." Her brow rose in slow preparation. "As Mr. Barry put it, 'To live will be an awfully big adventure.' What better way to become armed than with thousands of stories?"

"What do you mean there isn't a deed for Blackwell's?" Clara couldn't remember one story she'd read in her entire life that armed her for Mr. Lawson's declaration.

She had hired Mr. Lawson to settle Dad's affairs, since the previous lawyer Granny Sadie had kept for years had passed his prime long ago and hovered on a century birthday in some beautiful retirement home in South Carolina. And despite Mr. Lawson's sharp navy suit, and his intelligent hazel eyes looking back at her from where he sat behind his desk, his statement didn't make any sense. No deed? How was that possible?

He braided his hands in front of him and steadied his attention on Clara. "I know Mr. Everett managed Sadie's affairs for years and even took over the transfer of Blackwell's to your father after her passing, but either by oversight or a belief that ownership could be somehow grandfathered in, he never secured the transfer of the deed. In fact, I've not been able to locate one for Blackwell's at all."

"What does that mean?"

He shifted in his chair before continuing. "We need to find legally binding documentation that Blackwell's belongs to you or your mother via Sadie Blackwell. If we can't locate the actual deed, we need secondary evidence as proof."

Clara rubbed the well-worn hem of her sleeve, attempting to quell the knot twisting tighter in her stomach. "Like what?"

"The deed would be preferable, of course." His tight smile did nothing to allay Clara's heightened blood pressure. "I've searched every place I can think of and it's nowhere within my resources, but anything that would directly link Sadie to the purchase of the property could build our case, especially, God forbid, if anyone ever contests your ownership or you wish to sell the bookshop. But if you can locate historic letters, bank statements, anything that will provide a link between Sadie and ownership, we can secure a new deed."

Clara pressed back into the chair, her palms up as if waiting for an answer to fall into them. "Where do you suggest I start looking?"

"Since the bookshop went directly from Sadie to your father, I'd recommend searching anywhere you think they would have stored important documents or historical information. A lockbox? Some special room in the house or within a keepsake? Is there any place like that?"

Clara knew every part of Blackwell's, from the books on the shelves to the files in the office, and she'd never come across a deed, but there was one place she hadn't been in for at least ten years. Blackwell's cavernous attic.

When she was a teenager, she'd gone up there once with her dad, and a half-clothed mannequin in a clown wig left her with nightmares for weeks. Her entire body cringed at the memory. "I can think of one place." She hoped her smile communicated confidence because between the possibility of losing Blackwell's and of getting locked in the dark and dusty unknown of the attic, hers had dropped to an all-time low. "But it may take awhile, and there's a possibility I may never return."

"Whatever it takes, Clara." His gaze bore into hers, sobering her attempt at humor. "Because if you don't find this deed, or something equivalent, there is the real possibility that you and your mother could lose Blackwell's."

Chapter 3

For the entire afternoon, I waited for a summons to meet with Mrs. Vanderbilt, but the fateful moment never came. My smile grew as the night wagon made its jerking descent into Biltmore Village with a few other servants on their way to the tidy houses lining the far street of the quaint village. Perhaps the grand lady dismissed the accusations without another thought. After all, I'd given the guests exactly what they were searching for, hadn't I?

My smile fell as another thought nudged the more hopeful one out of the way. Mrs. Vanderbilt could have been furious, but due to her guests, she didn't have time to sack me today, so she'd wait and do it first thing in the morning. My stomach vaulted and I gripped the side of the wagon bed as the horses came to a stop on All Souls Crescent, just behind the church, where a long line of limestone houses with their copper-colored slate roofs glowed pale in the gaslight of the streetlamps.

"Sadie, you gonna sit there all day staring at nothing, or are you gonna get home?"

I shook from my thoughts and turned to see Carrie Macon standing outside the wagon, staring up at me, bemused. Her husband, Eric, a dairy worker, looked on with a matching expression.

"I'm sorry." My face scorched hot. "I was just lost in thought, I guess."

Eric helped me down from the wagon, his wry grin growing. "I think you find a way to get lost there more times than not."

"Must be a mighty fine place to be then, if she gets lost there so much," Carrie added. She linked her arm through Eric's and winked at

Sadie as they said their good nights and walked down the lane.

Most of the folks paired off, husband and wife, each outfitted with married-servant housing offered by the Vanderbilts. A unique provision because as a rule, once a servant got married, it usually meant they lost their position, but the Vanderbilts seemed to be different from a lot of rich folks.

So maybe Mrs. Vanderbilt's differences and kindness would win out no matter Mrs. Potter's accusations. I took the sidewalk down the lane, beyond the village houses, to a small white clapboard cottage nestled in the trees outside of town. Though I had a room on the fourth floor of Biltmore, once a week I took the night wagon into town to be with my aunt and younger sister. Family time made the ache of missing Mama a little easier, though her work had always kept her late, with little opportunity for memories. I clung to the ones I had.

The well-planned streets of Biltmore Village, with its uniform houses and specially designed streetlamps, welcomed me down its idyllic lanes to the edge of town, but not before I took a little detour. A moment to nurse a dream.

Just beyond the village lights, I gripped two of the spindles on the black wrought iron fence surrounding Brick House.

A week ago, I heard Mr. Long planned to sell the place—a beautiful, two-story brick building with a large box window at the front beside a small portico-covered doorway. My heart lurched into a rapid pace and my fingers squeezed around the cold fence.

If I closed my eyes, I could envision a hand-decorated sign over the blue-painted front door and brightly-colored books on display in that box window. *Blackwell's.* My very own bookshop. Though it seemed as implausible as flying above the Blue Ridges, hadn't man already shown he could do the impossible more than ten years ago by Orville and Wilbur Wright?

I glanced into the night sky, beyond the rooftops and streetlamps, and prayed that this impossible hope in my heart somehow turned into a whisper God understood.

He didn't put this love in my heart for nothing, did He?

I gave the house one last look before turning away and returning to the reality of my future. At least I could take care of the Vanderbilts' books.

As I crossed the threshold of the cottage, Lark ran forward with her usual enthusiasm, her apron from her day working at Clarkson's Bakery still dangling around her thin frame. "Guess what special treat Mr. Clarkson taught me to make today!"

I slipped my coat from my shoulders, allowing the uncertainty of Mrs. Vanderbilt's reaction and impossible dreams to roll with it. "Biscuits."

"Biscuits?" My sister's face scrunched into a dozen wrinkles. She snatched my coat from me and hung it on the hook by the door, shaking her head as she did so. "Biscuits at Clarkson's classic bakery? *Mais non*, Sister-dear." She brushed her long walnut-colored hair over her shoulder with a flourish. "Chocolate éclairs."

"Chocolate éclairs?"

"They're real good, Sadie." Aunt Elaine walked in from the kitchen, her salt-and-pepper hair pinned back in her usual bun. "Some things Lark brings home from the bakery, I ain't too keen on, but this here?" She hummed her pleasure and raised the remains of a pastry for my view. "This is mighty good."

I took the offering and stared at Lark as I took a bite. She'd only worked at Clarkson's for a month, but she'd always shown talent in the kitchen.

The pastry melted in my mouth and gave way to the creamy sweetness. I'd had the opportunity to sneak some Biltmore leftovers before—not often, but a few times—and this was as good as anything I'd tasted there. "Did you make this all by yourself?"

Lark steadied her palms on her hips, her tipped chin giving the answer before she spoke. "I sure did. Came directly home from work and tried it out."

"Your baking skills have always amazed me." I finished the rest of the pastry and then reached to place my weekly allowance in the jar on the nearby bookshelf. Ever since Aunt Elaine had taken us in during Mama's illness, Lark and I had contributed to the cost of rent and other needs. There'd never been a great deal of money, but with Lark's new job, the funds had grown enough to keep Aunt Elaine from bearing so much of the financial brunt. "And I'm exceedingly thankful for it."

We made our way to the sitting room, taking what little time we had to visit before the wagon came to fetch me at six o'clock the next morning. My thoughts kept me awake long into the night, stirring to life a longing I couldn't quite define. Even before Mother died, I'd felt some restlessness in my spirit that only settled through prayer or reading. Long ago she had—unknowingly, I think—planted a little seed in me. We had traveled to visit my father's family a two-hour wagon ride away, and in that small town, she'd taken me to a tiny bookshop.

I've never forgotten the dusty shelves lined with hundreds of stories. The secret nooks, where avid wanderers found their hiding places to delve into imaginary worlds. The stacks of books lining the floors as if some readers had left their precious tales for an emergency with a promise to return later. Some quiet dream in my heart awakened that day, but I'd held the wish close because a dream like that was a dangerous thing for a low, working-class young woman in a professional world dominated by men.

Some dreams require hard work. Others require miracles.

And this one looked a lot more like the latter than the former.

I had barely entered the servants' hall on the second floor of Biltmore when Mrs. Potter found me and with the most condescending expression known to humankind, informed me that I was expected in the Oak Sitting Room at nine o'clock sharp.

Mrs. Potter's fierceness might have hearkened a weaker constitution—or imagination—to quell beneath her arrogant fury, but I fought my laugh. Despite her pristine appearance, one of the dark hairs on her unruly mop of wiry, short locks had come loose from its pins and poked northward toward the ceiling like a bedspring. Since her frown tripled the size of her chin on a regular basis and her beady eyes squinted to near slits at this particular moment, she resembled, if I dared acknowledge it, a toad with a spring bouncing atop its head.

My mother would have been horrified at my train of thought.

I was not nearly as horrified as I ought to have been.

With well over two hours before the appointment for whatever punishment Mrs. Vanderbilt deemed appropriate for my mirror misadventure, I made my way to the library to complete my responsibilities as long as I was allowed to do them.

Dawn hues streaked through the glass doors lining the eastern side of the room, bathing the room in golden morning. The hush of a sleeping house and an undisturbed space welcomed me, offering solitude with only fictional folks and realms to keep me company. My thoughts, paired with the ethereal glow of daybreak, only encouraged my whimsy and nearly had me imagining fairies dancing on the sunbeams slanting into the room.

I took quiet steps down the spiral staircase to the main level and, after checking the emptiness of the room, slipped by the fireplace to a small table that housed several discarded books. A quick look let me know that Mr. Oliver Camden had already finished two of the choices I'd sent him: *Dracula* and *Tarzan*.

Both in less than twenty-four hours?

Oh yes, he was a kindred spirit. Unless, he didn't like them or—I gasped—skimmed these magnificent stories!

Then he was very much *not* a kindred spirit.

But I could not match indifference with the enthusiast I'd observed yesterday.

I cradled the books to my chest and carried them to their particular shelves, but as I raised *Dracula* to its place, a piece of paper wedged between the pages caught my attention. Was it a bookmark?

Elegant script from a neat hand blackened the page.

Dear Library Fairy,
*   I've always believed in fairies and feel a library is the*
perfect abode for such a fantastical creature. Thank you for
your book recommendations. I beg for more.
*   With anticipation,*
*   The Visiting Book Goblin*

Library Fairy? Book Goblin?

My snicker shocked me and I glanced around to make certain the room still hummed with the vacancy of morning. I'd never had a guest write to me before. And *Book Goblin*? I covered my smile, as if the paintings above would care, and noticed another piece of paper lodged near the very back of *Tarzan*.

Dear Elusive Library Fairy,

I am inclined to believe that Tarzan must have been part fairy as well as part ape-man. How he learned to read English without ever having heard the language, as well as so readily picked up on French, I cannot say. French was not my favorite. Clearly, there was magic at work.

I'm curious for more.

As ever,
The Book Goblin

I tucked both notes into my apron pocket and immediately set out to retrieve a few additional books in the Tarzan series while also adding *The Island of Dr. Moreau* and, just to see what he'd think of a bit more romance, *Far from the Madding Crowd.* Would he be an Austen fan? Or enjoy something as classic as *Ivanhoe?* With his reference to fairies and goblins, maybe George MacDonald should be considered.

I nursed the fleeting thought of writing him back, if only to feed the fairy idea tumbling around in his head, but I felt certain Mrs. Vanderbilt would never approve of such interaction between people above and below stairs.

With quick work, I placed the chosen books on the table with Mr. Camden's name printed on a card perched atop the stack and then finished my cleaning before making my way to Mrs. Vanderbilt's Oak Sitting Room.

Elegance pearled in every main room of Biltmore. Even the servants' quarters boasted more space than most grand houses, from what other servants said, but the personal rooms of the Vanderbilt family carried an intimate ambience. Perhaps even more so since Mr. Vanderbilt's untimely death.

As I passed a few servants on my way, their gazes held mine, but they didn't voice a word, almost as if they wondered at my fate as well. I came to a stop in front of the massive door and wiped my sweating palms on my apron.

At my knock, a quiet voice bid my entry. I opened the door wide enough to slide inside. The room stretched into a long rectangle framed by ornate oak-paneled walls on three sides and windows displaying the distant Blue Ridge Mountains along the fourth. A beautiful and intricately designed cream plaster adorned the ceiling, and two massive fireplaces provided bookends on either side of the room. Behind a large desk at the far right of the room, sat the lady of the house.

Donned in an elegant blue day dress, she didn't appear to be the ruthless employer ready to dismiss me from service. Instead, she beckoned me forward with a gesture of her long, slender fingers, her lips tilted in a subtle smile.

"Please, sit, Sadie."

With a slight hesitation, I took the proffered chair and attempted not to fidget. Mother always expected outward calm amidst internal chaos, if possible. Especially in the presence of the Vanderbilts.

"I am certain you are aware of a situation Mrs. Potter relayed to me about your..." Her lips twitched. "Spying on the guests."

"In all honesty, Mrs. Vanderbilt, I only wanted to see if my book choices met with the readers' approval." I squeezed my hands in my lap. "I had no intention of being inappropriate, but the younger Mr. Camden shared his love of reading with such enthusiasm, I simply had to see if I got it righ—"

Her raised palm stopped my rehearsed explanation.

"I haven't asked you here for a reprimand, Sadie." Her lips crooked slightly upwards. "You have your mother's love of books and her gift of discernment in readers' tastes, which is one of the reasons why you hold the position you do."

My shoulders threatened to collapse from the sudden relief. I wasn't being sacked.

"When Mrs. Potter brought your situation to my attention, she unintentionally made me aware of your strategic position in the house. For this reason, I asked you to meet with me this morning."

My face must have shown my surprise, because her smile etched wider.

"It does all sound rather mysterious, doesn't it?" She chuckled and tapped an elegant finger against her chin, studying me with those intelligent eyes of hers as if weighing my ability to complete the task. I sat up straighter, accepting the challenge, regardless of the request, if nothing else to prove her faith in me correct. There was no little pride in being considered for a special opportunity by the lady of the house.

"As you are aware, we have several young people visiting us at present."

"Yes, ma'am."

"And I am quite fond of helping others, especially in regard to future happiness."

An understatement if one considered all the ways Mrs. Vanderbilt worked to improve the lives of those around her, servants and guests alike.

"Of course, ma'am."

"And it so happens that my dear friend, Mrs. Moira Withersby, arrived and unexpectedly brought her eldest daughter, Miss Lorraine Withersby, with her when she learned that our guest list involved both the Camdens of Derbyshire and the Dashers of New York."

I nodded, even though I wasn't certain how the information correlated with Mrs. Vanderbilt needing *my* help.

"It is Mrs. Withersby's particular wish that her daughter have opportunities to engage in. . ." Mrs. Vanderbilt searched for her word, ". . .*interesting* dialogue with the two single young sons during her stay since she has been particularly thwarted in her attempts at finding a husband."

Single young sons? Finding a husband? Understanding dawned with added heat in my cheeks. *Oh dear, what was Mrs. Vanderbilt proposing?*

"Would you be so kind as to use your excellent powers of observation and your keen awareness of others' personalities to help me learn of any mutual interests among the young people?"

"To help Miss Withersby find a. . .a husband?" First impressions of Miss Withersby were not highly impressive, especially since she didn't seem to enjoy reading.

"That would be the hopeful result, if at all possible." Mrs. Vanderbilt's expression sobered, her brow wrinkling ever so slightly. "She's a darling, but perhaps not as readily engaging as some other young women. I think with a bit of encouragement she could find the right match."

My brain spun through the library's inventory, attempting to locate any books which might include guidance on engaging conversations or increasing winsome dialogue. I pulled up dozens of fictional examples, but it didn't seem that Miss Withersby's needs ran in a fictional direction. "There are a few articles on the art of conversation I noticed recently in some of your subscriptions, and I believe we have some psychology books—"

"Actually, Sadie, I hoped you might spend some time with her and help her along. She isn't much for reading."

"I don't think I understand."

Mrs. Vanderbilt sighed, as if she wasn't too comfortable with the prospect either. "I know this isn't what you would choose and it adds to your responsibilities, but apart from your mirror incident, I know you are the embodiment of discretion and would keep the situation private, for Miss Withersby's sake, if not for mine. Lorraine needs a nudge or two in the right direction, I think. Help with where to start in a conversation with men who enjoy reading."

I swallowed a lump in my throat as I nodded, my fingers pinching together in my lap. "I don't mean to contradict you, ma'am, but I. . .I'm not a. . .lady. How am I supposed to—"

"Didn't you help your cousin, one of the shyest of girls, find a husband two years ago?"

"But that—"

"And, as I recall from below-stairs rumors, you have been the matchmaker of at least two couples who have moved on from Biltmore to begin their own families?"

How had she heard of those incidences? "Those were all servants, ma'am."

"And"—she raised a finger as if to make her final point—"a well-read woman always carries wisdom to impart. It is a byproduct of reading. And you are an avid reader, are you not?"

"Yes, ma'am, but I'm not certain—"

"Shall we give it a trial? For a week or two? And if it isn't a good fit for you or Miss Withersby, I will recall my request." She leaned forward, the quiet entreaty in her voice drawing me forward also. She could command it as my employer, yet she requested. Trusting me to do something I felt fairly certain I had no expertise to complete, but I *had* read a great deal, so perhaps I could locate some help in my beloved world of fiction.

"If. . .if you think I am the right choice."

"I do." She relaxed back into her chair, her smile flared. "And I will give you a hint. She already has her sights set on one of the young men in particular, which is another reason your insight may help the poor girl."

Something quivered in my chest, as if Mrs. Vanderbilt were about to confess that she was going to get rid of the entire Austen section of the library. I braced myself for the coming revelation.

"I would like you to help Miss Withersby woo Mr. Oliver Camden."

Chapter 4

What could be better than an arrival of new classically bound books?

Clara unpacked the editions with care. A Dickens here, a Brontë there, even a few Hemingways, Eliots, and Twains. All part of a newly released collection of similarly bound books to tempt those readers, like herself, who prided themselves on a beautifully ordered and uniform personal library.

A rush of cold air seeped around the window, cooling her arm as she steadied the last book in place on the original shelves. Her father had made repairs throughout the years, but there were certain things this family heirloom-of-a-shop needed. New windows. Updated heating. Clara sighed down at the hardwood floor, scraped and scarred from years of foot traffic.

Windows first. Repairs were supposed to start in a week. She and Mother had saved two years to make it happen. But she had to find a deed first.

This shop carried with it the history of her family, and she'd promised herself she'd take care of it. With Robbie at the helm of some of the renovations, Clara had been freed up to work out the finances and marketing. Until now. Now everything came to a stop in order to save the bookshop from something much worse than a leaky roof.

With a final look at her work and a few adjustments of the white Christmas lights nearby, she scanned the empty bookshop, the quiet hum of the closing day only interrupted by Robbie's whistling from the second floor. She'd never been so grateful to have him in her life as now, with the uncertainty of Blackwell's existence. He'd offered his usual humor and calm, assuring her they'd search the entire place until they found the missing deed. With a quick prayer of gratitude and a hope Robbie's optimism proved true, she turned off the lamp lighting her corner of the shop and followed the sound of his whistle up the stairs.

The sight of a fully assembled Lego Star Wars' Millennium Falcon atop the sci-fi bookshelf brought her to a stop. "You finished it?"

Robbie's whistling ceased and he stood from his crouched position by the thriller section, arms filled with hardbacks. His lips took an easy stretch into a grin. "You've known my Lego fetish this long and you're surprised?"

"But this?" Clara took a few steps closer to the intricate creation, examining his handiwork. "I mean, how long did it take you?"

"A few days." He shrugged a shoulder and narrowed his gaze at her. "Isn't this your night off? You're allowed to take one, you know?"

She squeezed her eyes closed, stifling a whimper. "I have to venture into the dreaded attic to begin my frantic search to save Blackwell's from possible destruction."

"Ah, the daughter of a fantasy writer is coming through with exaggerative detail."

The wry tint in his words spurred Clara's smile. "It's coming in particularly handy right now."

He put his books down and stepped closer, his gaze searching hers. "You're not in this alone, Clara. I love this place as much as you do." His palm covered her shoulder, confirming their comradery. "I'm here to help."

Tears stung her eyes and she covered his hand with hers. "It's just right now, with all the uncertainty and the rainy weather and the smell of pine on the breeze—"

"You miss him."

Robbie's simple understanding—the ache she felt for her dad—pooled a warming comfort through her. "He loved rainy days."

"And Christmas." Robbie nodded, his gentle expression melting into a mischievous grin as he gestured with his chin toward a door in the corner of the room. "Then I think we need to get started on this attic search."

Clara narrowed her eyes at him in mock annoyance, but he knew her too well. There were times to dwell on her father and the loss of his colorful personality, and then. . .there were times to take a deep breath and turn her mind to something else. "We?"

He wiggled his auburn brows. "You don't think I'd let you face the clowns alone, do you?"

Her stomach squeezed at the mention of her childhood attic fear. She followed his gaze to the locked door and, almost without thinking, slid her hand into her pocket, which held the store keys. How long had it been since she'd ventured there? And never had she plumbed the depths of the rubbish-lined room with a century of knickknacks and papers.

"Besides, the sooner we put this behind us, the sooner you can redesign the store website like you've wanted to do for six months, but. . ." He waved a hand toward the shelves of books. "Books happened."

"I'm really not afraid of clowns anymore." She tipped her chin a little to add credence to her declaration.

"Riiight. . .and dog-earing pages is your favorite bookmark."

She snatched a pillow from the nearby reading chair and chucked it at him.

"I'm glad that wasn't a hardback Dostoyevsky!" His grin widened to show almost all his front teeth and he returned the pillow to its chair.

"I'd never throw Dostoyevsky." Her smile pressed for release. "I wouldn't want to damage the book on your hard head."

"Ah, I see that as a yes on the attic question." He gave his brows a shimmy. "You may not know this, but I'm a great sidekick for dark, attic-y spaces."

"Attic-y?" She pulled the keys from her pocket.

"What can I say, I'm better at reading words than using them."

She chuckled, releasing her anxiety and replacing it with purpose. "Sounds like you're the perfect person for the job. Hard head. Big heart. And doesn't mind *clutter-y*, dark places."

"Or adventure," he offered, his index finger pointed high as if he'd transformed into a detective with a brilliant idea.

"Okay, Chief Inspector, I hate to disappoint you, but I don't think an adventure waits on the other side of this door." She unlocked the old-fashioned brass handle and pushed the door open with a dramatic squeak.

"Well, that noise sounds exactly like the start of an adventure." His comment followed her across the threshold as she flipped a switch to illuminate the stairs.

"Or the proclamation that the hinges need oil."

"You really should stop being so practical right now, Clara." The stairs creaked beneath his feet behind her. "As I recall, you were actually the one who invented all of our adventures as kids. The magical places. The dangerous escapades. You were the mastermind behind them and I. . .well, I was like your faithful dwarf or something. The Gimli to your Eowyn."

She'd been that way once. Spurred on by her father and his massive imagination. And then, her mother's health started changing, followed unexpectedly by her father's. Somehow, the magic of those memories dimmed with the barrage of medical appointments and dim prognoses, and she'd not only tucked away her own stories, but the very dreams she'd once nurtured like breath. There'd been no time, no space in her mind. They'd failed to find their way back into the everyday work of being a daughter and helping run a bookshop. Besides, she was too old for fairy tales, right? Maybe because it stung a little too much to dream about romance when her dating life fizzled to nonexistent and any magic hid between the spreadsheets of the daily grind.

In her beloved books, she knew the ending came with a happily-ever-after, for the most part. At least, in the books she loved best.

The scent of pine and that unique aroma of "old unvisited place" thickened along with the heat as they climbed the stairs, and the strangeness tickled the edges of her imagination. An adventure? She shook the thought away. No, finding a deed.

At the top of the steps, to their left, the angled attic roofline stretched the length of the bookshop. The dusty floor was littered with various boxes, from cardboard to wooden chests, some pieces of old or broken furniture, a clothes rack with black bagged garments hung in a row, and one shelf running the full length of the space.

"No clowns," Robbie whispered from behind.

She shot him a glare.

"Can you imagine playing hide-and-seek up here?"

Her faux-annoyance melted into a chuckle. "You really are the biggest kid in the world."

"Actually." His index finger rose again. "I was one of the shortest guys in my class at school. If I'd just had two more inches." He winced and shook his head. "Height matters, Clara. Even if the girl doesn't care, the guy does."

"You make up for it in personality."

He stood a little taller, matching her height, and tilted his chin out as if she'd given him the compliment of the ages. "Okay, that helps." He shrugged. "A little."

She chuckled at his pun as he nudged past her into the room.

"Why is it that your dad didn't go through these things years ago?"

Clara scanned the cluttered space. "Mom says that Granny Blackwell had set up the business so well, that all he needed to keep the everyday workings of the bookshop going was in the office downstairs. This place just kept gathering storage." She ran a hand over an old rocking chair. "Right after Granny died, the economy started a downward shift and Dad had to do some extra editing work to keep things afloat, so the attic was the last thing on his mind."

"Oh right. That's when he started writing his kids' books."

"Yep." Tears tingled at the bridge of her nose at the acknowledgement. "He found his new dream, I guess, and it worked for him."

New dream? The idea prodded an unsettling discomfort, like an itch just out of reach. After a year of finding her rhythm taking care of the bookshop and her mother, could she even consider having her own dreams?

"What would your dad care for an attic full of—" Robbie waved a hand toward the room. "This, when he had imaginary worlds to create."

"And a bookshop to run." She followed behind him to an old rolltop desk situated halfway between the stairs and the far window. "I remember Dad saying that some of Granny Sadie's things were in an old desk up here."

"Great, you check that out." He walked in the opposite direction toward a box of old-fashioned toys poised on a shelf across the room. "I'm going to explore in this direction."

The old desk opened with hesitant budges, scraping wood on wood to reveal a conglomeration of various nooks and crannies filled with papers, trinkets, and other paraphernalia reminiscent of another time.

The first papers she uncovered were simple receipts for bookshop repairs, some dating back to 1959. She shook her head with a grin. Her father had been notorious at keeping paper trails, even as a late teen. "You never know when you might need to prove something important," he'd quoted after his grandmother, the mysterious Sadie Blackwell.

Boy, did she feel the sting of that truth now.

A small tin revealed a collection of beautiful pens, all engraved with the Blackwell name. She ran her finger over the gold lettering of her father's name carefully scripted onto one of them, and with a steadying breath, she slipped the pen into her pocket. . .just to have him a little closer.

A green-covered ledger showed a beautiful calligraphic hand, carefully marked within the rows from a date as early as 1954. Could that be her great-grandmother's writing? Simple, with small curls at the ends of the words. A strange sort of emotion swirled through her chest, as if she had some connection with this woman she never really knew. Clara's only tangible connection was a photograph of Granny Sadie holding her as a newborn, but her father had shared countless stories of his kind yet courageous grandmother.

Otherwise, not much was known about Granny Sadie's younger life, except she'd once worked as a maid at nearby Biltmore and basically created Blackwell's bookshop by herself. A powerful energy came from the memories her father shared about this woman, and the mystery of how she became who she was spurred a niggling curiosity. What sort of woman—a single mother at that—began her own business at a time in history where few women owned much at all?

In the far back of the desk stood a long, rectangular wooden box with a notched lid. Clara drew it forward, her movements resurrecting the scent of cedar. After a few attempts, the lid slid open to reveal some age-worn papers carefully folded inside. The first few appeared to be some communication between Sadie Blackwell and a Mr. Long regarding the use of the building as a bookshop. Dates placed them in the autumn of 1916.

Clara's breath whispered between her closed lips. 1916!

"Clara."

Clara jumped at Robbie's voice, so close. When had he moved to her side? "Yes?"

"I found something you might want to see."

He held out a small metal chest, about the size of a boot box, the glint in his hazel eyes undeniable.

"The deed?" She kept her gaze on his expression as she took the box from him.

"Nope, but I think your history-loving heart will like it anyway."

She narrowed her eyes at him and then placed the chest down on a closed box nearby. She slowly twisted the golden clasp until the lid clipped open. Inside lay a careworn, black leather Bible, a few yellowed papers, and a simple string of pearls. "Whose is it?"

"The only name in the Bible is Evelyn Blackwell." Robbie tapped the cover of the Bible. "Have you ever heard that name?"

"No." Clara smoothed her fingers over the pearls and then drew the Bible out of the box. She carefully peeled back the first page. In a less elegant hand read the phrase: *Presented to Evelyn Patterson Blackwell on the 20th day of May in the year 1900 by Reverend Anderson Clark of Hope Baptist Church.* "Who do you think she was?"

"You're asking me?" He chuckled and peered closer, as if the yellowed pages held more information than the inscription.

"I don't recognize any of the names in this stuff except Great-grandmother Sadie's." She leafed through a few of the Bible's pages, and a flash of white caught her attention. "Wait, here's something." She flipped back to the spot and drew out a small slip of paper, less yellowed than some of the others. An unfamiliar hand, beautiful in its flourish and style, wrote in what appeared to be a hasty script.

Dear Library Fairy,
I've always believed in fairies but feel a library is the perfect abode for such a fantastical creature. Thank you for your book recommendations. I beg for more.

With anticipation,
The Visiting Book Goblin

Clara slowly turned her gaze to Robbie, whose expression reflected less confusion and much more humor. "I've always suspected your family had some wackos in it."

"Hush." She nudged him with her elbow and reread the note, mind swirling through a zillion questions. "Like your side is any better."

"Didn't Granny Sadie live to be a hundred or something like that?" His words lathered with a hidden laugh. "Your dad said she was just trying to outlive everyone to make sure they took good care of her bookshop."

"Then you'd better be careful." Clara needled him with a glare. "I may live that long just to pester you into eternity."

Granny Sadie had raised Dad after his father had been killed in World War II and his mother returned to live with her family in Georgia, only to move back to Asheville seven years later with a new husband and a newborn Julian. And though Robbie didn't have an ounce of true Blackwell blood in him, his heart pumped with every bit of love for Clara, her parents, and this shop. . .and by proxy, Granny Sadie, even though he liked creating a whole slew of wild stories about her enigmatic past.

Further exploration revealed another hidden piece of paper.

Dear Elusive Library Fairy,
I am inclined to believe that Tarzan must have been part fairy as well as part ape-man. How he learned to read English without ever having heard the language, as well as so readily picked up on French, I cannot say. French was not my favorite. Clearly, there was magic at work.
I'm curious for more.

As ever,
The Book Goblin

"I like this guy. He's funny."

Clara grinned and replaced the note. "This library fairy sounds as if she was supplying books for the goblin to read, but when? How?"

"You know, when you say sentences like that, it makes me really happy. I love fantasy."

A clock chimed from below, interrupting Clara's laugh. She checked her phone. Eleven? Already?

"It is getting pretty late, and I need my beauty sleep." Robbie ran a hand through his mass of hair in a dramatic flourish. "Besides, this place will be here tomorrow and we can do some more research then, especially since I've scared away all the clowns."

Clara closed the desk and pulled the box with the papers, Bible, and pearls into her arms. "You're my hero."

"I'll claim that title until you meet Mr. Wonderful." Robbie snickered and tugged the box from her hands. "But promise me one thing."

"What's that?"

"Let me in on the discoveries too." He turned toward the stairs. "I'm excellent at knowing random facts. Everyone needs someone like me on their adventures."

Clara followed him down the steps, sending one more look over her shoulder before turning out the attic lights. Pearls? Library fairies? For some reason, she felt she'd just opened a wardrobe door to the entrance of a story that could change her life.

Chapter 5

Dear Library Fairy,
 Do you actually read the books you suggest or is it merely some clairvoyance on your part? Because if you are the sort of fairy who reads Sir Arthur Conan Doyle, I should very much like to discuss Sherlock Holmes, Watson, and the various mysteries in which they find themselves. I had only read one book by this author before arriving at Biltmore, and now you've sufficiently hooked me on my third. I am determined that Mr. St. Clair and Hugh Boone have a lot more in common than a shared opium den. Do fairies talk of opium dens? It doesn't seem a very fairy-like topic.

               Sincerely,
              The Book Goblin

My teeth bit into my bottom lip in a vain attempt at reining in my grin. If Oliver Camden knew I was a servant in this house, would he still speak so freely of opium dens and stories? Of course, he must suspect I was a servant, mustn't he?

Oh, how I itched to write to him. I looked behind me in the vast recesses of the empty library, as if someone could overhear my thoughts.

With soundless movement, I slipped from my place by the bookshelf and walked to the large library desk. Pen and paper waited in abundance for any guest who wished to write a letter or take notes on the books they were reading. I'd replenished the materials dozens of times, touched them without hesitation, but now, my intentions took a new turn.

Write him back? Would it truly be so wrong? He'd asked for my response, after all.

With another glance toward the library's various entry points, I took up a pen and scribbled out a quick note.

Mr. Book Goblin,
    No self-respecting library fairy would dare give away the ending of a book to the reader. I should most certainly lose my wings.

Sincerely,
The Library Fairy

P.S. Fairies talk of many things, but only when pressed.

My pulse pounded in my ears as I slipped the note into *The Adventure of the Blue Carbuncle* and left the book on the table near the juncture between the long gallery and the library. In a few hours guests would meet in the gallery for tea and then, perhaps, retire to the library. That had been the pattern for most of the guests over the past few days. Maybe I would attempt a peek at Mr. Oliver Camden's response to my little missive. . .but now, I had an appointment with Miss Lorraine Withersby, and had no idea what to expect.

"I don't need to know every detail of the book, Miss Blackwell." Lorraine Withersby pushed a loose strand of golden hair back from her heart-shaped face and reached for her teacup. The young woman had clearly taken great pains with her toilet, for even the curls brushing the sides of her face appeared to have been placed there with as much purpose as the rose color on her cheeks.

Respectable women never admitted to wearing makeup, even if the whole world recognized the pretense. I'd even heard from visiting maids how their mistresses forced them to secretly purchase cosmetics so no one would suspect the lady. Of course, the maids I knew rarely had interest or funds to spend on such a frivolous and disreputable indulgence. There was no denying Miss Withersby was pretty, and as the daughter of one of the richest men in South Carolina—or so the house gossip went—I felt certain she became even prettier, but she did not care for books.

I stifled a sigh. Despite the impossibility of the venture for both parties, Miss Withersby and Mr. Camden, I would do my part, and perhaps they'd find mutual ground in other areas.

Mrs. Potter had arranged for me to meet with Miss Withersby in the sitting area of the Sheridan Room, one of the bedrooms not in use at present *and* nearest to the library, which allowed easier access for me to return to my duties. The housekeeper took to the assignment with a scowl I felt to my bones.

With very little to go on in preparation, I had gathered several books Mr. Camden had enjoyed and brought them with me to the meeting, proceeding to read a bit to Miss Withersby in an effort to help her gain a sense of the author's voice and style.

I've always found it rather fascinating how those two elements—voice and style—can color a story. . .or detract from it.

"Just tell me what the story is about." She sipped her tea and offered a lackluster smile. "If you're worried about my ability to take what information you give and use it to its fullest extent, have no fear. I possess an excellent memory and have always excelled at theatrics, from what my mother tells me."

Though sarcasm was generally frowned upon in good society, my mind tended in that direction without assistance. In fact, at that moment, I wondered if Mrs. Withersby employed a bit of sarcasm on her own, because Lorraine Withersby embodied every ounce of high-bred, shallow-character theatrics I'd ever seen.

I immediately reprimanded the turn of my thoughts, as contrite as if the bishop had stared at me from the high pulpit of All Souls. Few people are as they appear at first, and it behooves the heart of a Christian to see with gracious eyes our fellow humans, whether of high-bred means or low. After all, I'd been a servant, or the daughter of a servant, my entire life, and certainly hoped, if given the chance, people would see me for more than a quiet worker with nothing of interest to say. I had plenty to say—too much, really, for my occupation. Loud enough to beat a steady rhythm against submissive servitude. I wondered how long it would take for those words to pound through my self-control in this situation.

Oh, what would it be like to have someone truly see me? And appreciate what they saw?

I softened my expression and readjusted my approach. "It is my understanding that you wish to impress Mr. Camden. Is that correct?"

Her gaze darted from mine and she took a piece of shortbread from the offerings on the table. "He appears to be the best option of the two men here."

I couldn't disagree with her. From what I'd observed, Mr. Ezra Dasher, though quite handsome, kept his words few and his smiles even fewer. Though his reading choices proved more along the lines of gothic horror and crime thrillers, he also read psychology-based books as well. His family, though wealthy, wasn't nearly as prestigious as the Camdens, it appeared, and, well, to be honest, I liked Oliver Camden better because he liked my favorite books.

"And what characteristics about Mr. Camden appeal to you most?"

"He's a highly respected and rich gentleman's son." Her pink lips tipped into a saucy smile. "And he has an estate in the Lake District of England, which will assure me an escape from here." She waved a palm to the room as if encompassing the entire country.

"You don't care to stay in America?"

She scoffed and straightened her posture. "I have experienced three failed seasons, two in New York and one in Charleston. It is a humiliating endeavor to have your hopes dashed and to be viewed as a failure by all polite society." At this declaration, her bottom lip quivered, and compassion doused my previous assumptions. "I do not pretend to be clever, but I am not unkind." She blinked a few times and then seemed to rally. "So, I don't mind trying for either man, but Mr. Camden offers me an escape that Mr. Dasher cannot."

I attempted to understand, but the upper-class social dance of husband-finding usually induced a headache, if I thought about it too long. Maybe there were some benefits to being poor with fewer expectations to marry for position instead of marrying for love. "Don't you want to at least like your husband a little?"

Miss Witherby's brown eyes grew wide. "Liking him is all well and good, but what I want more is to secure a place for me and a name for my family. If talking books and being friendly are the means to my end, then I shall do that."

My previous compassion dimmed a little in light of her confession. I sighed. But I had a job to do, so after summarizing two books that Mr. Camden had just finished, as well as explaining one of the books Mr. Dasher had found interesting, from what I could discern, I shared that Mr. Camden would be in the library around four that afternoon and Mr. Dasher would take a walk along the library terrace around six, if she should wish to venture in those directions.

A sadness stole over me as I left Miss Withersby's presence. Whether from the fatalistic view she held of her future marriage or the fact that I'd helped her deceive Mr. Camden in believing she loved all those fictional characters as much as he, I wasn't certain, but I felt as though I'd betrayed the beloved characters as much as I had Mr. Oliver Camden.

I had second thoughts about the note, especially after my conversation with Miss Withersby. I would have removed it from the book and tossed it away if I'd not been called, along with several other servants, to help Mrs. Idlewild, a rather eccentric guest, find her wayward and somewhat intoxicated cat. It took nearly two hours before either the drunkenness wore off or the cat got tired of running, and the animal and its owner were reunited. Unfortunately, this meant I missed the opportunity to remove my note, because when I finally returned to the library, *The Adventure of the Blue Carbuncle* and my clandestine correspondence were gone.

So, with a sigh of resignation, I continued my work. There was nothing to be done about it. Most likely Mr. Camden would find it amusing, tuck it away, and never think of the Library Fairy again.

I had just finished returning a stack of twenty books to their respective places and was preparing to slip through Mr. Vanderbilt's secret study to the loggia, when the sound of feet on carpet brushed close behind me.

"Are there any good books in this library at all?"

I turned and looked down to find a pair of pale blue eyes staring up at me from a face wreathed in golden curls. A pink bow sat among the gold and somehow matched the blush of the little girl's cheeks in an almost porcelain doll way. My shoulders relaxed, and with a smile I lowered to a chair at my right so I'd meet her height. "Well, I imagine it all depends on what you consider a good book."

The girl, maybe eight or nine years of age, measured me with those powder-blue eyes and nodded. "Yes, I suppose so."

"What sorts of books do you like? If you tell me, perhaps I can help you."

She drew in a deep breath and perused the vast room of bookshelves then turned back to me, chin at a confident tilt. "What would you recommend?"

I barely kept my grin in check at the girl's clear desire to be viewed as more grown-up than she was. "Well, I'm not sure." I tapped my chin as if contemplating the question. "But if you're interested in such things as architecture and theology, we have a rather extensive collection."

Her nose curled into a dozen tiny crinkles.

"And, of course, there are a few books on gardens and animals."

The crinkles became less defined, but I still hadn't won her over.

"And, I suppose..." I looked up toward the bookshelves as if thinking, but cast a quick glance at her from my periphery. "There are always adventure books and fairy tales."

Her smile stretched into two dimples which she quickly quelled when I turned my full attention back to her. "I don't think I'm keen for gardening books today, but I should very much like to see your fairy tales."

"Ah, a reader after my own heart."

Her eyes grew wide. "You read fairy tales?"

"Oh yes, they're some of my favorites."

"But aren't you too old for fairy tales?"

"Too old?" I pressed a palm to my chest as if shocked. "The only people who are too old for fairy tales are the ones who've forgotten their imaginations."

Her gaze turned thoughtful. "Grown-ups forget a lot."

"You are right. Unfortunately, they do."

"I suppose that's why they look sour so often too."

I barely caught my laugh. "We should at least feel a little sorry for them, don't you think? How dull and gray it must be to live without an imagination."

She nodded, and I searched her cherub face. "But you and I are kindred spirits because we both know the best way to manage the real world is to keep a firm hold on an imaginary one." I grinned and crooked my finger to beckon her to follow. "I think I have just the place to look."

Her airy giggle hit me in the heart and I grinned as she followed me with dancing steps through Mr. Vanderbilt's secret study, down the loggia, and up a back stair. Before stepping from the stairwell, I searched the hall. Empty. With silent movements, we slipped to the center of the bookshelves that lined the hallway leading from some of the guestrooms to the first-floor sitting room.

"Here is where we keep our fairy tales," I whispered, opening the glass door to reveal rows of various sorts from *Beauty and the Beast* and *Peter Pan* to collections of Andersen, Grimm, and MacDonald.

"Why aren't they in the library?" Her quiet voice matched my own.

"Mr. Vanderbilt always wanted them nearby because he loved them so well."

Her pink bottom lip dropped. "Do you mean he loved fairy tales too?"

"Oh yes, he had one of the best imaginations of all, even though you couldn't always tell it from his very proper behavior. Sometimes, my mother said, he'd get a far-off look in his eyes as if he was dreaming something wonderful, and we knew he was likely thinking about one of his very own fairy tales filled with these mountains he loved so much."

"You know a lot about books." She sighed as if I'd won some sort of award in her mind.

This little girl and I would get along quite well. "It's my job to know about the books at Biltmore. I tend them." I leaned close, lowering my voice. "And I love books too."

Her dimples emerged again and she studied me quite intently. "Who are you?"

"My name is Sadie Blackwell and I tend the library."

She studied my uniform. "You don't act like a servant."

"Don't I?"

She shook her head. "All of our servants are either sad all the time or have nothing to say. I've tried to talk to them for years and they barely answer with one word."

"Ah, well, not all servants know what to say to people."

"How come you do?"

"You and I are kindred spirits, so I think we understand one another better. And, I daresay, we both believe in magic." I offered her a wink. "What do you think?"

Her grin emerged again and she turned to the bookshelf. "My name is Victoria, like the queen, but my brother calls me Vicky."

"You have a very special name then, don't you?"

She nodded and reached for two of the books, both with the most elaborately decorated spines. My lips twitched into another smile. Yes, I would have chosen those exact ones for her. The illustrations were unparalleled.

"My brother says I am the princess of the house."

"It sounds as though your brother has an imagination too." I closed the glass door and tapped the top book in her hands. "This one happens to be my favorite because it holds twenty entire fairy tales, all with some of the best colored illustrations I've ever seen. You can practically feel the ocean breeze blow off the page in the story of *The Little Mermaid*."

Victoria's wide eyes sparkled. "Oh, I can't wait to read it straight-away. It looks very magical."

"I should like to see that book too, I think."

The male voice, soft to match our whispers, emerged from behind me and sent a wave of warm tingles up my spine. I squeezed my eyes closed. Being "seen" by a child was one thing, but by an adult?

"Sadie helped me find the best books in the whole house." Victoria's exaggeration kept to a whisper. "With color illustrations. She knows everything about all the books because they are her special work."

"Are they now?"

I stood from my crouched position and readied my rebuttal, but when I turned, I stood face-to-face with Oliver Camden, the Book Goblin.

My throat closed around my breath. Victoria was *his* little sister? Oh dear, how much had he heard of our conversation?

"Perfect books are difficult to find." His eyes narrowed, slightly. "It takes a special sort to uncover them."

I attempted a retreating step but my body failed to comply, so I stood frozen like one of the marble statues in the Italian garden outside. Guests rarely spoke to me. Male guests even less. And young, handsome ones? Never. My mind went blank.

"I can't tell you how grateful I am that you helped my sister locate one." He took a few steps forward, his gaze searching mine, his smile slipping from his lips. "It's easy for young ones to feel left out in a party such as this."

His words failed to match his expression, as if he meant to convey something else, something unspoken. I lowered my gaze, my face aflame at how long I'd stared at him. "It is my pleasure, sir." I slid my attention to Victoria. "Our conversation was delightful."

"She loves fairy tales too. Just like you and me, Ollie."

I felt his gaze on me. My throat burned with awareness.

"And what are her thoughts on Sherlock Holmes?"

My attention came up at the question, which was a mistake, because those ghostly blue eyes, so much like his sister's, captured mine. His lips crooked into a grin and, for some reason, my breathing squeezed to a stop all over again. *Look away. Look down.*

The dinner bell rang in the distance and voices murmured from the sitting room in response.

"Come, Vicky, run on to dinner." Oliver Camden nudged his sister ahead of him, but his feet didn't move. He stood so close, I caught scents of vanilla. "I think we deserve a proper introduction, don't you?"

My gaze rose against my will, curiosity overriding propriety. One of his brows rose. "Oliver Camden, The Book Goblin." He offered a hand, and when I didn't immediately move, he took my limp fingers into his own. "And you are?"

Should I answer? Victoria could tell him, but the entreaty in his gaze pulled against my sensibilities. "Sadie Blackwell."

His teeth flashed with his smile before he returned to a more neutral expression. The little hint of his delight inspired something beautiful and deep to awaken in my heart. "Sadie Blackwell," he repeated and offered a slight bow. "It truly is a pleasure to meet another…kindred spirit."

And with that, he disappeared around the corner of the hall and I collapsed back against the bookshelf, only noting a few minutes later that his comment about *kindred spirits* was a parrot of my conversation with Victoria *near the very beginning of our discourse.* So the clever Book Goblin had been following our conversation for longer than a few seconds.

I wasn't quite sure how I felt about that.

About any of it.

And what exactly I was supposed to do with the feelings I wasn't supposed to feel...especially when I was trying to help Miss Lorraine Withersby win Oliver Camden's heart?

Chapter 6

C lara, I know it sounds odd, but I'm only going off what the birth and death records say."

Clara looked down at the phone in her hand as if she could see Mrs. Pinkerton's teacher-like glare piercing through the receiver to hammer her point home. "There's no husband or marriage mentioned at all?"

"I checked all my sources, *as usual.*" The librarian's voice flattened on the last two words and Clara bit back an apologetic groan. Clearly, Mrs. Pinkerton hadn't recovered from the previous half a dozen or so calls Clara had made about Sadie Blackwell. "All of my information confirms that Sadie Blackwell was born Sadie Blackwell on May 7, 1895 and died November 12, 1994. She was the daughter of Amos and Evelyn Blackwell. She had one sister, younger, named Lark, who married a Mr. Ralph Wolfe."

Evelyn Blackwell? So the Bible had belonged to Sadie's mother.

"She gave birth to one child, a son—"

"Grandfather John Oliver," Clara supplied, knowing the trajectory from there. Grandfather John married Eliza Arlington just before setting off to fight in World War II, leaving Eliza expecting her firstborn, Christopher John Blackwell. Her father.

When Grandfather John died in 1945 in combat, never having seen his son, Eliza left her child with Granny Sadie and disappeared back to her family in Georgia, returning seven years later with her new husband and one-year old son, Julian. Granny Sadie had adopted Clara's father as her own, which, as her father recalled, likely helped her heal from the loss of her only child to the war.

The few photos Clara had seen of Sadie held no mystery. A frail woman with wiry black-and-white hair, kind eyes, and a broad smile. All the stories her father had told her of Granny Sadie warmed Clara's heart enough to make her believe she knew the woman, or at least made her feel some strange connection she couldn't really explain.

Perhaps, if Clara knew more about her, she'd have a better idea of where to look for the deed. The attic had only revealed two more Book Goblin notes—one about *Ivanhoe* and the other related to a discussion about Sherlock Holmes—and a birthday card from a woman named Helen. At least this Book Goblin and Library Fairy had excellent tastes in books.

Not only would searching help with finding the deed, but if there was something else to uncover, something more, Clara's father would have wanted her to discover it—to *know* Granny Sadie's story. A desperate curiosity about this woman who'd started a bookshop, raised her son and grandson on her own, lived a long life without ever marrying, and held such favor in Clara's father's eyes burned to life. They'd lived with a building full of books, but had anyone ever learned Granny Sadie's story? It all hinted of a tale much more intricate than she, or even her father, seemed to know.

Sadie's mystery—her life—knotted an uncomfortable awareness in Clara's chest and unearthed a question which had lurked in the back of Clara's mind for years. *How long will you breathe in the life of other people's stories, but not step out into your own?* Her mother had asked that once. Clara had written it into her journal.

"It seems Sadie Blackwell was a woman who got into a bit of trouble." Mrs. Pinkerton's voice on the other end of the phone pulled Clara back to the conversation. "And, she decided to do the hard work of keeping the baby herself. From all I can tell, she rose above her circumstances like few women of her station could have done in that time, despite being an unwed mother. There is no mention in any of my records of a father to her child. I suppose it's one of those stories that has disappeared with time."

"And no reference to other properties she owned or lived in?"

"Nothing that is still standing. Her aunt rented a home near Biltmore Village, but it was torn down decades ago."

Clara stifled her sigh. "Thank you for all your hard work on this,

Mrs. Pinkerton. If anything else comes up, would you let me know?"

"Of course."

Clara ended the call and slumped back on the stool behind the counter. If they weren't able to discover the deed in one of the boxes they'd uncovered in the attic, where else could Sadie have placed it? She'd worked at Biltmore and lived in the apartment attached to this bookshop. That's all the information Clara had to go on.

"Ms. Blackwell?"

Clara looked up from the notes she'd taken during Mrs. Pinkerton's call to find a tall man in a black suit peering down at her from an astronomical height. His lean frame made him appear even taller.

She stood just to decrease the intimidation factor, if nothing else. "Yes, may I help you?"

His gaze roamed over her face and then trailed to the books on the shelf behind her before returning to her eyes. "My name is Douglas Kemper. I believe you had a phone conversation with my associate, Lars Duncan, last month."

Clara steadied her palms against the counter, a sudden tension twisting like a rubber band in her stomach. Duncan's Books. "I remember." She offered a smile. She hoped. Maybe. "I don't suppose you're here to admire our Christmas display?"

His angled jaw tensed and he cleared his throat. "I thought perhaps you'd reconsidered Mr. Duncan's offer about purchasing your inventory and buildings. It's a substantial offer, Ms. Blackwell, as you well know."

Insanely substantial. "Please let Mr. Duncan know how much we appreciate his generous offer, but my mother and I are still resolute in providing the people of Asheville an independent and historic option for acquiring their books."

"Ms. Blackwell, I've been in this business for five years and I can assure you in more cases than not, independent shops are not equipped to compete with our business long term. I'm trying to help you get the best opportunity while the shop is still seen as competitive and vibrant. In two or three months, I cannot promise the same generosity."

Why did she feel she'd lived through this scene before? Except with Tom Hanks? Aha, *You've Got Mail*! Though Clara still didn't know what "going to the mattresses" really meant when fighting against a big chain mogul, and she had no real desire to find out. *Sorry, Joe Fox.*

"We'll take our chances on the future of Blackwell's. She's survived so much already." Her words squeezed through a quickly closing space in her throat as she held his gaze. She snatched up one of the home-made flower pens for sale, provided by a local artist, and offered it to Mr. Kemper. "Have a great day."

He grimaced down at the bright yellow papier mâché sunflower and, with an ungentlemanly grunt, turned and left the store.

Blackwell's had made it through the Great Depression. Two World Wars. A fire in the 1950s. Time. Age. Fluctuating economy. Would it survive a lost deed and a mega bookstore?

"Okay, okay, I have a design idea for the new website. How do you feel about a dragon—" Robbie slid to a stop at the counter and lowered the paper in his hands. "Whoa, are you okay? You look pale as a ghost."

Clara glanced around the storefront, noting a few people just beyond earshot by the classics section. "Duncan sent one of his men by again." She lowered her voice. "Same spiel as last time."

"Determined, I'll give them that." Robbie shrugged. "Are you worried?"

"I don't know. Besides this stuff with the deed. . ." She sighed and leaned a hip against the counter. "Business is staying consistent, but it's an old building. We don't have a lot in savings to cover if something big breaks and, well, sometimes—"

His face softened into a gentle smile. "Sometimes you get tired of it all?"

She cringed. "Does that sound awful? I mean, my dad loved this place. It was his heartbeat. Granny's too. And I *do* love it, but recently, I've just realized. . ." She pulled a breath in through her teeth, trying to place her feelings into words he might understand. "This has been my life. I went to school nearby, graduated college nearby, and have every significant memory of my life somehow associated with this shop. What if I'm supposed to do something else?"

His grin didn't match the crash of loyalties in her chest. "What do *you* want, Clara? It sounds like that's what you need to figure out. Not what you think your parents would have wanted. But you. And it's okay for your dreams to be different than what you thought they were going to be." He winked. "That's called growing up."

"You're hilarious." She swatted at him with a copy of Adelise Newsome's newest mystery. "Now what's this about the website design?"

He raised the paper and showed her some of his ideas to modernize the defunct page in hopes of moving her parents' dream into the twenty-first century. Despite the fact that he'd not been encapsulated in the life of Blackwell's as a child, once he joined the team, he'd joined from the soul out, and the bookshop seemed to ignite his creativity in the most amazing ways. Displays. Designs. Marketing. The old building with the creaky steps didn't bother him at all.

And, most days, it didn't bother Clara either.

But her father's death had ignited buried questions in her heart, and Sadie's unfinished story fueled the flame. Something in Clara's life felt unfinished. . .like only reading half of a book and then placing it on the shelf. Had she shelved the part in her own story where she was supposed to *do* something with her life?

Her gaze dropped back to her notes from her phone call with Mrs. Pinkerton. Granny Sadie had started a bookshop while being a single mom. Had she taken hold of her own story or been thrust into it by circumstances?

The idea haunted her throughout the day, dogging her steps as she reshelved a collection of hardback fairy tales, updated some of the bookkeeping, finished decorating the shop Christmas tree, and added twinkle lights to the display window in the front of the store. Her gaze caught on a couple walking hand in hand down the cobblestone street, iconic in historic Biltmore Village. Warmth branched up her neck into her face and nearly pricked at a surprising rush of tears. Taking care of her parents and the bookshop had been her life, but was the bookshop what she wanted for her future? The answer dangled on a brink onto which she didn't dare step, because she wasn't sure if she'd be brave enough to jump. . .and then have to live with the "almost." If those dreams of happily-ever-after fell apart, or worse, never came.

"Clara, I found something in the papers you brought down from the attic." Her mother's voice drew her from the window, the wintery view, and the twinkle lights. "I waited until we closed to show you, but I think it's a clue."

Mama's eyes sparkled as she waved a small piece of yellowed paper in the air, all those rewatched Miss Marple Mysteries gleaming in her massive smile. Clara's grin responded, her thoughts righting themselves on the present. She had things to do now. She didn't have time for "almost." "I think we're in front of the wrong bookshelf for this revelation, Mom." Clara gestured toward the little sign to her right. "Mystery would be more appropriate than aquatic animals."

Mom paused and glanced to the bookshelf sign as if trying to sort out Clara's joke before shaking her head. "I found this postcard and a key."

Clara took the proffered card and small silver key. One corner of the postcard bent inward, another had been nearly torn off, but the black ink displayed a clear, though short, message from an almost calligraphic hand. In the top right corner, a faded insignia of Biltmore's name and logo marked the origin of the note.

Brontë is excellent, but I prefer Austen. Humor is a key to life. And who doesn't want to read a good romance now and again? Though I'd prefer to live one. What about you, dearest fairy?

Your Book Goblin,
Oliver

Book goblin? Oliver? Was this the person who left the notes in Evelyn Blackwell's Bible? Were Oliver and the Book Goblin the same, then?

Clara looked over at her mother who had leaned back against a bookshelf, her face flushed, palm pressed to her chest. "Mom?"

"I'm all right." She waved a hand, attempting to dismiss Clara's concern. "Just got a little overexcited with all the research." Her smile spread wider despite the perspiration on her brow. "I'd always told your father there was more to Sadie's story than she ever mentioned to us. She kept quiet about her younger life, but I just knew she'd loved deeply. You could see it in her faraway glances."

"Faraway glances?"

"When you fall in love, you'll understand, my dear." She stared at Clara in the tender way she often did when she was thinking of Dad. "There are conversations Sadie had with your father and me that have been resurrecting in my mind since we discovered these papers. I wish I'd written things down." Mom shook her head and waved a book in front of her like a fan. Then suddenly she pointed the book at Clara. "Which is all the more reason you need to write things down, so you won't end up regretting it like your mother."

"You think this Oliver was romantically connected with Sadie?" Clara slid a chair over to her mother's side and gestured for her to take a seat. She leaned against the wall and examined the postcard again, though keeping a close eye on her mother's demeanor. Her breathing was slowing by degrees. Good. "Oliver, from who knows when?"

"Your grandfather's middle name is Oliver, Clara." Mother tsked, her lips taking a playful turn.

"Which was and *is* a common name, *Mother*," Clara exaggerated the word. "It doesn't provide a direct link."

"But you can't rule it out as mere coincidence, or the fact that this Oliver was at Biltmore when Sadie was there." Mom gestured toward the postcard. "I checked with my friend, Marlana Carter, who works in Biltmore's archives. The Vanderbilts stopped making those particular postcards, the ones with the smaller trees featured near the house, the year after Mr. Vanderbilt died. 1915. So our Oliver had to have been at Biltmore some time between Sadie's mother's death and the end of 1915."

"Sadie's mother's death?"

Mama nodded, her pallor and breathing returning to normal the longer she sat. Congestive heart failure loomed like a strange sort of constant waiting. "Sadie took over her mother's place at Biltmore after her mother died. Granny Sadie mentioned it once when I was determined to find out more about her early life."

"Well, you are notoriously stubborn when you set your mind to it." Clara eyed her mother, who refused visiting the doctor any more than absolutely necessary despite Clara's urging. "Especially about your health."

"There's nothing else to be done, Clara." Her mother held her attention, almost as if trying to brand her words into Clara's head. "Except to *live* all the days of our lives, however long or short those may be. And I have, dear girl. I have."

Tingles stung at the bridge of Clara's nose, so she glanced back at the postcard, embracing the choice she'd made. Loving her parents well because they'd needed her. Their example had been one to pedestal. A quick certainty of the right match. A deep affection. A lifelong friendship surrounded by laughter, books, tea, and music. A relationship like that probably only happened once in an entire family history. In those faraway glances, did her mom long to be with her dad again?

"What about this key?" Mom gestured toward the small item in Clara's hand. "It looks like one of those lockbox keys."

"An old one." Clara raised the key for closer examination. "Have you ever found a lockbox among Dad's or Granny's things?"

"Nothing." Mom shook her head, her bun bobbing. "But if your granny kept it all these years, there has to be a reason."

But what? And where else could she possibly look?

She shifted her attention back to the postcard, a frown pulling at her lips. "So, some man by the name of Oliver left this note for Sadie?" She sighed. "Mom, can you imagine how hard it would be to find one Oliver in all the Olivers that worked at Biltmore?"

"Or visited?" Her mother's pale brow rose. "To use a postcard would suggest—"

"A houseguest?" Clara reached for a chair of her own and slid down into it. Austen and *Downton Abbey* swirled through her thoughts. "That would mean Granny Sadie may have had a forbidden romance. Servant and houseguest?"

"Maybe." Her mother's grin emerged. "Only one way to find out, my dear." She tapped the card with her finger. "I've set up an appointment for you with Marlana at Biltmore."

"What?"

"She's the one who suggested that the years could be narrowed down based on the postcard we had, and of course she'd want to see anything related to the house's history." Mom chuckled and pushed herself to a stand. "It's what historians do."

"Mom, Sadie's name isn't even on this card." Clara stood and slid her arm through her mom's as they walked to the back of the room where their little apartment joined the shop. "This Oliver guy could have sent this to anyone."

"But why would Sadie have saved it, if it was meant for someone else?" They slid through the adjoining door to their quaint little living area. Her mother squeezed Clara's arm. "You must start thinking like a sleuth. What happened to the girl who devoured Nancy Drew books when she was eight?"

Clara's feet faltered in following her mom. What had happened to that girl? She'd stopped looking for clues in imaginary mysteries and started watching for physical signs of her parents' health and future needs. Imaginary mysteries seemed too trivial. Her attention fell back on the postcard and key. Was there a place for mysteries, adventure, and even romance in her life? Could she release her hold on her fear long enough to try and find out? She drew in a deep breath and for the first time in a long time prayed that she'd be hopeful enough to search for everyday magic, and brave enough to step into her own story.

Chapter 7

Dear Library Fairy,

Have you truly read The Island of Dr. Moreau*? I can tell you without hesitation that this fatalistic and morose tale is not one of my favorites. Please provide a lighter fare, if you will, with as few half-man, half-beast creatures as possible. I trust your guidance and understanding on this matter, since you outfitted my sister with such an excellent choice as the* Finding Ever After *collection.*

Besides fairy tales, which seems appropriate for a fairy, what other type of books do you enjoy?

Curiously,
The Book Goblin

P.S. Forgive me, but you are nothing like any servant I've ever met, therefore I've determined you truly are a fairy.

Book Goblin,

I hope you'll enjoy the three offerings I've selected for you, but if not, I feel certain I can locate something else. Biltmore has many literary adventures to offer.

Fairy tales are my favorite type of book, but I find that many fiction books hold fairy-tale elements without being categorized in that genre. A world of wonder reveals itself in many different ways through literature—magic in everyday sorts of ways if one has the eyes to see it.

It rarely takes pixie dust for the true book lover to locate magic between the pages of a well-written story.

The Library Fairy

After another "tutoring" session with Miss Withersby, I'd reluctantly informed her that Oliver Camden's habit was to take a stroll about the gardens after breakfast, usually with a book in hand. A pastime I'd have happily indulged in as lady of the house. But even though I was a servant, Biltmore offered the opportunity to read and provided an endless supply of stories as long as the reading didn't interfere with my work.

As I passed by the window overlooking the library terrace, movement caught my attention. Two figures walking in synchrony along the terrace wall, which opened to a vast view of the mountains on the horizon. Miss Withersby and Oliver Camden.

They walked along the path, the late summer sky a deep azure behind them. I braced a hand against the window frame and watched, as Miss Withersby's lavender coat blew in the breeze and Oliver walked with his hands behind his back, his profile turned in Miss Withersby's direction. They made a lovely pair. Picture perfect. Exactly as everyone expected, I suppose.

A sickening pain lurched in my stomach and I took my silly emotions firmly in hand. At least impossible romances became possible, quite regularly, in fiction. And in fiction—I turned back to the dozens of library shelves surrounding me—I would remain. But a little extra daydreaming about a bookshop might be necessary.

My attention flittered back to the window, the nausea resurfacing.

"I *finally* found you."

I spun from my spot as if Mrs. Vanderbilt herself had caught me mooning over Oliver Camden, only to find Oliver's little sister staring up at me. Garbed in lovely green, complete with a ruffled collar, she arrived at the perfect time to afford my wayward thoughts some pleasant distraction.

"Have you been trying to find me?"

"For hours and hours." Which likely meant thirty minutes to a curious child.

"Well, look what an excellent finder you are." I clasped my palms together. "How may I help you?"

"Father doesn't like reading books and Ollie is with Miss Withersby." She scrunched up her face as she said the woman's name, and I liked the cherub even more. "There are some words I can't read."

"Are you asking me to read to you, Miss Victoria?"

Her dimples emerged again and she bobbed that head of golden curls. "Would you? Please? The pictures only make me curiouser, especially the one with the witch and the apple."

I lowered myself to her level and almost said yes right away, except I remembered the errand Mrs. Vanderbilt had specifically assigned to me. "I would love to read to you, but I cannot meet this afternoon because I must run an errand for Mrs. Vanderbilt in the village. What about tomorrow?"

She turned her tiny chin northward, as if in thought, and then her smile bloomed. "Tomorrow morning? I wake up early."

I stifled my chuckle. "That sounds perfect." I leaned close and baited her with a whisper. "And perhaps I can sneak some pastries and tea from the kitchen for our very own private tea party? Tea and books go very well together."

Victoria's dimples nearly deepened to dime-size. "And biscuits," she whispered back.

"Of course, as long as it's not *too* early."

And without warning, Victoria lunged forward and wrapped me in her warm little arms, her soft curls brushing my face with the scent of roses. I didn't have a great deal of practice with hugs, though I loved experiencing them. The sweetness nearly unraveled my emotions and my heart trembled with the hint of a desire I didn't fully understand. Motherhood? Touching children's lives?

I squeezed back and let the moment linger like the ending of an excellent book. God knew my story. I prayed the next chapter would hold more possibilities for the impossible. I was determined to make a way.

I'd never been an admirer of surprises. They usually came packaged in bad news, or that had been my experience, so when I entered the bakery where Lark worked, I wasn't exactly thrilled to find her engaged in an intimate conversation with a young man.

Mind you, by appearances, the man held a fine quality. Gray suit. A pair of shiny wing-tipped Oxfords on his feet, and a likeable face. But his eyes? Something about them grated against my sisterly heart. Not so much their color, which was a dark brown, but more the *way* he used them. Or, to be precise, the way he used them on my sister.

Lark saw me and, with sobering expression, parted from her conversational partner to cross the bakery to me. "Sadie? You're here in the middle of the day."

"I had a package to collect for Mrs. Vanderbilt." My gaze never wavered from my sister's face and she finally sighed, took me by the hand, and pulled me to a quiet corner of the shop.

"His name is Ralph Wolfe, a banker." She straightened to her full height, still a few inches shorter than me, and I readied myself for the blow. "And I'm going to marry him."

Clearly, I'd not readied myself sufficiently, because the declaration stole my breath.

"He fell in love with my cream puffs, first." Her smile kept growing the more she spoke, her hazel eyes nearly beaming. "He's been into the bakery every day the past three weeks and he told me last week that it's because of me."

"And your cream puffs?"

"Sadie, he's not one of the factory workers." Lark grabbed my hands. "He can provide me with a good and proper home. I can have store-bought dresses and bake because I want to, not because I have to."

"Has he asked you to marry him?"

Her smile faded and she looked away. "Not yet, but I know he will soon. He's already spoken to me about how delightful it would be to have a wife who knows her way around the kitchen to help entertain his business associates properly." Her attention fastened back on mine. "Entertain them? The hostess of my own house where dinner parties happen! Sadie, you know how much I want this."

Yes, I did. Lark had always wished for a wealthy husband, or at least one that could provide all the "necessary" things she couldn't afford now. "Have you spent time together, other than here?"

Her cheeks darkened and she released my hands to grab her own, nodding like a guilty child. My heart squeezed. But she wasn't a child.

Nearly nineteen. A perfectly marriageable age.

"Twice." Her gaze shot back to mine. "But nothing scandalous. We merely walked along the street and talked."

My mind immediately went to Miss Withersby. "What did you talk about? Mutual interests?"

"Well, mostly he talked. He's very passionate about his job. He *did* compliment my hair." She looked around the corner to where he still sat staring out the window with his Apollo-like profile. No wonder he turned Lark's head. The man had a way about him that commanded attention. "And he spoke of his townhouse and his expectations for the future."

"And he appreciated yours as well?"

"Mine?"

"Your expectations for the future?" I searched her face, so young, so certain.

"Sadie, I just want to be married and not have to work as hard as Mama did her whole life. That's all."

"Marriage is much more than a townhouse and house parties, Lark."

"If I'm lucky enough to have more than that, then it will be like the cream on top of a strawberry pie, but I don't need that. I've never needed that."

How could she even know what she needed after their childhood? An absent father. A mother who worked such bone-wearying hours she barely had time to see her daughters, let alone talk to them. At least, when her mother had been assigned to the library from house-maid, the workload had lightened a little, but she still traveled back and forth to Biltmore Village every day and they'd rarely seen her during daylight hours. Lark's reasoning made painful sense if logic and indifference served as the only predictors of future happiness. "Don't you *want* more?"

Lark's bottom lip quivered with her deepening frown and I imme-diately redirected my concern with a smile.

"Perhaps you could introduce me to him? If you like him so much, I'm sure I will too."

Her smile resurrected and she took my hand and pulled me toward Mr. Ralph Wolfe, a man whose eyes matched his name a little too much for my peace of mind.

My feet walked toward a dream, even an impossible one.

After collecting Mrs. Vanderbilt's newest book package from the post office, I took the long route back to the Biltmore's Gate House. If Lark married, Aunt Elaine would move to live with her daughter in Waynesville, and then what? No one to watch after except myself.

My gaze traveled over the Brick House, re-envisioning what it could be, what I could make it, if given the chance. Lark's perspective of logic tugged against the dreamer inside of me. Couldn't I have both the dream and the reason? The imagination and the reality?

If I worked hard enough, was it possible?

"Well, what a pleasant surprise this is."

I spun around and came face-to-face with Oliver Camden, who looked dapper in his light brown sack suit and straw bowler atop his head.

"Mr. Oliver."

"Vicky said you planned to be in the village this afternoon and look, in your civilian clothes, no less." His grin etched into a playful turn and he scanned me from my simple navy hat to the bottom of my blue skirt. "I wouldn't have recognized you from such a distance if Vicky hadn't pointed you out from across the street."

I scanned the sidewalks along the way but didn't see the golden-haired girl anywhere.

"She's inside the toy shop with Father." Oliver shifted a few steps closer. "I feel certain she'll be there for quite some time."

"And. . .and you didn't want to visit some of the other shops?"

"Actually, I was in search of a fairy."

His answer nearly drew my gaze to his face, but I quelled the impulse and remained quiet. Writing harmless notes was one thing. Having private conversations was quite another.

"What is it about this house that held you so spellbound a moment ago? It looks rather vacant?"

My throat tightened around my response. How should I answer him when we shouldn't even be conversing at all? "Mr. Long plans to sell it soon."

I closed my eyes and pinched my lips together. What sort of response was that?

"And you plan to buy it?"

A laugh burst from me before I could stop it. "If Mr. Long can wait another five years with an added price reduction, perhaps."

He grew quiet and I chanced a glance at him from my periphery. His head tilted back and he studied the Brick House with such intention, I actually felt as though he'd taken my confession seriously. "What would you do with it? Live there?"

The question, so innocently asked, prodded my hopes into words. "And perhaps. . ."

He didn't respond, so I continued. "Open a bookshop?"

His hearty laugh pulled my full attention his way. "That's an excellent idea, Sadie." He dipped his head with a grin. "I. . .I mean, of course, Miss Blackwell. What a wonderful bookshop it would make too."

Sadie. He'd called me Sadie, as if a chasm of social expectations didn't stand between us. I nearly dropped the package of books. And I wanted to hear him say it again.

"It's clear you have a gift for books and matching them with people." His grin crooked as he kept studying the Brick House. "Yes, I can see it now. Books in the windows. A sign displaying the name. Happy readers pouring from the doorway, their giddy laughter peeling down the streets at their literary discoveries."

"Portable adventures," I whispered, allowing his words to resurrect the pictures in my mind.

"Yes, so true."

We stood quietly, side by side, the wind tossing a cool breeze against my cheeks. The air bit with the taste of coming rain and I still had a long ride ahead of me back to the estate house. Speaking my dream aloud made it come alive in a different way. A. . .possible way.

"Your suggestion of Wilde's *The Canterville Ghost* was just the medicine I needed after Moreau," Oliver stated, turning toward me. "See, you have a gift."

I glanced back at the Brick House and away from his blue eyes, so similar to his little sister's, yet so different in the way they looked at me.

"And, though not as happy an ending as I'd hoped, *The Lost World* was much more hopeful than Dr. Moreau as well. Though, I prefer happy endings. They make the world less gray, don't you think?"

I tugged the package to my chest, myriad memories pressing in upon me of hungry nights and hopeful mercy. "I like happy endings, but the world is filled with gray and light. One helps us measure the other, to find gratitude for the light when compared with the gray."

I felt his stare on my profile and attempted to lighten my much-too-philosophical admission. "But I love books of all sorts. If it is bound, I will read it."

"*Any* sort of book?"

"Most of them. I try to avoid ones that keep me from being able to fall asleep because I'm envisioning terrifying things in my head, but otherwise, I just enjoy the journey. The ability to be other people and see other places that I'll never have opportunity to be or visit."

"What makes you think you'll never travel?" He spread his palm forward as if spanning the street. "See the world?"

My smile tempted to release. "How many of your servants travel the world with you, Mr. Camden?"

"I do wish you'd call me Oliver, or at the very least TBG."

At this, I turned my full attention on him. "TBG?"

He lowered his voice and winked. "The Book Goblin."

I raised a brow. "All pretense has fled, I see."

He shrugged a shoulder, his ready grin emerging with such gleam mine responded without reservation. "Actually, I'm rather horrible at pretense anyway. My mother continually scolds me on the subject."

"Your mother?" There had been no mention of a Mrs. Camden; I'd come to the conclusion she'd passed away.

"She is not fond of travel, but felt it a social devastation to keep Father from visiting the Vanderbilts at their invitation." He shook his head slowly. "I'm afraid my mother is quite wrapped in the webs of expectation and high demands. Unhappily so." He pushed his hands into his pockets and looked back at Brick House. "Most of my childhood friends were village children or servants, which, thankfully, my mother didn't know about and my father didn't care about. My older brother took many of the 'proper' expectations with him. It was quite liberating."

A gentleman's son who befriended village children and servants?

His knowing gaze fell back on my face. "It's important to be seen as a person instead of a position, isn't it?"

I shifted my attention away, but his words still lingered between us, as if spoken directly from my head. My family had been involved in service for as long as I could remember. Being seen for who I was? Truly? Beneath the apron and the cap? Like a real heroine in a story? I squeezed the books closer to my chest.

"It makes one feel more confident in following dreams and truly living life for all the reasons and gifts God has given to us, don't you think? Those pesky class boundaries are so limiting, not only in aspirations but also in"—he tipped his head in my direction—"friendships."

I really wasn't certain what to think. His words pierced me, resonated with my soul. It was like being a child lost in the woods and suddenly hearing a mother's call nearby.

Hope. Awareness. Some inextricable link to another human.

The sense that, in all my internal conversations with the Almighty, someone else understood. Could Oliver Camden truly "see" me, when I'd spent most of my life, even as a child, being taught to be "unseen"?

"You don't speak like an upper-class English gentleman, Mr. Camden."

"Is that unfortunate? That class creates such limitations on excellent friendship possibilities." His smile re-emerged with an added twinkle in his eyes. "*If* we let it, that is."

My face warmed at his direct stare and I lowered my eyes as I should have been doing all along, but he kept making it so difficult. He annihilated the usual distance between my class and his with the ease of a kind word and a smile.

"But I suppose you are right. The only servant of mine who travels with me is my valet." He sighed. "I haven't considered how very confining your place in the world must be, and I am sorry for that." His gentle response pulled my attention back to him. "You are the sort of dreamer who deserves a chance to see and experience the world and all its wonders."

"And I do." I gestured with my chin to the package in my hands. "Through books."

"Yes, you do." His voice softened, tender, and its entreaty drew my gaze back to his. "You are a singular young woman, Sadie Blackwell, and I say that with the greatest admiration."

"Is that what you meant by your note?"

He shifted a step closer, and the scent of vanilla along with the quickening of my breath accompanied his approach, "Which part?"

I shouldn't say it, but his personality, his interest, made it so easy. "Me not being like any servant you've ever met."

His gaze held mine, probing so deeply with such a look I swayed toward him before catching myself. "Well, none of the other servants I know are fairies, of course."

My lips split into a grin.

"And," he added, his voice low, close. "You're rather wonderful, aren't you?"

Had he truly spoken those words aloud or had my ears played tricks on me? But from the earnestness in his expression paired with his nearness, it had to be true. He thought I was wonderful? The tug to sway forward whooshed through me again and I blinked as if coming awake. I had to think of some diversion from this train of thought because the temptation to hang a hope on this dream bordered on overwhelming. "You and Miss Withersby seem to be getting on well."

I pinched my eyes closed. That? That was the diversion I needed to voice? *Lord, help me!*

"Ah." He walked alongside me down the main street of Biltmore Village as if a highborn man being seen in public with a female servant was the most casual thing in the world. What would Lark think if she happened to see? "So you think I should set my cap at Miss Withersby, do you?"

My face flamed with heat. "I can assure you that I don't *think* about it either way."

"Yes, of course." His expression smoothed with mock innocence. "But it does make one wonder if the very fact you asked the question denotes that it is taking up space in your thoughts."

I opened my mouth but couldn't think of a clever enough response, especially since he was right.

His grin provided a slight balm for my embarrassment. "I'm glad I'm in your thoughts, though I do wish you wouldn't think about me with Miss Withersby."

"And exactly how should I think about you, Mr. Camden?" Clearly, his teasing had usurped my clearheadedness, because a servant did *not* speak to a guest in such a way.

"Oliver? TBG?" He corrected me with a raised brow. "A friend, even?"

"A. . .a friend?" Was that my squeaky voice speaking? "I'm. . .and you're. . ."

"Charmed, is what I am, Miss Blackwell." He held my gaze for much longer than proper, until I heard my heartbeat thrumming in my ears. I quickly lowered my attention to the sidewalk ahead. "But, if you truly wish to see me with Miss Withersby, I suppose you could train her to love books as well as you've trained her to parrot them. It may make me like her better."

"Parrot?" All heat fled my face. "How did you know?"

"My valet." He leaned close. "He's an excellent spy among the servants, and servants know everything about everything."

This servant certainly didn't, especially at the present moment.

A drop of rain hit my cheek quickly followed by another. I raised the package above my head in protection.

"I shall collect my brolly just there in the motorcar." Oliver gestured toward a Model T down the street. "And rescue you without delay, Miss Blackwell."

He rushed off in the direction of the car and my breathing returned to normal. What was I thinking? Whatever it was, it had to stop. I would not become one of those heartbroken servants who fell prey to the charm of a houseguest only to lose her virtue and her position in one night.

But Oliver didn't seem that sort of houseguest.

Not at all.

Which meant that nothing along the lines of my imagination could ever happen between the two of us.

I sent a glance toward the nearby shops just in time to see Victoria emerge from the toy shop, her purple coat and hat a lovely frame around her little body. She hugged a package to her chest and looked up, meeting my stare.

With a little squeal, she waved and began to run toward me into the street.

A motorcar bounded down the lane from one side. A carriage from the other. And Victoria plunged forward without heed to either.

Dropping the bundle in my arms, I set off at a sprint toward her. She froze when she noted my approach, her eyes widening. A car horn sounded. Horses reared. And in one desperate action, I lunged forward and wrapped the little girl in my arms.

Chapter 8

Clara knew Biltmore as well as any annual passholder. She walked the path around the lagoon at least once a week, if more for the nostalgia of being near her own local castle than exercise. And anytime the estate offered special tours, Clara was first in line to take in the fashion displays or historical nuggets.

Living in Asheville and loving history equaled loving Biltmore.

And now, the estate held a part of *Clara's* history.

Clara entered the house by way of the beautiful double front doors, breathing in the magical step from modern life back to the elegance of the early nineteen hundreds. But she'd not expected their new display. Books! Upon entry, a massive table greeted her, laden with decorative glass cases filled with unique bookish celebrations. One globe featured a spyglass, a vintage-looking map, and a copy of *Treasure Island*. Another showed a miniature pirate ship, a little bottle of something labeled "fairy dust," a thimble, and a copy of *Peter Pan*. A half dozen other cases—each celebrating various classics—surrounded a centerpiece designed to look like a tree made out of books with twinkle lights hanging from it.

What a wonderful way to celebrate the Vanderbilts' love of stories and reading.

The famous cantilevered staircase twisted up and out of sight around the colossal black steel chandelier suspended from the roof three floors above. Morning light streamed in through myriad windows lining one side of the staircase, haloing the limestone steps with an almost angelic light. Clara stifled a giggle, embracing the magic that was Biltmore, and cast a glance toward the Winter Garden to her right. Various flowering plants encircled a glass-roofed court with a marble fountain in the center crowned by a statue of a boy with two geese. A pianist, tucked in the Winter Garden near a display of poinsettias, regaled the room with classical versions of Christmas carols, the sound reverberating off the high ceilings and adding sweeter Christmas ambience to the festive estate house.

Clara sighed like a little girl in a daydream. *Magical.*

"Clara?"

Clara turned to find a middle-aged woman approaching from the stairs, her reed-like silhouette elongated all the more by her black trousers. The pale blue of her blouse brought out the almost translucent hue of her eyes—a color even lighter than Clara's—and her shocking head of auburn hair made the vision even more stunning.

"Mrs. Carter?"

The woman's smile spread and she offered her hand. "Yes. I'm pleased to meet you." She gestured for Clara to follow as they stepped toward the direction of the Banquet Hall. "As one of the archivists at Biltmore, I treasure any story or artifact associated with the house or family." She slipped through the archway into the Banquet Hall, maneuvering around guests as she did so.

The largest room in the house, the Banquet Hall featured a wall of medieval tapestries, a massive triple fireplace at one end, and a table to seat over sixty people when fully extended. Clara nearly stumbled from looking up at the vaulted ceiling, seventy feet above her. This room never failed to impress, especially with a fifty-foot Christmas tree on display. Mrs. Carter unhooked one of the rope barriers blocking passage of visitors and ushered Clara to follow.

Clara's breath caught. Mrs. Carter was taking her into places at Biltmore she'd never seen.

"I must say that your great-grandmother and this Oliver fellow have given me a bit of work to do." She continued talking as they slipped up a narrow servants' stair. "But I believe you'll be very pleased with my discoveries so far."

Discoveries? Clara pulled her attention away from an unfamiliar passageway to her right and caught up with Mrs. Carter as she stopped before a simple wooden door.

"My office is next to the archives." She nodded toward a door on the opposite wall. "I think we'll be more comfortable in here away from all the machines that keep the archive room at optimal conditions for protecting our documents."

Clara entered a small room that looked like any other office except for the oak paneled walls on one side and vintage blue wallpaper on the other. Mrs. Carter sat behind a desk and offered Clara a chair across from her.

"Did you bring the postcard?"

Clara opened her purse, removed the postcard she'd placed in a plastic bag, and handed it to the historian. Mrs. Carter tugged her glasses from around her neck and placed them on the edge of her nose, taking her time examining the card. "It's in good condition for its age. As I told your mother, these particular postcards were used during a limited time, 1914 to 1915, and we only have one other copy in our archives." She looked up from her perusal. "As you will note, the line drawing of the Biltmore is unique for this particular card."

Clara had no comparison, so she merely nodded.

Mrs. Carter smiled and placed the card on the table before relaxing back in her chair. "Getting information like this is always like a treasure hunt for those of us who are into archives, and thankfully, Mrs. Vanderbilt kept a great many correspondence and detailed documentation throughout her life."

"Does that mean you were able to find something about my great-grandmother?"

The woman's Cheshire cat smile slipped into perfect bloom. "Not a full story, but enough to get you started, I think."

Started? Clara sat up a little straighter. A real mystery? A true adventure? Even if it all started in order to save the bookshop, the story triggered a dormant place in Clara's heart. The little girl who believed in fighting dragons with Robbie or embarking on untold adventures with a handful of imaginary friends slipped from behind a closed place in Clara's heart and tiptoed back into the light.

Clara braced her elbows on the desk and stared back at Mrs. Carter, pulling a bit of her childhood spunk to the surface. "I'm listening."

"From what I've been able to uncover, it seems that your love for books is hereditary." She chuckled and tapped at a few pieces of aged paper lying on the desk. "Mrs. Vanderbilt's meticulous records show that after her mother's death, Sadie took over her mother's position as primary servant in charge of the books of the house, which includes the library, of course."

So, the Library Fairy must have been either Sadie or Sadie's mother. "What exactly would a library fair. . .servant do?"

"Well, it was her job to not only keep the library tidy, but to provide options for the Vanderbilts' guests by leaving books out for them they may have requested." Mrs. Carter lifted a note from the desk and began to read. "Our stay at Biltmore was remarkable. Besides the beautiful surroundings, as well as the excellent company and food, we also found your library almost magical. Books we'd discuss, or speak of, would appear on display soon afterwards. Whoever, or whatever, you have taking up residence in the library, is excellent at his occupation."

Clara's smile bit into her cheeks as she leaned forward to see the note. "Was that about Granny Sadie?"

"It was written by a guest who stayed at Biltmore in late 1915, and Sadie was our resident library servant at the time."

Clara attempted to read the signature on the note without touching the dainty paper. "Who wrote that?"

"That's the exciting part. It appears to be from a Mr. Heathcliff Camden, a friend of George Vanderbilt, and a man whose only visit to Biltmore took place in 1915."

Camden? Clara had heard that name before too. Had it been on one of the letters she'd found in the attic? "And that's exciting?"

"It is if Mr. Camden's son's name is Oliver." Her pale eyes twinkled as she pointed to a part of the letter. "As referenced here to show he'd accompanied his father and little sister on the trip to Biltmore."

The same name as the letter. "And was there a direct link to Sadie?"

Mrs. Carter's smile took a broader bend. "Indeed there was." The woman's gloved finger slid across the page as she read. "I have no words of gratitude large enough to thank your servant, Sadie, for saving my daughter's life. What reward I attempted to bestow upon her was graciously refused, so I am including a small sum for her, as a gift, and entrust she will receive it more readily from her mistress than from me."

"Granny Sadie saved his daughter's life?" Clara reread the sentence. "How?"

"It doesn't say, but having Sadie specifically noted in a letter is indeed unique. There have been hundreds of servants in this house, and most are only in the archives as a name listed in a row of other servants. This gives us a bit more."

"A lot more." Clara shook her head. "I'd always heard what a good woman Granny Sadie was, but I'd only thought of her as the frail and kind ninety-something-year-old I saw in photos." She gestured toward the letter. "I've never really imagined her as anything else."

"Perhaps I can help you even more on that score." Mrs. Carter stood and led Clara from the room, through a series of corridors, narrow ones for servants, and finally up several flights of stairs to where the ceiling lowered and the decor became less elaborate and more practical.

Biltmore's fourth floor? The place where all the single female servants lived?

The implications began to fall into place as Mrs. Carter and Clara skirted down a long hallway with uniform doors on either side, a few open and on display to tourists. Mrs. Carter stopped in front of one of the closed doors and drew a set of keys from her pocket. Without a word, she unlocked the door and stepped inside. It was a small room, similar to the other servants' rooms, with a simple iron bed on one wall and a washstand, mirror, and modest oak wardrobe along the other. A small window offered a view of the French Broad River as it snaked in the direction of the distant blue-tinted mountains already alight with sunset's gilt glow.

"This was Sadie's room."

The simple declaration resonated through Clara with a strange sense of awareness—as if she'd stepped to a veil between time and if she reached out her hand she might touch some unseen ancestor. Clara moved a few steps to the bed and smoothed her palm over the cool curve of the iron footboard. Sadie had lived here. This had been her own space for the few hours each evening she had to herself.

"This is one of the handful of servants' rooms we haven't placed on the tour or turned into a storage space." She stepped toward the wardrobe and tugged it open. Inside hung two maids' uniforms with their black base and white aprons, pressed and pristine as if they'd been worn the day before.

"I plan to keep looking for more information. These sorts of stories are wonderful additions to our tours. Visitors love to hear the true accounts, and this one is even more fascinating because it may end with a clandestine romance between a guest and a servant."

Clara's fingers smoothed over the sleeve of the dress, another strong sense of awareness—of connection—squeezing in her chest. Had Sadie worn this? "We can't be sure there was a romance between them. Maybe it was just the idea of one." She'd watched *Downton Abbey*. Upstairs guests could use their influence to sway servants. Had that happened with Oliver?

"But I believe there's enough there to speculate." Mrs. Carter started for the door and then sent a grin over her shoulder. "And I am counting on you to share what you learn. I shall do the same."

Clara felt a sudden loss as the door closed behind them, separating her from her great-grandmother's room. Did some mystery hold the truth behind the bookshop and Sadie's past? A clue, somewhere, to the deed for the bookshop? "That letter from Mr. Camden?"

Mrs. Carter turned at Clara's words. "Yes?"

"Did it have an address listed?"

Mrs. Carter's expression lit with a grin. "Of course it did."

For some reason, Clara couldn't shake the idea that Oliver Camden had more to do with the bookshop than a name, and maybe, by learning more about him, she'd find out more about how the bookshop started.

Clara gave her mother the name and address of Oliver Camden's family and sent her doing what she loved to do best—Google—and then got back to work at the bookshop. Robbie had things well in hand, as usual, and while they reorganized the suspense/thriller section, she told him of her findings at Biltmore.

"So, this Oliver Camden was an Englishman who came as a guest to Biltmore?"

"It appears so."

He paused, looking down at a copy of Stephen King's newest. Just the cover made Clara cringe. She loved books, but not *that* kind.

"Do you think Granny Sadie was trying to move up the social ladder by wooing this guy?"

"Wooing this guy?"

"Hey." His palm came up in defense. "Poor servant. Rich Englishman. Sounds like a great novel."

"Exactly." Clara waved a Colleen Coble book at him. "A story. Stuff like that doesn't happen in real life and if it does it's *very* rare. Like love at first sight and marrying royalty."

"But it *does* happen." He shook a book right back at her and raised a brow. "Don't you remember your very own parents said it was love at first sight for them. They met in April and married in October, I think?"

Clara rolled her eyes, but the reminder of her parents' sweet romance brought a sudden sting to her eyes. Oh, how they'd adored each other. "Well, they're an anomaly, and—" She snatched the next book Robbie raised from his hand. "Granny Sadie didn't go about wooing some man named Oliver Camden. That would have put her position at Biltmore in jeopardy, and she respected the Vanderbilts way too much to do something like that. Remember how Dad said she talked about Mrs. Vanderbilt in particular."

He shook his head and placed the last few King books on the shelf in beautiful order. They looked less terrifying in a straight line on a shelf with only their spines showing.

"I just wish I knew where she put that deed, Robbie. If it had ever been in Dad's possession, he would have filed it away with extra care and order as he did every other document."

"Well, what else can you do? It's been over a hundred years since Granny Sadie purchased this place."

"I've made a few phone calls over the last week, leaving messages with several people who might have some idea. I even contacted Stephen Long, the great-grandson of the guy who supposedly sold the bookshop to Granny in the first place, just to see if he has any record of the transaction."

"Maybe you should be a little more discreet on sharing that kind of info, Clara." Robbie's freckled brow pinched into wrinkles. "Especially with Duncan's trying to purchase the place. If they found out you didn't have the deed, well, I don't know what that might do to you or the bookshop, and. . ." He pressed a palm to his chest and stood. "This place is as much a part of my history and heart as yours."

She took his outstretched hand, and he pulled her to a stand. "Do you really think someone would try to steal it from us?"

His expression relaxed and he placed a palm to her shoulder, taking his role as the "big-little brother" in her life seriously. "Just be careful. For our sakes and—" He glanced around the upstairs, bookshelves lining almost every wall. "For this place."

They walked down the stairs to the main level, where Mama had just turned the sign to CLOSED. The quiet after a flurry of early Christmas shoppers settled over the empty rooms, a time Clara had always believed signaled to the characters in the books to come from their bindings and visit the world beyond the pages. Or at least, her father always said so.

"I couldn't wait to close up tonight, you two." Mom rushed forward and gestured for them to follow her. "Come, come. I want to tell you about my research."

Robbie sent Clara a bemused smile, and between the three of them, they finished locking up before retiring to the apartment, where Mom had laid a plate of cookies on the coffee table beside her laptop. Oh yes, she had a plan.

"Sit, sit." She waved toward the chairs and pulled her computer onto her lap, her eyes glimmering. "I know you're laughing inside, but I haven't had so much fun in a long time."

Robbie's snicker burst out.

"Fun?" Clara stared at her mother. "Mom, we can't find the deed to the bookshop."

"Oh, I know, and we're all looking for it, aren't we?" She typed something into her laptop, totally ignoring Clara's gaze. "But there's also this wonderful mystery about Granny Sadie that I think she meant for us to find."

Oh dear, Mom had resorted to her Agatha Christie days. Despite Clara's concern, she couldn't tame her own smile. It had been over a year since she'd seen her mother this sprightly, this engaged. Father's death had taken such a toll on her heart, this glimmer of excitement hearkened back to their family outings to discover history and relive the journeys in books.

Clara almost sighed. It had been years and years since those times. "All right, Mom. What have you found?"

"Well. . ." She adjusted her glasses, but they almost immediately slid back to the end of her nose. "Not only did I locate Camden House from the address you took from Marlana, I've also been in contact with the current owner."

Clara sent Robbie, who'd crammed a second cookie into his mouth, a look and sat up straighter. "You spoke to Oliver Camden's descendant?"

"What?" Mom looked up over her computer, her eyes lit by the screen. "No, not his descendant. The Camdens don't own Camden House anymore. Actually, they haven't for over seventy years. I corresponded with Gillie Weston. She and, I suppose her husband, Maxwell, purchased Camden House from a previous owner and have turned it into a bed-and-breakfast."

Her mother paused, studying her screen.

Clara sent another look to Robbie, who was chuckling behind his napkin. He wasn't any help at all.

"Mom?"

She looked up and her eyes widened. "Yes, sorry. I was rereading the email." She waved away concerns no one voiced. "It seems that the Camdens sold the house so suddenly that they left many of their belongings there. The previous owners moved the items into the attic of the main house and Gillie said that neither she nor Maxwell have had time to sort through them yet."

"Why would Oliver Camden have anything to do with the deed for this bookshop?"

"Bookshop?" Mom blinked and stared at Clara as if she'd lost her mind. "I'm not wondering about the bookshop. I want to know if the Camdens have any information about this romance of your granny's. Your father asked her about it over and over, and she never gave any real clues. She told me a few vague things once, but I can't recall them now, and your father would have loved trying to uncover this mystery."

"Well, Mom, sounds like we should divide and conquer, then. You put on your Nancy Drew hat to uncover what happened in Granny's past, and I'll try to find this missing deed. I still have at least three boxes of papers and notes to go through from the attic." Though Mom's research sounded much more fun.

"Oh, notes!" Robbie popped up from his place on the couch. "That reminds me, a note was dropped off for you this afternoon, Eleanor. I left it on the counter near the cash register."

Robbie slipped from the room and returned with a small envelope. "Who sent it?" Mom asked as Robbie placed it in her hand.

"I don't know. I just saw it lying on the counter when I was checking out a customer."

Mom began peeling open the envelope and Clara turned to Robbie. "You wouldn't mind bringing the last of the boxes down from the attic in the morning, would you?"

"As you wish." He flourished a bow and crooked his grin, his attempt at an English accent rather appalling. "Besides, we've got to save our bookshop."

Our bookshop. Yes, that was how she thought of it too. He'd become such a pulse to the place, she couldn't imagine him not being as involved as she was.

A gasp from the other side of the room stilled Clara's chuckle. Mom's palm pressed against her mouth, her face two shades paler than a minute before.

"Mom?"

Without answer, Mom raised the card to them, her hand shaking. Robbie took it and turned so Clara could read along with him. The words splashed a chill through her chest.

Blackwell's isn't yours. I'll have it. Soon.

Chapter 9

I remember three things: a rearing horse in my periphery, Victoria cocooned in my arms, and a sudden jolt of pain reverberating down the left side of my body as I crashed to the ground and awaited the hooves to finish the job.

A collision of voices echoed around me. Victoria wiggled against my chest, her little voice confirming she was alive. I attempted to move, but my arm wouldn't respond. When I tried to push myself up, sharp pain sent me crumbling back to the cold ground.

Victoria was taken from my arms, her cries forcing my eyes open. She reached for me from her father's arms. I attempted to move again, blinking against the rain splashing my face, but nearly fainted as the pain knifed all the way from my elbow into my head. My vision blurred.

"Careful there." The soft voice sounded warm, familiar, and soon I was gathered up into strong arms and completely lifted off the ground.

"Get her to the car." Came another voice, older. "We'll take her to the house."

"I think it's a dislocated shoulder, Father." The words resonated near my ear, and I was enveloped in the scents of vanilla and. . . chestnuts? The urge to nuzzle deeper into his warmth nearly took the last of my energy. I was moving, floating.

"Sadie!" Victoria's cry resurrected my fading consciousness and I forced my eyelids open again, only to find myself staring into the face of Oliver Camden.

I was in *his* arms.

"I do believe, you brave girl, that you've dislocated your arm in the process of saving my sister's life."

My fuzzy brain attempted to make sense of his sentence. Dislocated my arm? The throbbing in my shoulder confirmed his statement.

"I can walk," I whispered.

He tsked, his grin slanting. "Now where's the fun in that."

If I'd had more mental clarity, I would have argued with him, but instead I relaxed back into his arms, attempting to siphon through my pain to brand the moment into memory. I'd never been held by a man, except hugs from my uncle when I was a child, and this was altogether different. His warm vanilla scent, the sturdiness of his chest against my side, his hands beneath me.

With a slight shift, I soon found myself seated inside an autocar, Oliver Camden at my side, with Victoria on the other side of him peering around her brother's arm.

Mr. Camden joined the chauffeur in front.

I attempted to adjust my body to reduce the pain, but nothing worked. Nausea roiled with unpredictable warning. I pulled in a slow breath, forcing my mind to alert.

I'd never been inside an autocar. Looked at them from a distance, but ridden in one? Not the servants' lot. Still, I wished I'd had more wits about me to investigate the lush interior.

"I don't see any wounds on your face or head." Oliver leaned close and brushed some of my stray hair from my eyes. "Does anything else hurt?"

I shook my head and moaned as I moved, surprised at how my neck muscles connected to the ache in my shoulder.

"The doctor is to meet us at the house." This from Mr. Camden.

"No." I shot up straight and nearly buckled from the shock of pain. "No, we don't need the doctor, surely." How much would a doctor cost?

"No worries, dear girl." Oliver held my gaze, almost as if he read my concerns. "Didn't you know that doctors never charge fees for valor? It's in their contracts."

Valor. I looked away, stifling an eye roll that would likely hurt my shoulder too. But the sight of Victoria's smiling face, even if she had a few smudges on her cheeks, made me feel a little better. She was safe. That was the important thing.

"Have you ever set a shoulder dislocation before?"

Oliver's brows rose. "Well, yes, for a friend or two during horse riding and such."

I'd reset my mother's shoulder once. And helped the teacher with a boy at school. It was a simple procedure. Excruciating, if memory served, but fast and efficient, and proving no need for a doctor. "I can brace myself against the side of the car."

His eyes rounded as comprehension dawned. "No. I will not hurt you that way."

"I'm going to hurt at any rate, and this way we won't have to include the doctor."

"I can't." He shook his head, gaze pleading with mine. "No."

"You know that as soon as the shoulder is set, I'll stop hurting as much, don't you?"

His expression took on the look of a trapped rabbit.

"You'll help me much more by setting my shoulder now instead of allowing me to ache all the way to the house." I knew I baited him. He knew it too, but there was truth in my words. Each bump in the road jostled my arm. And each time, my stomach lurched against the pain.

Emotions warred over his features. Agony as he watched me grip my stomach when the car rumbled over uneven ground. Something in the tenderness of his struggle broke through the barrier his presence had attempted to dissolve since our first conversation.

"Oliver," I whispered. "Please."

If a person could touch a soul with a look, something in his touched mine. He firmed his expression and, after another hesitation, took my hand in his. "It's going to hurt. Badly."

I nodded, swallowing the lump gathering in my throat. "And I'll likely faint from the pain."

"That's all right." The tension in his face quivered for an instant. "You're in good hands."

I almost returned his smile but another shudder from the car produced a wince.

"Brace your good shoulder against the side of the car, Sadie." All playfulness had fled from his face and he tightened the grip on my left hand. "It will steady you."

I shifted to lodge myself in place.

"What are you doing, Ollie?" Victoria's pale blue eyes shifted from her brother to me and back again.

"I'm helping Miss Sadie feel better." His stare bore into mine, uncertainty wrinkling his brow with an unvoiced apology. "I hope."

I held on to the compassion in his eyes and braced myself as much as I could.

"On the count of three." His Adam's apple dipped with his swallow. "One, two, three—"

In one swift movement, one palm pressed up on mine and the other guided my arm. I cried out, pain riveting up through my head and then...all went dark.

"Tyger Tyger, burning bright,
In the forests of the night;
What immortal hand or eye,
Could frame thy fearful symmetry?

In what distant deeps or skies.
Burnt the fire of thine eyes?
On what wings dare he aspire?
What the hand, dare seize the fire?"

The voice rumbled over the words, quiet and constant, ushering me to the brink of waking. Who read Blake aloud in the library? And with an English accent?

I forced my eyes open and found myself lying quite comfortably in an enormous bed. Cream walls surrounded me on every side with the satin hangings on the tester bed a glistening shade of pale peach. Where was I? Ornate satinwood furnishings? Hand-carved, muted clay tones of the mantel? A portrait of children hanging over the fireplace?

My eyes shot wide. What was I doing in the Sheraton Room?

I pushed to a sitting position, only to moan at the ache in my shoulder. But when I reached to touch it, I found it wrapped and in a sling at my side. I blinked and raised my gaze to meet the amused expression of Oliver Camden sitting to my left, book raised in hand.

"What are you doing—"

"Shh…" He raised a finger to his lips and gestured toward the book.

"What the hammer? what the chain,
In what furnace was thy brain?
What the anvil? what dread grasp,
Dare its deadly terrors clasp!"

"Why are you here?" I glanced down, grateful to still be in my regular day dress. "And why am I in a *guest* bed? I don't belong—"

"Do you mind, Miss Blackwell, I am trying to read." The annoyance in his tone failed to match the glimmer in his eyes as he rattled off the last two stanzas of Blake's famous poem.

I could only stare. The man clearly had no sense of propriety whatsoever.

He finished and clipped the book closed, crossing one leg over the other to stare at me. "I am under strict orders from the lady of the house to ensure you do not move from this bed for the remainder of the day."

"I don't believe one whit of it." I huffed and pushed back the coverlet. "A dislocated shoulder doesn't make a person indisposed for an entire—"

"You would forgo your mistress's specific orders?" He tsked, taking up another book from the bedside table. "That is not a very good employee."

"Once she knows I am quite well, she won't expect me to stay abed."

"Her distinct orders were for you to remain in this room until supper, at which time you could retire to your bedroom, if you felt able to do so." He tapped the book in his hand. "In the meantime, I'm to regale you with excellent literature and force you to accept the reward of saving a young girl from being trampled."

I succeeded in unraveling myself from the many blankets and produced one stockinged foot.

"Stop this instant, Sadie Blackwell." His voice rose and he waved the book at me, his brows bunching to center. "Be a good patient and return to your bed, or I shall be forced to tell Mrs. Vanderbilt how ungrateful you are."

My mouth dropped open.

"And poor Victoria will be positively heartbroken."

"Victoria?" I gasped the name. What was he talking about?

"She said you were to have tea and read together this morning, but, since you are currently indisposed—" He gestured with the book to the bed. "She has gone off to see to the tea for today in the hopes of helping you feel better."

"I will be happy to have tea with your sister, but in a room more appropriate for my station."

"Are you always so troublesome?" He studied me with such intensity, warmth began climbing up my neck into my cheeks. "You were not so troublesome when unconscious, I must say. As a matter of fact, you behaved with the utmost reserve, though you did almost take my hand."

"I almost took your hand while I was unconscious?"

He raised a brow. "Subconscious desires and all."

Heat soared to oven proportions in my face. "I can assure you that I did not—"

"Please, don't try to explain it away. It only proves my point." He waved away my words, a playful tip to his lips. "Hush now, and be a good patient."

"I feel certain the doctor will—"

"The doctor has come and gone and, in fact, has ordered you to bedrest, of which I am the enforcer." He raised the book. "Hearing me read aloud is excellent medicine."

"Mr. Camden, I have a job to—"

"Oliver," he corrected in a whisper. "And if you don't lie still I shall be forced to bring out Poe as punishment."

I couldn't usher up a reply so I dropped back against the pillows and stared at him.

"So, what shall it be?" He raised the book I'd loaned to Victoria. "Fairy tales?" He brought out another, his eyes dancing with an unleashed smile. "Or Shakespeare?"

"Mr. Camden, I truly am much better."

"I am glad to hear it, Sadie." His gaze softened into mine and my breath took a decidedly shallow turn. "I was sorry to have hurt you."

The gentleness in his entreaty stole my fight. Oliver Camden possessed a nearly intoxicating ease about him, a characteristic that swelled an ache through me to enjoy his company. Miss Withersby could only offer him shallow, heartless conversations, but I. . .I knew the books he loved. I craved the same joy of stories. And there was something inexplicable that bid me to linger a bit longer in his company with each new meeting.

He had an infectious playfulness that nearly distracted from his . . .what was it? His grin softened as I stared, and my heart trembled beneath his admiration.

Kindness.

"I shouldn't be here," I whispered, waving toward the room. "This is not the place for me."

"Right here?" He shrugged a shoulder, some awareness dawning in his expression. Something I couldn't quite interpret, but my pulse tripped into a higher beat as he continued to hold my attention, as if it understood. "I believe it may be the exact place for you."

"Sadie!" Victoria burst through the door followed closely by Mr. Camden. Trailing behind came Dolly, one of the housemaids, carrying a laden tray of tea and cakes. "You're awake. I'm so glad."

Without hesitation, or intervention from either her brother or father, Victoria bounded on the bed and snuggled up to my good side. "You were asleep ever so long. Like the cursed princess."

From the shadows falling over the room, "ever so long" couldn't have been more than a few hours, but even the knowledge of Oliver Camden watching over me for any length of time had me nearly burying my head under the plush pillows.

Victoria's little face tipped back to stare up at me, the slightest scratch running down her left cheek. Had that been from one of the buttons on my dress? Or a loose rock, maybe? I brushed a thumb against her skin without thinking. "Were you hurt at all?"

"Not a hint." Mr. Camden closed in a few steps, his hands folded in front of him in solemn stance. "You wrapped yourself around her. I. . .I can't tell you how grateful I am." He gestured toward Oliver, his lip quivering. "*We* are."

The vulnerability on the man's face, aging him, quelled my fight for propriety, and I resigned to live these next few hours as if I belonged on the other side of the stairs. "I am happy I was there, Mr. Camden."

"You. . .you have a special place with our family, Sadie." He cleared his throat. "We shall always see it that way."

"Ollie said that listening to someone read made people feel better, so I told him to read until you were better, and you look so much better already." Victoria touched a loose strand of my hair, its dark sheen a contrast to her pale skin. "Your hair is very long and lovely. Just like a princess."

I reached up, horrified to find my hair completely loose from its usual bun. With my good hand, I snatched up a handful and pulled it to one side, making a poor attempt of twisting it back. Dolly sent me a sympathetic nod as she placed the tray on the table at the end of the bed, but everyone else appeared utterly ignorant of my unkempt state or the complete inappropriateness of this entire scene.

Having tea with an English family in the Sheraton Room of Biltmore was not remotely typical in the life of a housemaid. Dreaming about it, perhaps, but not living it.

"And here is my thank-you." Victoria snuggled closer and pulled a gift from behind her back, placing it on my lap. "Ollie helped me choose it for you."

My attention swung to Oliver, who merely tipped his head, his eyes glittering like the goblin he was.

"It's only a small token of our appreciation, you understand," Mr. Camden added. "There is no possible way we could adequately thank you for saving Victoria."

"Open your present." The little girl giggled, tugging at the red ribbon on the white, slender package. "Then we can have tea."

"I'll need your help because I only have one hand right now."

Victoria delved into the package without a moment's hesitation and unveiled a copy of *Finding Ever After*, the fairy tale book I had shown her on our first meeting. "It's your very own copy since you love fairy tales so much."

I blinked down at the book. I would never have been able to afford such an extravagant purchase for myself, with its rich color illustrations and golden lettering on the front. But now I had my very own copy? What a treasure.

I looked to Mr. Camden. "This is very kind of you, but I. . .I can't accept it."

"Of course, you can." Mr. Camden rushed forward. "It's just a book. You saved Victoria's *life*."

Just a book? He had no idea. No one had ever given me anything as precious as this. "I appreciate your kindness, but my station won't allow it." I smoothed a hand over the book's cover and then held it out to Victoria. "Mrs. Vanderbilt would frown—"

"Sadie." Mrs. Edith Vanderbilt's tall, lean figure filled the door-frame in a lovely royal blue day dress. "This situation calls for special consideration. I couldn't think of a more fitting gift for our resident literary heroine. Of course you may keep it, along with my gratitude for taking such excellent care of my guests."

"Thank you, ma'am." I pulled the book into my chest, unable to hold my grin any longer.

"George used to say that stories carry their own special magic every time you turn a page." Her smile softened and for the briefest instant, she appeared to send a deliberate look from me to Oliver Camden. "I would say that you've earned a little extra magic today of the most authentic variety."

I gave the book another squeeze, embracing this gift and the gratitude that accompanied it, without giving in to the desire to glance in Oliver's direction. My act may have come with a little extra magic, but I doubted it produced enough fairy dust to breach the distance between a house servant and an English gentleman.

That sort of fairy tale only happened between the pages of a book.

Chapter 10

After alerting the authorities of the note that had been left for Mom, Robbie decided to stay nights with the Blackwell ladies for the next week just to help ensure their safety, or at least help Clara's mother feel safer. With nothing to go on but a piece of paper, the police could do little except keep an eye out. Clara shared with them the whole situation about the deed and gave names of people she'd contacted in regard to it in hopes the information might lead to some answers, but all of it would take time.

Time.

And if someone from Duncan's, or whoever, thought a note would scare them into selling Blackwell's, they didn't know the owner of the shop. Oh no! In fact, the threat thrust Clara into an even more dedicated search.

Clara poured out another small box from the attic. For the last several days Mom had remained vigilant in her communications with the Westons at Camden House as well as in her attempts to find out information online about Oliver Camden. She'd discovered a file that documented his admittance to a hospital in France during World War I. And she'd become quite chummy with the English bed-and-breakfast owner, even referring to Gillie as her Brit-buddy.

Robbie took over most of the workings of the bookshop while Clara devoted her time to searching for the deed. With the help of their two best teenage employees, the pre-Christmas rush moved like clockwork.

"Mr. Claflin, you can't go back there." Faith's southern drawl was unmistakable. "Like I told you, I'll be happy to take a message to Clar—"

"I'm part of this family, am I not? And I can speak to my niece whenever I choose." Uncle Julian's trumpetlike response blasted down the tiny hallway.

Clara barely had time to stand before he burst into the office. His gaze skimmed over her, likely mentally criticizing her navy blue 1950s rockabilly dress with adorable checkered buttons up the front that matched her headband.

"Uncle Julian." Clara spoke before he could beat her to it. "I hope you're doing well?"

"I'm grieved, Clara. Grieved about this news." He wiped a hand across his brow in dramatic fashion and dropped into the chair across from her.

News? Clara kept her breath controlled. "And what news is that?"

"The deed, of course. You have no deed for Blackwell's, if we can even call the shop Blackwell's anymore."

How had he found out? Robbie? No. But who? Her hands fisted at her sides as she sat back down. "I don't see why we can't. It's still our bookshop."

He gave her a pitiable glance, shaking his head of slicked-back dark hair. "Without a deed, can you really say that?"

"Uncle Julian, Granny Sadie would not have lied about owning this shop all these years. Everyone who knew anything about her praised her for her kindness and good—"

"I hate to say this so bluntly, Clara, but you need to remember Sadie Blackwell was a fallen woman. There's a good chance she did whatever she could to make ends meet as an unwed mother, and whatever she did to convince Ezra Long to let her use the building—"

"How can you say that? I know she wasn't your biological grandmother, but she took you and your mother in without hesitation when you moved here." Clara hated the way her voice rose into Minnie Mouse squeaks when she grew angry. "She helped you find a house and provided money for you to start your law business." *Such as it was.*

He had the decency to look away and tug at his collar. "Be that as it may, the truth is the truth, and, despite my family ties with her, I must seek to support my client."

Clara's face cooled forty degrees. "Your client?"

He released a heavy sigh and produced a paper from inside his suit jacket. "Sadie, I'm truly sorry that you and your mother find your-selves innocent victims in the middle of all this. Especially as it appears there is no deed of record for Sadie Blackwell's procurement of this building."

Oh no! Clara's defenses spiked. He'd turned on his lawyer voice. Not that he'd ever been a very successful lawyer. Most people who hired him either knew him, wanted someone cheap, *or*—Sadie's pulse ratcheted up a beat—needed someone who didn't mind skirting around the law a little here and there. Surely, he hadn't—

"Mr. Stephen Long, great-grandson of Ezra Long, the owner of this building before Sadie Blackwell took residence here, has asked me to approach you about coming to an agreement regarding the building so that he will not have to pursue formal legal action."

"Formal legal action?" Clara choked out the words. "Over what?"

"Over ownership of this property." He peered at her over the paper.

Clara's bottom lip dropped. No! Why, oh why, had she ever contacted Mr. Long about the deed in the first place? He'd twisted it for his own gain. Or hopeful gain.

"The fact is that legally this property belongs to the Long family, and Mr. Long would like it back."

Clara shot to her feet, heat rising up her neck to nearly explode in her head. "Mr. Long does not own this bookshop." Or at least Clara hoped not. "And I can't believe you'd represent someone who is trying to take it from us."

"Stephen is a friend of mine. He knows of my connection with you and your mother, so he thought I'd be the best one to approach you about coming to some sort of agreement."

"Agreement?"

He gestured for Clara to sit, and after a slight hesitation, she complied, although her body remained rigid.

"I'm working with Mr. Long on your behalf, Clara." He unfolded the paper. "Hoping to ensure some sort of financial benefit for you and your mother. With her medical diagnosis, the bills and expectations of future expenses must be significant."

Clara's eyes narrowed. Low blow. She'd not validate him. "We're not discussing my mother's health, Uncle Julian."

"But if it's uncovered that Granny Sadie never officially purchased this building, rightful ownership would resort to Mr. Long, and there's a possibility back rent could come due."

"Back rent." Clara's jaw dropped. "For what? A hundred years?"

"No one wants a big scene. Mr. Long wishes to ensure you can leave the shop with something, so he's willing to offer an out-of-court settlement, seeing as you had no way of knowing Granny Sadie never purchased this building. Here is what he is offering you."

He placed the paper on the desk. Written on it was such a low amount that Clara laughed before she could stop herself. She knew quite well the value of property located near Biltmore Village. Mr. Long and Julian knew too, which was probably the entire reason all this started. The offer wasn't even half what Blackwell's was worth. She stifled the urge to rip the paper in half. Her uncle had been waiting for an opportunity to take Blackwell's since her father's death.

"Can you prove Sadie didn't own it?" Clara pushed the paper back at him.

"Now see here—"

"I don't know what you and Mr. Long have in mind, but I can assure you, I'll pick through every part of this bookshop and travel wherever I need to go to find proof you are wrong."

"I'm giving you a chance." He stood, a sneer beneath his infernal mustache. "If Mr. Long can prove that Sadie Blackwell never owned the property, and you're not willing to take a generous offer for property that's not even yours, then the amount you'd have to procure for back payments would be substantial." His brow rose with threatening slowness. "And you own a bookshop, my dear, not a gold vault."

Clara pressed her palms against the desk and stood, refusing to give way to her wobbling knees. "You may leave now."

"I know this is all new for you, so I'll give you another chance to come to your senses." He pushed the paper back toward her. "Mr. Long and I will be talking to Judge Linden in two weeks, at which time we will make a formal complaint. This amount would allow you and your mother to start over without court costs and the real chance of losing everything you love."

A darkness hovered over his words, seeping through her with a chill. Clara held his gaze, daring him to offer another threat. She would not cow to him, the villain.

He lowered his eyes first and backed toward the door. "It's the best choice for everyone."

"Everyone?" Her question drew his attention back to her face. "And what exactly do you get out of all this?"

He didn't answer, but with a tip of his head exited the room. If she knew her uncle Julian and his past at all, she'd wager he was charging Mr. Long much more than a usual lawyer's fee.

She stared at the closed door, her forced breaths pulsing her chest to keep the tears at bay.

How could this have happened? And how could her own uncle be part of the shadow falling over Blackwell's? *Traitor.*

She slipped back into her chair and buried her face in her hands. *First Dad and now this? God, what are You doing? Don't You care about me and my mom?*

Her gaze drifted over the myriad papers on her desk to land on Sadie's Bible, the cover bending up at two ends and pages crinkled with use. Clara slid the book closer and opened it to the first page. A handwritten message was there. . .no, wait, it was a set of verses. The reference marked the bottom of the script. Isaiah 43:1–3.

But now thus saith the Lord that created thee, O Jacob, and he that formed thee, O Israel, Fear not: for I have redeemed thee, I have called thee by thy name; thou art mine. When thou passest through the waters, I will be with thee; and through the rivers, they shall not overflow thee: when thou walkest through the fire, thou shalt not be burned; neither shall the flame kindle upon thee. For I am the Lord thy God, the Holy One of Israel, thy Saviour.

The middle part had been underlined. By Sadie? Or Sadie's mother, Evelyn? The passage was followed by a short note. *Help me to walk with courage. You know my real name.*

Walk with courage?

"I am the Lord thy God. . .thy Savior," Clara muttered, rereading the verse. Savior? Yes, she knew Christ saved. She had responded to His call on her heart when she was ten. But the reference in this verse hinted toward saving even through other things too. Suffering. Pain. Fear.

"Like losing my livelihood, Lord? Will You save me from that?"

"*Or bring you through it stronger. . .*" The thought pressed through her like a whisper to her soul. Her breath shivered out. "But Lord, if it has to hurt, I don't know if I want to be stronger."

Her life hadn't been filled with loss like Sadie's. Yes, she'd put her dreams on hold to care for her parents, but she loved them. She *wanted* to care for them. Yes, she'd lost her father. Her chest ached with constant reminders, but Sadie had lost her son, her sister, her reputation.

"*I know the way.*"

But her heart pulsed. What would that way look like?

The door burst open and in stumbled Robbie, his face almost as red as his hair. "Are you okay?"

She groaned and ran a hand over her eyes. "I don't know."

He closed the door behind him and rounded the desk. "Faith told me about Dad stopping by, and being the stellar employee she is, she eavesdropped on the conversation, but only enough to give me the gist."

"Great." Clara squinted up at her cousin. "Now it'll be all over town."

"No." Robbie patted her shoulder. "You underestimate Faith's maturity." He winked. "And my blackmailing skills." His expression sobered and he scanned the messy desk as he moved to the chair his father had vacated. "What happened?"

She relayed the details of the visit, keeping her tears in check.

"I'm sorry, Clara." He shook his head and pushed a hand through his thick hair. "I know Dad's gotten himself into some financial messes lately, but—" Robbie growled and stood. "How could he do this?"

"He must be desperate."

"You mean selfish." He paced the room, his breaths pumping his chest in increased rhythm. "He's not only betrayed you and your mom, but me too. And why should I be surprised? The only person he's ever put first in his life is himself."

Pain creased his face and he held her gaze, almost as if he wanted her to confirm his loyalty.

"I know he's wrong about Granny Sadie. We can't let him take the bookshop."

"Of course we can't." His words ground out, low and tense.

Clara set her jaw, refusing to give in to the impossibility of the task. "Then we must keep looking. Everywhere. Take any lead. Even the crazy ones." She looked back at the scripted verses. "And pray for a miracle, Robbie, regardless of how the miracle shows up. We need one, and we only have two weeks to find it."

The old grandfather clock struck in the front of the bookshop, customers' murmurs filtering down the little hallway to the office.

Three o'clock.

Clara stretched from her hunched position over the desk, her workspace much the worse for wear after almost four hours of careful investigation. One box left after this one and then. . . ? Where would she look next? The attic had been turned inside out. Mom had scoured through all of Dad's things, and though Mrs. Carter had found another entry of Sadie's time at Biltmore, nothing shed light on the lost deed.

A worn ledger near the bottom of the box revealed purchases from the oldest dates Clara had been able to find so far, 1917, one year after Granny Sadie opened Blackwell's. One note from a local family praised Granny for her shop, thanking her for bringing such a delightful building to their town. Just as Clara placed the book aside, she noticed a piece of paper stuck to the back of the ledger as if stamped there by time's hand. As she carefully peeled it from its home, the letterhead snagged her attention first. *Biltmore.*

Clara nearly gasped when she noted the signature: Edith Vanderbilt.

November 17, 1916
Sadie,

What a delightful shop you've added to our village! I write "our village" even though it borders the outskirts of Biltmore, because you are a part of Biltmore and thus your shop belongs to our village, as I know you meant it to. I am so pleased to see how you've taken such a painful experience and turned it into something that will bring joy to not only others but yourself as well.

Those of us who live with grief must still live. One breath at a time.

With your love for books, stories, and people, I am certain the future of Blackwell's will prove much brighter than its beginnings, especially with someone as capable as you at the helm. Thank you for serving so many in both outward and secret ways. God knows your heart.

I look forward to visiting Blackwell's again and bringing Cornelia with me.

Sincerely,
Edith Vanderbilt

Clara sat back in her chair, studying the letter. So Blackwell's opened some time before November 1916, which means any documentation of a deed should reveal a purchase before that time. At least that narrowed the timeline. And what sort of secret service was Sadie doing?

Clara rubbed at her aching forehead and flipped through each page of the ledger, looking for anything else. In the middle, a piece of paper protruded.

Clara carefully pulled the yellowed page free from its confines. A well-worn crease created a definitive line down the middle, as if someone had opened and closed the page many times. Pushing back some of the clutter from the desk, she placed the paper on the flat wood and peeled it open.

A typed letter. Dated August 10, 1916.

Mr. Ezra P. Long
109 Main Street
Asheville, NC

Dear Mr. Oliver Camden,
    I am writing to confirm that I received your payment for 9 Elm Street in Asheville, NC, locally referred to as Brick House. Enclosed you will find the key as insurance until I can have the deed mailed to you. As requested, I have added Miss Blackwell's name to the

deed as co-owner. The legalities involved in trans-
ferring the deed with such particulars may take a few
weeks, but my lawyer has assured me you should have it
in hand by the end of September at the latest. Thank
you for offering such a fair price and I hope you and
Miss Blackwell will enjoy the old place.

Sincerely,

Ezra P. Long, Esquire

Clara closed in to reread the note, her shallow breath spurting.

A deed?

There's a deed.

She reread the letter.

Yes. Somewhere. Money was paid for this building. And Sadie's name had been on the deed with Oliver Camden. The same Oliver from Biltmore. . .and England!

Clara's laugh echoed in the room. This was proof Sadie had owned Blackwell's.

But how did a man who was only mentioned in a letter by his father come to have such a close relationship with Sadie that he'd purchased a building for her? Uncle Julian's accusations came back to mind. Had Granny Sadie been his lover? Was this payment for her services? A love gift from a wealthy man who would never marry her?

Clara shook her head, grabbed her purse, and pushed up from her chair. It didn't matter. All she needed was proof that Blackwell's belonged to her and Mom, not Mr. Long.

She rushed from the office, alerted Mom and Robbie of her plans, and headed directly for Mr. Lawson's to see if the letter was enough to document ownership.

"Clara, I understand how important this is for you and your mother, and this document certainly helps your cause." Mr. Lawson placed the paper on the desk that separated them, his kind eyes offering an apology he didn't voice. "But I don't know that it's enough to stop an investigation."

Clara leaned forward. "But doesn't it prove that the building was purchased for Sadie? That a deed was forthcoming because payment had been made? Ezra Long's signature is on the paper—a little faded, but still clear."

He nodded, reviewing the paper again. "I'll have to do more research, but usually we either need the actual deed, proof of registration of the deed, *or* more than one official piece of documentation to prove ownership."

"Like what else?"

"Another correspondence with Mr. Long about the sale? Copy of a receipt of payment, if possible?" Mr. Lawson rolled his narrow shoulders in a shrug. "Something more that will link the two."

After another encouraging comment or two from Mr. Lawson, Clara left the building, her mind spinning with questions about where else to look.

The darkened windows of the bookshop alerted her to the lateness of the winter hour. She glanced up at the sign hanging from two iron chains over the door front. Blackwell's. Her family name. But how much longer would it be there?

With a long sigh, she slipped through the side door of the building into the apartment.

"Oh dear, from the look on your face, the news wasn't as good as you'd hoped." Mom stood from the table nestled at the juncture between their kitchen and living area. "What did Mr. Lawson say?"

"Please don't share any news that will ruin the chocolate cake your mom just served up," Robbie quipped, patting his flat stomach as he leaned back in his chair. "It was too delicious for bad news."

She feigned a look of annoyance at her ridiculous cousin, who ate like a pig and still kept some semblance of a slender physique, and then she dropped down into a chair across from him. "The letter was certainly helpful, but he wasn't sure whether it would be enough to prove ownership on its own." Mom placed a glass of iced tea in front of Clara and a sudden weariness slid from her arms. "Thanks, Mom."

"We need more?"

"He says we need some way of proving a solid connection between Oliver Camden and Sadie to strengthen the validity of the document. Whatever the connection was." She reclined back in the chair with a sigh. "Were they married? Lovers? Did he give her Blackwell's as a gift to keep silent? What?"

"And you've looked in every known place here." Mom placed a slice of cake in front of Clara, the sympathetic tilt to her lips not as convincing as usual. "The attic. The storage room. Biltmore."

"Yes."

"Are there any other options? Even unexpected ones?"

"Right, like thinking outside the box," Robbie added. "Or the country."

Clara's gaze shot to Robbie's face. "What are you talking about? Outside the country?"

"Be quiet and eat your cake." Mom nudged a fork into Clara's hand. "And then go pack your bags."

"Pack my bags?" Clara stared at her.

"For England, of course," Robbie said, reaching for Clara's uneaten cake. "If you're just going to sit there with your mouth open, can I have a bite?"

"England?"

"I've thought it through, Clara." Mom needled Clara with a stare while Robbie took a bite of Clara's cake. "You have two weeks before Julian turns this into some atrocious legal battle. By the time you get to England, you'll have. . .what? Maybe ten days, at most?"

Her mom was going crazy. "Mom—"

"It really makes great sense." Or that's what she thought Robbie said with half a cake in his mouth.

"The Westons have already agreed to it. Gillie and I sorted it all out, so you can do research—"

"I can't just leave the country to go—"

"Do you have any other suggestions?" Mom folded her arms across her chest with one of those "you're not as smart as me" looks.

"I can't leave you here alone."

"Hey, I'll be here with her." Robbie forked the last bite of cake. "And we have Faith and James helping with the shop, not to mention Kayne. I know he's only been working here a week, but he's catching on fast."

Clara shook her head, the idea refusing to lodge into reality. "I. . .I have the children's story contest."

"Robbie can send the entries to you." Mom waved her hand in the air as if her words worked like a magic wand. "You can judge them from there, and you'll be back in time for the Christmas party."

The two closest people in her life were insane. "It's almost Christmas."

"Almost only counts in horseshoes and hand grenades," Robbie quoted, inciting an eye roll from Clara. "You'll be back for Christmas. That's what matters."

"And just think of all the lovely decorations you'll see while you're in England. Fenwick, to be exact." Mom tugged a small envelope from her wallet. "Isn't that perfect?"

Clara opened her mouth to respond then snapped her lips closed before rallying again. "I can't just take off to Eng—"

"Why not?" Robbie the rebel interrupted.

"I. . .I don't do things like that. Besides, what do we know about this couple? You've talked with them for a little over a week and now you're best friends?"

"They own a bed-and-breakfast, Clara. They're used to taking people into their house." Robbie pushed the empty plate back to her side of the table with a wink. "It's kind of their job."

"And all their reviews are marvelous," Mom added. "Gillie would love to have you. She said she doesn't have time to go through all the rubbish in the attic at Camden House, not with how busy they've been and now that it's Christmas rush. But she'd give you free access to whatever you needed."

Clara looked from her mother to Robbie and back, the idea still floating just out of reach. "This is crazy."

"A flight leaves tomorrow at noon." Robbie looked up from his phone. "Which gets you to Carlisle's Lake District Airport before breakfast."

"Book it, Robbie." Mom answered before Clara could even put words into a sentence in her mind. "Use the business card."

"Tomorrow?" Clara pushed herself to a stand and forced words into motion. "Fly to England tomorrow?" She stretched her palms forward as if one of them might come to their senses. "Tomorrow is. . . tomorrow."

"How very clever of you, dear."

And her mother was usually so sweet. "I need to pack and plan. And I need to go through some of our book inventor—"

"There is nothing you *need* to do that we can't communicate through email, if at all." Robbie waved his phone at her. "I've handled Christmas here before, Clara. Years of it. I'd advise you to get to your room right now and start packing, if you're so worried about it, since I just confirmed your flight."

"This is crazy." Maybe if she kept repeating it, someone would believe her.

"You said whatever it takes to find that deed, right?" Robbie reminded her.

If looks had power, Robbie's hair would be on fire.

"Exactly." Mom chuckled. She took Clara by the shoulders and directed her toward the stairs that led to her room. "Now go pack. You'll feel better *doing* something instead of sitting around here *worrying* about it anyway."

Clara stiffened at her mother's prodding but couldn't deny the truth of her words. If making a crazy, spontaneous trip to England helped save Blackwell's and gave Clara a focus in rescuing this family heirloom and securing her mother's financial future, then maybe insanity proved the best option?

Because despite good numbers for the bookshop over the past few months, Uncle Julian was right. They didn't have the money of heiresses to fix the past if they couldn't locate the deed to Blackwell's.

And just maybe…the secrets to Sadie's past lay in Oliver Camden's.

Chapter 11

Mrs. Vanderbilt ordered me on at least three days' rest, which Victoria interpreted as daily afternoon tea with her, and by his own invitation, Oliver. As much as I attempted to remain indifferent to the charming Englishman, he made it practically impossible.

When I insisted that I shouldn't join them for tea in rooms used for guests, Oliver used his effervescent charm to persuade Mrs. Potter into letting the two of them join me in the servant's dining hall, where he engaged in conversation with anyone from Mrs. Cox, the cook, to Mr. Leeds, the gardener, as if he didn't belong on the posh side of the green baize door. It became almost expected to hear his laughter in the below-stairs hallways. And conversation after conversation, a tremulous acceptance weaved its way into my hesitations with the frail hope that perhaps impossible things may not be as impossible as I'd imagined.

No! Even contemplating a relationship with Oliver placed me on an inevitable path of heartache and unemployment. I had an obligation to Mrs. Vanderbilt, though the very idea of Oliver with Miss Withersby irritated like a novel with the wrong ending.

With a little help from Mrs. Vanderbilt, I orchestrated an afternoon stroll between the two of them in the walled garden and watched them disappear across the library terrace, an early autumn breeze rustling the trees along their path.

My work had accumulated during my convalescence, but with only one available arm, returning books to their places in the two-story library took much longer and more energy than usual.

"I see you need a. . ." Oliver appeared in front of me and surveyed my arm. "Left-hand man to help with those books."

I nearly dropped the ones I held cradled in my right arm. "What are you doing here?"

He leaned close, his lips teasing a grin. "Well, in case you don't remember, I'm a guest, but please don't hold that against me."

Then, with his usual charm, he swept in and began helping me replace the books.

"You are supposed to be on a stroll with Miss Withersby."

"Oh no, my dear." His face flushed with false innocence as he placed a palm to his chest. "Mr. Dasher happened by, and I mentioned the theater."

"What?" The word burst out on a laugh.

"Didn't you know that Mr. Dasher is a lover of the theater?" He placed another book on the shelf above my head, his shoulder touching mine. "And Miss Withersby is not for me."

His attention dropped to my lips for the briefest touch, and my throat constricted as if he'd breached the distance. Did he want to? *Could* he want to? His gaze returned to mine and I suddenly realized I wanted him to want to.

I quickly shifted my attention to the books in my hands.

"But"—he continued, clearing his throat—"Mr. Dasher is morose enough to love theater and Miss Withersby is dramatic enough. So I think they may be a perfect match."

Despite my best attempt, my lips slipped into a grin. "You're not the theatrical sort, Mr. Camden? I find that somewhat surprising."

"Sarcasm?" He stood so close I could almost feel his smile spreading. "Now I know you're relaxing from all this pomp and stuff."

I raised my gaze to his.

"Don't give me that innocent shocked bit. You've lathered our conversations with plenty of sarcasm the past few days, so I won't allow you to resort to your shy servant role. Or do you want me to take you for the dramatic sort too?"

I scanned the empty room and lowered my voice. "I'm supposed to be invisible to you."

"Impossible." He tugged another book from my arm and studied the nearest shelves. "Besides the obvious, we've already engaged in too many personal conversations to remain distant. You speak in book language, love the great outdoors, have an imagination, are kind, brave, beautiful, should I go on?"

I pressed my cool palm to my cheek, each compliment increasing the temperature of my face. "B–beautiful?"

His sudden focus nearly drilled me into the bookshelf. "Don't you know it?" He tilted his head as he studied me, his gaze never leaving my face. "Has no one ever told you?"

I had no reply, and his expression gentled. "I'm glad to be the first."

The look on his face, his nearness and words, ushered a visceral acceptance. "So am I."

His smile creased the corners of his eyes and then he pulled in a deep breath and looked back at the bookshelves. "Now, let's put these books away so we can enjoy another tea with excellent company and conversation. Miss Withersby should be engaged on her walk for quite a while yet, and I'm sure Vicky will be coming down very soon with great expectations of biscuits and pastries galore."

The conversation moved from the virtues of the Reverend James Buchanan's writings—of which I'd only read a few works, but Oliver found them both devotional and stimulating—to the humor of Don Quixote, and finally to the unlikely romance, if the word *romance* could even be used in their case, of Romeo and Juliet.

All of which led to a deep discussion of the beauty of friendship and kindred minds in the development of the most intimate of romances. When the tea arrived, along with Victoria, we turned to discussing why most fairy tales should include dragons, at least in mention, and, of course, beautiful dresses—Victoria's addition.

"Mother never talks of dragons," Victoria said, opening her current fairy-tale book to an amazing illustration of a unicorn near a waterfall. "Or books, unless it's the Bible, and she talks about the Bible a lot when I disobey."

I poured her more tea and cast Oliver a grin.

"Mother isn't fond of reading," he explained.

"And Ollie said she outgrew her imagination a long time ago."

I caught my snicker before it emerged. "Well, I think you and your brother make up for the lack."

"That's what Ollie says." Her grin spread to double dimples. "And Grandmama."

"Oh yes, Grandmama would love Sadie," Oliver added. He turned to me with a raised brow. "Helen Camden, one of the few sensible women in our family, which automatically means she possesses an excellent imagination."

"She reads to me too, Sadie." Victoria took another cookie. "And does the voices like you do."

I failed to rein in my laugh.

"Sadie is one of us, Vicky." Oliver leaned forward, elbows on his knees, but his gaze traveled to mine. "It's not often that you find kindred spirits, so when you do, you make certain to keep them if you can."

"Then there's only one thing to do," Victoria said, reaching for another cookie. "We must keep her."

My brows shot northward. "Well, I don't—"

"An excellent idea, Vicky." His attention never left my face, the humor in his tone not reflected in the soberness of his eyes. "But she would have to be willing. We're not the sort that go around stealing perfectly good people. And for Sadie's part, it would take a great deal of imagination."

"Oh, Sadie has plenty of imagination."

I barely heard Victoria's response because the wordless request Oliver offered reverberated through me as if he'd shouted. Be with them? Him? Leave Biltmore? America? But I knew he meant it, and I wanted what he promised. Love, and friendship like I'd never known. A world of which I'd only read. A chance to be seen and see in return. What an opportunity! What a risk!

Did I have enough imagination? Was I brave enough?

Dear Library Fairy,

You were right about Anne of the Island. *Of course, I had to read the first two books to appreciate the entire story of Anne and Gilbert, but their friendship is an excellent example. I must say that I'm not certain I would have had the tenacity of Mr. Blythe to chase after his stubborn friend's heart, but he is portrayed in such an exemplary way, I am inclined to approve of anything he does.*

While reading these stories, I found myself wondering what a man would have to do to convince a woman of his intentions, especially if she's inclined to doubt his sincerity. Let's say she's a highborn lady and he's a valet in a grand house, yet at heart they are very much the same. Is there any hope for him? Or if the roles were reversed? What would it take for the young gentleman to convince the housemaid of his regard for her?

Since you are a fairy with magical abilities, I feel certain you would know.

Affectionately,
The Book Goblin

"She's done what?" I stared at my aunt, shaking my head to clear the words she'd just spoken. Surely, I hadn't heard correctly.

"I tried to talk her into waiting until you could be here, but she was determined." Aunt Elaine wrung her hands, her simple blue gingham dress falling loose against her thin body. "*He* didn't want to wait."

"He." I dropped down into the chair next to my aunt's small kitchen table and ran my palm over my forehead. "What do we know about him?"

"It doesn't matter now." She smoothed her hands over her skirt and sat across from me. "She's married to him."

"Married." The word raked over my throat in a rasp. Only hours before, I'd cradled the word with a whisper as I thought of Oliver and his most recent note. His intentions, though cloaked, had been unmistakable. He cared about me, much more than a passing flirtation. Enough to step over all social lines and make a way. Was it even possible?

But now, the tender word carried barbs. Lark had married Ralph Wolfe in a private ceremony and gone off on her honeymoon without so much as a note to me. Everything about the choice brewed with foreboding.

"Don't take it too hard, Sadie." Aunt Elaine placed her hand over mine. "She wasn't the sort to make things easy. Never has been, with that passion of hers." She chuckled. "The two of you as different as fire and rain. Her, so headstrong and impulsive, and you with your quiet strength and tempered emotions."

Too much like Austen's Marianne and Elinor?

My stomach squeezed at the notion, especially in regard to Marianne and Lark. But was I like Elinor? I'd admired her patience and honorable responses, but had nearly thrown the book across the room when I thought she'd lost her chance at love from such a good man.

I blinked. An unequal match, even.

"I'd wager your sister will be happy." She gave my hand another squeeze. "You should have seen her when she came by to tell me the news on her way to the train depot. She fairly glowed. And he looked so handsome and gentlemanly." Aunt Elaine nodded with a little too much excitement. "He'd bought her a string of pearls to wear for their wedding day. She looked lovely. So much like your mother."

My eyes burned with the warning of tears, but I swallowed the grief. What point was there in grieving now? I couldn't stop what had happened. All I could do was pray. Pray for her happiness. Pray that her rash decision ended in a good match. A happy home.

"I'm glad she seemed happy."

"Oh, she did, and he doted on her too. Wouldn't leave her side for a second." She tsked and walked to the stove, retrieving her teapot and a dainty, chipped cup. "This frees you to find your own way now." She set the cup in front of me and filled it with the light, amber liquid. "I know you were waiting to make sure Lark was taken care of before you looked for your own beau, and now you can."

I raised my eyes. The careworn ribbons over her forehead creased into deeper grooves as she searched my face. She'd worried over our futures and tried to take care of us after Mother died, though we'd been old enough to manage our own affairs. She never spoke of her story, of the childless home and her husband's untimely death, but the ache lingered in her worry lines.

She'd taken every opportunity to encourage both me and Lark to "settle down" and "not wait too long" for marriage, love or not, because "a woman belongs in her own home with her own family."

I wanted those things, but not at the expense of my heart.

Lark had made her choice. I couldn't influence my sister's life anymore. Nothing held me back from stepping into the impossible.

I kissed Aunt Elaine goodbye and walked out onto the street. The Brick House was settled among the trees at the far end of the street, as impossible a dream as a future with an English gentleman.

"*I've believed as many as six impossible things before breakfast.*" The Lewis Carroll quote teased into my mind. But a more treasured verse sank deeper into my spirit. "*With God all things are possible.*"

Even this?

I looked up into a sky of early autumn azure and offered an impossible prayer, because if hope lived anywhere, it was with the One who wrote the stories in the stars.

Dear Book Goblin,

I have been called to another part of the house to assist other fairies, but I've left you with a dearly loved book of mine. Cinderella. *The illustrations in this particular version are rather breathtaking, especially the next-to-last one. I hope you will find it especially meaningful, considering your earlier analogy of wealthy bachelor and poor housemaid.*

Fairy tales carry with them a unique ability to unfurl deep truths in a whimsical way. They also, this one especially, offer hope for those who feel magic is out of their reach. Being a goblin yourself, I'm sure you know that humans have lived outside of magic for so long that they've forgotten how to believe in it. You might have to help them.

The Library Fairy

I'd barely made it to the walled garden entrance when the sky opened up in a full downpour. With a look over my shoulder toward the gardener's cottage, where I'd just delivered some landscaping books to Mr. Leeds, I weighed my options. Dash to the conservatory to wait out the storm or attempt to make it back to the house.

Dampness seeped through my dress, chilling me to my bones, when my attention landed on the weeping willow just around the corner from the garden. Its thick branches draped to the ground and left a dry space beneath its canopy. I ran for it.

Barely had I made it within the haven of the branches and taken a seat against the tree's dry trunk, when another form pushed through the boughs.

"A library fairy's hiding place?" Oliver's golden hair curled in wet ringlets around his face, his smile in full bloom. "Is this where you've been all morning?"

"What are you doing out here?" I laughed, taking in the sight of him after missing opportunities to speak with him over the past few days.

"Well, I badgered enough servants until someone finally told me you'd gone to the walled garden." He nestled down beside me, dusting at the droplets on his coat. "Then, when the sky opened, I saw you dart in here, so I followed."

"You didn't have to risk the rain for me." I rubbed my arms, wishing I'd taken the time to grab my coat before leaving the house, but I'd only planned a quick visit to the cottage and back. "You're soaking wet."

"Not as much as you." He shrugged out of his coat and draped it over my shoulders. "Besides, after not having seen you for two whole days, I was determined."

"I had to take over another housemaid's duties."

"I know. I badgered that information out of the servants as well."

"Oh Oliver, what will they think of you searching for me?" I pulled his coat more closely around myself, sinking into his warmth and the scent of vanilla. Actually, at the moment I didn't care if the whole house learned I cared for Oliver Camden. All I wanted to do was sit beside him, wrapped in his coat, as the sound of rain pelted the world outside this little fairy space.

"I like it when you call me Oliver." He nudged my shoulder with his.

"It's a pleasant name to say." I tucked my chin low as heat soared into my cheeks from my declaration. *Oh Lord, help me. What am I doing?*

"Sadie." He pressed closer, his voice low. "I found your message."

"My message." I barely uttered the words, searching his face.

"And I want you to know that I brought my own magic." He took my cold hand into his warm one, his gaze locked with mine. "Enough for the both of us, if we need it."

His certainty trembled through me with the hint of hope. Yes, he cared about me. And I him. But how could this work? "I want to believe you, but it doesn't seem real. I'm a servant. I've never even owned a pair of new shoes. You live in a world so different from mine. Don't you think those differences will eventually pull us apart?"

"Are those differences the ones that really matter?" He brought my hand to his lips, and my breath weakened. "All I've ever wanted in life is a well-stocked library, a warm place to sip my tea, and a special person with which to share it all. I'm not afraid of hard work or meager beginnings. Things are just that, things. Magic makes the smallest meals a feast if love is a part of it."

"Love?" I barely worked the word through my throat. "You love me?"

"Can't you tell?" His smile gentled with the look in his eyes. "Don't you realize, we're two halves of the same whole. We understand one another at the heart level. No amount of money or prestige can deny such kinship as this. I know you feel it."

My bottom lip trembled against my best efforts. "We don't even live in the same country, let alone the same social class."

He released a long sigh, allowing the pitter-patter of the rain a pause within the conversation.

"What if we'd just met, you and I. You walking along the street in Biltmore Village and I coming in from work at the. . ." He looked up at the branches overhead.

"Sawmill."

His eyes lit. "Yes, sawmill, all covered with dust but still rather dashing." He patted his chest and continued. "I would approach you and ask if you'd take a walk with me. Of course, you would reply with. . ."

His brows rose, waiting for my response. He was so close, his pale eyes near enough to view the sunburst of gold around the irises. "Yes, I'll walk with you."

His smile flashed wide for an instant. "And we would talk for hours about books and our love for nature and the virtues of excellent tea and how ridiculously clever Shakespeare's Falstaff is."

"Or Dickens's Dodger."

"Exactly." He searched my eyes with such tenderness, it soothed like a caress. His words rasped, "Or Dodger."

"And we'd walk until the lanterns light on the street," I whispered, envisioning the conversations, the shared life.

"And then I'd accompany you to the door of your house and ask if I could see you the next day, and the day after that." His thumb brushed my cheek. "And every day for the rest of our lives."

With the slightest hesitation, his gaze holding mine, he crossed the inches between us and touched his lips to mine. Vanilla, fresh rain, and moist earth mingled in waves around me as he lingered, his palm rising to warm my face. I'd read of kisses, but nothing prepared me for how the touch of his lips against mine somehow reached my soul. All the hints of attraction and kinship his nearness had encouraged the past three weeks settled into a deep, sweet bond.

The chasm between upstairs and downstairs, the rift of our worlds, even the schism of an ocean, evaporated into the tenderness of such affection. My breath shook, my chest quaking as if this fragile connection bound my life to his and I would never be the same...would never wish to be the same.

With trembling fingers, I rested my palm against his chest and embraced this exquisite love, this whole acceptance, of one person for another.

He drew back first, a beautiful tenderness reflecting in his eyes, and I blinked back tears at the sweet realization: not only did he see me, but he embraced me as I was. His companion, his friend, his lover. His equal, capable of believing in this impossibility or hoping for a reality beyond my reach as much as he did. Love did that. It gave me courage.

"I have three days before I return to England to start my fall term." His thumb slid to rest on my chin. "May I write to you?"

My hand squeezed around the lapel of his jacket. Three days. So soon. "But send the letters to my aunt's house." No one could know. Not yet.

He pushed back a damp tendril of my hair. "I cannot be certain how long it will take and what I must do to make this happen, but if I send for you, would you come?"

I pinched my quivering lips tight, a wave of tears blurring my vision. "I don't understan—"

"To be my wife." He spoke the words on a soft laugh as if he could scarcely believe it as well. "I *will* find a way, Sadie."

How? When? Those questions dispelled beneath the confession that he wanted me to be his. "If you send for me." My breath quaked out the words. "I will come to you."

"Not if, my dear girl." He grinned, wiping at my tears. "When."

I laughed and hesitantly touched his cheek. "You sound so certain."

"I've never been more certain of anything in my whole life." He kissed me again, longer, sweeter, and my soul ached closer to his. "I will send for you, Sadie. I promise you, I will make a way."

Chapter 12

Clara stepped toward the tall glass windows after retrieving her bags from the claim area at Carlisle Lake District Airport. The small size, so much like the regional airport in Asheville, reduced some of the stress of trying to locate Maxwell Weston among the strangers.

Green hills, as if moss covered the ground all the way to the ridges, rose into the blue-tinted horizon. Clara wasn't sure what she'd expected to see. Rain. A foggy day, from what little she'd been able to read about northern England during layovers, but not this.

And since she'd had to leave in such a hurry, she didn't even know what Maxwell Weston looked like. There was no photo of him on the Camden House Bed-and-Breakfast's website, just Gillie's, but the view out those windows held almost enough reward to discount the Pilates-hold tension she'd felt in her stomach all the way across the ocean.

This land bloomed with fairy magic. These hills looked much too otherworldly, in all their emerald splendor, to only stay in the real world.

As she stared, the emerging sense of someone watching her began to permeate her imaginings. She pulled her attention from the beautiful countryside and turned toward the waiting area. People dispersed in various directions, meeting their parties or rushing to waiting cars outside, until the number had grown much thinner.

Clara's attention finally settled on a lone figure in one of the nearest corners of the room, half in shadow. She couldn't make out his face, but his form didn't resemble a contemporary of Gillie, who was in her late fifties.

He shifted a step closer, his face turned in a strange way so that the light shone on his right side. His derby pressed low over his forehead, shadowing his eyes. Sandy curls escaped from beneath his hat and covered his ears. He reminded Clara of a superstar who was trying to stay incognito. He dipped his head. "Clara Blackwell?"

His voice rumbled over the distance between them, soft and low. She'd never heard her name pronounced that way—a softer touch to the *A*'s and a curl to the *R*.

"Yes?"

He shifted a step closer, keeping his body still turned slightly to the left. Clara's grip tightened on her suitcase. She had enough clothes in there to at least knock the man backwards a few feet.

"I'm Max Weston." He offered his hand. "Mother sent me here to collect you."

His mother?

"You're Gillie's *son*?"

He raised his face then, his brows disappearing beneath his hat, and the first thing she noticed was his eyes. Warm and golden-brown, like tea with just the right amount of milk. Followed quickly by an unnatural discoloration of his skin down the left side of his face. The left corner of his mouth stretched down ever so slightly in an abnormal tilt. Either that, or he was as uncertain of her as she was of him.

Her gaze flipped back to his and he shifted to the left again, showcasing the right side of his face in profile.

This was crazy. Going with this man she didn't know to a place she'd never been to research a woman she couldn't remember was crazy.

She gripped her suitcase tighter and nearly whimpered. *But losing the bookshop was even crazier.*

"I can arrange for a taxi if you'd rather." The warmth in his voice had cooled to a growl.

"Of course not." Clara stepped forward, hand outstretched to stall his retreat. "It's just that. . .well. . .I wasn't expecting you to be—"

He raised a brow, almost as if daring her to finish her sentence.

"Young."

At this, his other brow joined the first beneath his hat and his jaw slacked.

"I mean, my mother has been the one corresponding with your

mother and since she always referred to Gillie and Maxwell Weston, I just assumed you were. . .not her son."

He snapped his lips closed into a fine line that puckered at the left corner where the skin took an unusual and reddish turn. Clara flipped her gaze from his lips and found him staring at her.

"I'm ready." She smiled to cover her embarrassment. "If you are?"

He reached for her bag and, with the slightest hesitancy, she released it to him.

"This way." He turned and took long strides toward the doors.

Thankful she wore flats, Clara rushed to keep up with his pace. He stood at least four inches taller than she and, despite the leanness of his silhouette, there was a strength in his stride. Of course, he may have been trying to put as much distance between the two of them as possible.

Oh, what had her mother and Robbie gotten Clara into?

The cool December air hit her cheeks as soon as she stepped from the protection of the airport. The horizon boasted a line of flowing mountains, so much like those back home, and yet, even at a distance something seemed different about them. Not as blue. More of a hazy brownish-blue, perhaps. Green hills spread up to meet them, as well as some sheep-dotted pastures. She chuckled. Sheep pastures? Right beside the airport?

Someone cleared his throat.

Max stood by an adorable red-and-white Fiat, staring at her with raised brow.

She stumbled to catch up to him. "Sorry," she murmured as she slid her carry-on into the trunk beside the suitcase he'd placed there. "It's all so beautiful here. And those mountains remind me of the ones back home."

He followed her gaze to the horizon, the tension in his lips relaxing ever so slightly. "You've never traveled to England?"

"Only in books." She offered a grin which he didn't reciprocate, but at least the frown around his eyes lessened.

He studied her a moment, as if he wasn't quite certain about her, and then rounded to the passenger side of the car without a word. She froze. She'd never driven on the wrong side of the road before, and especially not in front of a complete stranger. How could he expect her to even try? Didn't she need a special license or something?

When she didn't move, his gaze came up, the late morning light falling on his full face. Her attention flipped to his left side where his twisted skin looked pieced together in various shades of Caucasian with a few pinkish-red streaks. Burns?

She felt his stare, and volcano-like heat burst into her face. "Aren't you going to drive?"

He blinked a few times and the right corner of his mouth rose ever so slightly. "Yes."

He opened the door where he stood and continued to stare at her, and then she realized, this was England. And he *was* standing by the passenger door.

She released a groan that bent her shoulders before she moved to join him. "I'm not inane. I promise." She tossed him a look she hoped portrayed an apology. Conversations in a bookshop, particularly one she'd spent her entire life in, flowed much more easily than conversations in the real world. Or at least that seemed to be her experience, especially with her peers. "It's all just wonderfully distracting, if you know what I mean."

His forehead creased as he narrowed his eyes and stared at her for another long moment. "Welcome to England, Miss Blackwell."

He closed the door and circled the car to take his place behind the steering wheel, which put his left side in clear view. Definitely burns. Bad ones. From beneath his coat collar all the way up to disappear into his hair. She could make out the connected lines of the skin grafts, even though someone had worked to smooth out the skin tones so they weren't as obvious.

She pulled her attention away as he started the car. What had happened to him? Those weren't new scars. Did he remain in the shadows in the airport to keep from scaring her? Or others? Or was he that sensitive about his scars? Her heart squeezed in her chest. Could she put him at ease?

"I can't wait to see the Christmas decorations at Camden House. The photos online are spectacular."

He didn't so much as turn her way.

She waited in the silence before trying again. "It was very kind of you and your mother to allow me to come."

More silence.

"My mother can be very persistent when she puts her mind to something."

"From what I understand, she has reason for persistence," came his quiet response.

"So much so that we booked a flight two nights ago and here I am today." Clara shook her head at the dizzying sequence of events. "All the way here." She sighed as the horizon pulled her gaze to it. "England."

Scattered houses and buildings lined the road. White, flat-fronted houses. Typical metal structures for some of the buildings, but most of them were different in style than back home. She grinned as a house slid into view on a distant hillside. A dusty road led between two rock walls up to the rock cottage as some sort of green vine arched from one side of the blue front door to the other.

Enchanting.

Her heart quivered with a sense of familiarity she shouldn't feel.

But she'd been here before. How many literary journeys had she embarked upon where England provided the backdrop, and yet, even with all the images in her head and online, nothing could rival the real thing.

They drove away from the hills though the faint silhouette of mountains teased on the horizon. The buildings and houses became fewer, but many of the houses they passed still looked like something from a storybook. Stone. Tan brick. White limestone. Many with stone fences around them.

Though the gas stations mirrored those in America. A little pub cradled the roadside here. A small inn there. She nearly squealed when they passed a red double-decker bus, but felt certain Max heard her quick intake of breath before she pressed her fingers against her lips. A red double-decker bus. *Iconic England.*

And the cars seemed so much tinier. Or was it the road?

She snickered and garnered a glance from Max's periphery. Her face warmed. "The cars are so cute."

His eyebrow rose but he remained quiet.

"Like little ladybugs of different colors, you know?"

The corner of his lip twitched. "I'll take your word for it."

Quiet branched between them again to the point Clara pushed beyond her discomfort for another try at conversation. "How long have you and your mother had the inn?"

"Four years."

"Mom mentioned what a popular spot it is." She cleared her throat, attempting to keep the silence at bay for a little longer. "I'm glad you decided to stay with a more vintage style of decoration."

His gaze flipped to her, sliding from her burgundy wool bowler hat down her plaid wool skirt, thick stockings, to her vintage leather Angelique-cut shoes. She brushed at a nonexistent something on her skirt in response.

"Mum thought guests would enjoy a sense of history."

More silence.

He straightened, his shoulders tensing as if readying for some sort of battle. "Your travels went well?"

Clara blinked. A question? "Yes, thank you. It's been a long time since I've flown and never so far. I love the wonder of it."

"The wonder of it?"

"Humans arched above the clouds, flying through mist and sunlight, looking down at the changing landscape of ocean and earth. A God's-eye view of the world."

He tilted his head toward her as if considering her words but remained quiet.

Well, she supposed a few exchanges counted for something. He didn't seem the friendly sort, and she, as usual, blurted out odd things that most women her age wouldn't voice for fear of sounding as peculiar as she looked. Might as well complete the expectation in full authentic style.

Max steered the car away from the highway onto a narrower lane. The road weaved over hills and through hedge-rowed alleys, passing into little villages with quaint names like Bothel and Bassenthwaite.

"The towns are so small," she whispered as they passed another splattering of fieldstone and limestone structures, including a church, pub, inn, and restaurant of some sort.

"Were you hoping for a city?" came his quick response.

"Oh no, I much prefer this to a city." She nearly pressed her nose to the window to stare at the stone church nestled up on the hillside nearby, a graveyard to one side like something out of a Brontë novel. "As Anne of Green Gables says, 'there's so much scope for the imagination.' "

He made some sort of noise. A growl? A grunt? She couldn't tell, but she fisted her hands in her lap and attempted to keep her thoughts inside. Figuring him out required too much work for her comfort. Besides, she'd come to England to save her bookshop, not engage in awkward dialogue with a clearly reticent Englishman.

Just then, the forest fell away and unveiled the mountains, much closer than she'd expected. Not as tall as her Blue Ridges, but familiarly rolling one over the other.

"Oh, they're getting closer."

Max's forehead crinkled with a look of confusion and Clara offered an apologetic smile. "The mountains." As if that explained things perfectly.

He tilted his head, studying her, before returning his gaze to the road.

"I've lived around the Blue Ridge Mountains my whole life, so there's something comforting in seeing a similar sight in a new place. It makes one feel. . ."

"Safe."

She looked over at him, but his attention remained forward. "Yes." She turned back to the view, examining the landscape. "But yours have more of a brownish-blue tint than mine. I wonder why?"

Quiet responded for a few seconds and then. . . "There are much fewer trees on mine."

The way he said the word "mine" caused her to cast him a second glance. He merely raised his brow, sending her an unconvincing look of innocence. She squinted at him. Who was this guy? She reached up to straighten her very straight hat and turned back to the window. Somehow Maxwell Weston suddenly took up more space in the car than he had before.

Clara had barely kept her gasps under control.

The last half hour of the drive proceeded with back-to-back beauties, from white limestone villages tucked at the base of smooth-curved hills to rock-built hamlets nestling along crystal-blue lakes.

The only frightening part of the entire trip so far had been passing other cars on the narrowing road. Any time they neared another vehicle, Clara pasted her body against the door from fear of sideswiping the other car. She closed her eyes completely when they met a truck.

They turned off the main road and a beautiful gatehouse came into view, except it wasn't like any gatehouse Clara imagined from medieval history. Three stories of gray stone filled with tall windows covered both sides of the gate with miniature spires pointing into the sky at every corner. Her grin bit into her cheeks.

"It's like a miniature castle."

"And overgrown like one too," came Max's reply. "We opened this entrance back up when we bought the house, but for decades the owners used a back entrance as their main drive."

"And miss this? What a shame," Clara whispered.

"Exactly."

His simple agreement nudged at her grin.

As they passed beneath the gatehouse, a sign reading CAMDEN HOUSE welcomed her onto a long, narrow lane lined by trees. Above the tree line one of the mountains rose so close, Clara could make out how the colors shifted from emerald green to pale green and then a brownish-black foliage, which, from a distance, looked like parts of the peak had been scorched.

And then the house came into view and Clara couldn't catch her ridiculous giggle in time to hide it. "It's perfect, isn't it?"

She didn't expect him to respond, didn't really care. Whitewashed in a pale cream color, the walls of the country house glowed in the afternoon light. Georgian style, if Clara remembered correctly from her online search. A white portico stretched out from the matching, double-doored entrance as a dozen windows flanked each level of the elegant structure. To the right, a short walk from the house and connected by a stone wall, stood a small cottage of the same pale cream, most likely Gillie's house, from what Mama had told her. And in the distance, on the other side of what appeared to be a walled garden, an even smaller rock cottage nestled beneath ivy.

To add to the charm with the mountain behind and the forest to one side, a field slanted down from the house to the edge of a lake, also surrounded by those same lovely mountains.

"Do you ever feel as if you've stepped into a storybook living here?" The question slipped out and Clara looked away, reaching for her purse as the car came to a stop in front of the portico. "That probably sounds silly."

"I suppose we're all part of a story, one way or other. I do prefer the view in this one." He exited the car, leaving her wondering whether he was teasing or serious or. . .whatever.

She pinched her eyes closed. It didn't matter. Maxwell Weston was just the sort of person she didn't have the energy or time to spend peeling back the deep layers to see if someone more interesting lived under the surface.

Conversations could be hard enough as it was. A reluctant communicator was the last thing she needed to worry about.

She stepped from the car, the deep blue of the nearby lake reflecting the larger snowcapped mountains on the distant side. They rose steeper, with more pronounced edges, than the smoother hills closest to the house. "What are those?"

Max looked from his place at the trunk of the car. "Those are the fels."

"Fels?"

He closed the trunk, careful to posture his left side away from her. He shrugged a shoulder and averted his gaze as he slung her bag over his shoulder. "Mountains."

Stifling her groan, she followed him toward the entrance.

"Oh, here you are." Strolling from beneath the portico, smile in full beam and arms wide, emerged Gillie Weston, her shoulder-length golden hair spun with bits of silver. "I thought you'd gotten lost."

Lost? Clara looked from Gillie to Max and then checked the time on her phone. Two hours from the airport? She'd measured the distance before leaving home. It should only have taken them a little over an hour.

"We went by way of Bassenthwaite and Lorton," Max answered, casting a look over his shoulder to her. "And the Skiddaws."

Gillie's brow rose as she turned her hazelnut-colored eyes toward Clara. "He took you the scenic route, did he?"

Clara's attention flipped to Max's retreating form as he disappeared into the house. He'd taken her a special way?

"Of course, most places in Cumbria are scenic, but a drive through the national park is especially so." Gillie linked Clara's arm through hers and tugged her forward. "I feel as though I know you already, Clara, with your mother and I hitting it off so well. What a pleasure to have you join us here at Camden House."

They stepped over the threshold onto a stone floor that led to a large room tinged with untouched history. A double fireplace with a darkly ornate mantel stood on the far left wall of the room and various large portraits and landscape paintings dotted the sage green walls. Persian rugs ran the distance of the stone, leading to a wood-paneled staircase disappearing out of view.

"This is the Day Room, where guests check in or seek assistance." Gillie waved toward a desk on the far side of the room. "There are pamphlets about the sites in the general area, should you should choose to explore."

Clara's gaze lingered on the colorful pamphlets but she quelled the curiosity. Deed, first. Exploration, later.

"The library is through there." Gillie gestured down an adjoining corridor where the corner of a book-laden room came into view. "But few people visit it, I'm afraid. Not with digital books and the vast outdoors as competition."

Clara bit back her delight and ignored the overwhelming desire to detour down the carpeted hallway and befriend some of the neglected books. An arched entry opened to a room on the right, its windowed walls framed by various tables, all covered with white cloths and lanterns decorated with festive holly.

"The dining room."

"It's lovely." With crimson walls complementing the striking white trim, the room gave off Biltmore vibes. "And you have so much room for guests."

"Oh yes." Gillie continued up the stairs. "We have seven rooms in this house, two on the ground floor and five on the first, along with our carriage house to hire for larger groups, plus two more rooms we're renovating on the second floor as well." They continued rounding the stairs as the windows showcased the magnificent view of trees, lakes, mountains, and sky. On the third turn, the ceiling narrowed to lead onto the "second" floor, which Americans called the third. Floor-to-ceiling windows opened for a view over the high-walled back garden and the emerald countryside.

Scenes from Burnett's *The Secret Garden* tickled in the back of Clara's mind and she leaned toward the windows to examine the space below. A lone figure moved among the greenery, a melody rising to greet them.

"That's Max's special place," Gillie said, joining Clara at the window. "The garden. He took the tangled disaster the previous owners left behind and completely transformed it."

A gardener? Well, she hadn't expected that. Her gaze followed his easy movements, attempting to pair the uncommunicative airport driver with the whistling gardener below.

"It looks beautiful."

"You'll have to visit it when you're not searching through our rubbish." Her laugh lightened Clara's musings. "But for now, let me show you your room and your. . ." Her blond brows offered a playful wiggle. "Your place of possible discovery."

Chapter 13

I rushed through the forest from Biltmore Village, moving as fast as my skirts allowed, along the trail toward the main house. Darkness hovered on the edge of sunset, lengthening shadows into crisscrossed patterns against the forest floor. I pulled my coat more tightly about my simple cotton dress and increased my pace.

I'd stayed too long at my aunt's house, holding on to each extra minute I could spend with Lark. Minutes which had been few and far between since she'd returned from her honeymoon.

I'd wanted to leave the house as soon as Aunt had given me a package from Oliver. Everything within me ached to read more of the words he'd penned so faithfully over the past two months of our separation. Sometimes I'd receive as many as two letters a week, each deepening this unfathomable bond only God could have designed. He wrote of school and books and silly things happening, and of war and the many empty seats in his classrooms. Though he wanted to join his comrades on the front lines, his mother had, as Oliver stated, "fallen into an emotional tirade" to persuade him to remain in school since his older brother already represented his family in the fight. I rarely appreciated what he shared about his mother, as she presented as a controlling, unhappy sort of woman, and someone from whom Oliver wished to create distance, but in this case, I was grateful for her persuasion. What news we received of the war always came with large numbers of casualties attached.

I had stayed for an early Christmas supper at Aunt's, hoping to curb the growing concern I had for my sister, to no avail. I'd seen Lark only three times since she'd returned from her honeymoon, but subtle shifts in her behavior put me on edge. Yes, marriage changed people, of course, but some undefined foreboding grew with her bright smiles and forced enthusiasm. With every shifting of the conversation away from Ralph Wolfe and back to simpler things. A careless comment here or there, such as "business has been overly taxing the past few weeks" and "everyone loses their temper sometimes" took on veiled meaning.

She couldn't veil her eyes, and those spoke volumes.

The entire meal had been a practice in avoidance.

Lark averted details about her marriage and I dodged any particulars about Oliver except to say "a friendly correspondence about books."

Even as we'd parted ways, Lark in her elegant burgundy walking suit and cloak and I in my simple cotton dress and wool coat, the wedge of secrets stifled our usually easy conversation. I wanted to tell her. To share with *someone* this enormous feeling of loving and being loved, but caution stole my confession. The fewer people who knew of the true nature of our friendship, the better. I couldn't afford to lose my position at Biltmore while we waited for a future.

The forest darkened just as I reached the top of a familiar hill and the world opened to one of my favorite views. The hillside sloped downward toward Biltmore, framed by trees on either side and with a molten horizon glowing behind the tawny hue of the house. Despite the many castles I'd seen portrayed in fairy tales or European architecture books, nothing compared to this breathtaking collision of two adored sites. The house with its spires and gleaming roofline cradled by the familiar flow of those blue-tinged mountains. Two completely different worlds, but fitted together as if they belonged to each other.

I squeezed my parcel closer to my chest and smiled at the scene. Had God offered the same type of unexpected but beautiful belonging between the two very different worlds of Oliver's and mine?

The breeze rushed up the hillside and blew against my cheeks, bringing the scent of pine. Lights glowed in the house's windows along with the faintest twinkle of electric Christmas lights. It was magnificent.

Christmas at Biltmore held no equal. I'd witnessed it my whole life. The wreaths adorning the dark-stained front doors, the holly strategically draped over mantels, the carefully placed trees of varying styles throughout the public rooms, and, of course, the icing on the yule log. Then there was the massive Christmas tree in the seventy-foot banquet hall, lit with electric lights and adorned with Mrs. Vanderbilt's gifts for all the servants' children.

Even as I slipped around to the bachelors' wing entry, the pine fragrance encompassed me and helped dampen my previous concern for my sister. Perhaps her behavior was related to going from the responsibilities of being a baker's assistant to those of being a banker's wife. The contrast must be astounding. My mind embraced the explanation. My heart failed to agree.

I rushed up the servants' stairs and avoided two other maids in conversation by slipping into the storage closet to let them pass before completing the last few steps to my room.

Two letters and a package. I opened the envelope with the oldest date first.

December 9, 1915

My dear fairy,

How can you write a letter in such a way that I feel as though you're sitting across from me? It helps with the distance, though I'd much rather have you really sitting across from me, talking of books or whatever we liked. Or not talking at all.

I received three of your letters in one collection today. I fear the war may have disrupted the post, but as long as your words arrive, I will not complain in what manner they do. Thank you for opening your heart to me through your letters. I feel as though I knew you in part while we could talk of stories and characters in Biltmore's library, or life and nature over tea, but now, as you reveal more of who you are, my admiration for you grows with each letter.

Thank you for sending your tintype. I can almost make out the flakes in your eyes if I stare at it hard enough. I carry it in my school jacket pocket to keep you near me as I sit through tedious lectures or long hours of study.

As I enter the end of this term, I am thinking more and more of what really matters. I can think of three things. My faith, you, and my country. Fewer of my friends will return to university for spring term. They are enlisting, and I am compelled to do the same, though I have not decided for certain. I covet your prayers, my dear girl, especially for my friends and my brother, currently fighting on various fronts.

There is talk of conscription. Father will not like it and Mother will fall into hysterics. They'd hoped to keep at least one son away from the battle, but how can I refuse the call to fight for my country. I'd hoped to wait to enlist until I'd finished my education, but the need is great and our forces are floundering at almost every turn.

Which brings me to my current endeavor. I have employed what workers I can find to secure us a home, though it will be a unique one to start. It's not a castle, but you might find it a bit romantic and castle-like. Or at least I hope so. It should meet our needs for both privacy and distance, from my mother more than anyone else, and give you ample access to Fenwick, should you need it. It's taking longer than I'd hoped due to having to correspond with the workers from university instead of being on-site with them. Also, the number of able-bodied carpenters is drastically reduced due to so many being enlisted.

Well, that is enough talk on wars for now, but do pray for me as I decide what is God's will. I seek to serve Him and love you in all of my choices.

I've heard that Christmas is beautiful at Biltmore. Could you describe it for me? Fenwick decorates a tree in the middle of town, and all the shops sport their finest festive decor. You would love it. It's a storybook place.

I cannot wait to know what you think of the little Christmas gift I've sent along with my letter. Victoria helped me choose the perfect collection of items for it. She giggled so much in the shop, the store clerk thought I was tickling her, but in reality, the delight of choosing a gift for you proved amusement enough.

I must say, my face was sore afterwards from grinning.

I hope your Christmas is a happy one and that this gift will help me feel closer even though I am far from you.

Yours,
Oliver

I wiped the tears from my cheeks as I placed the letter on my bed and brought the package into my lap. With careful fingers, I peeled back the paper and opened a small box. The silver gift blurred in my vision as something between a sob and a laugh escaped my lips. A simple note sat atop a beautiful charm bracelet, each charm carved with intricate detail. The note read, *A hundred memories for each charm.*

I drew the bracelet from the red paper and wiped at my eyes again. Each little charm held rich meaning. A teapot, a book, a weeping willow, a fairy, a goblin, and a castle. I rubbed my finger over the dainty spires and smiled. I'd never possessed anything so precious. What could I ever give him that he didn't already own?

I placed the bracelet on my lap and drew up the other letter, carefully breaking its seal. It was much shorter than his usual notes and the script looked hurried. I smoothed back the page as if to calm his hand.

December 15, 1915
My dearest Sadie,

It's impossible to keep my mind on my studies, especially with so few of my classmates returning to university for the spring term. The war's casualty list continues to grow and I am here, waiting. I must join. I must do the duty of an Englishman for his country.

My stomach curled into a knot. I knew it had to come at some point, but now? When we were so close to a future together?

I will understand if you do not wish to become the bride of a soldier, if you cannot travel to a whole new country to marry me only to have me leave for war. I will bear no hard feelings toward you, my dear girl, if you cannot embrace the future uncertainties that this choice brings us. I will still love you for as long as I live.

Not become his bride? I quivered at the very idea.

It is too much to ask, to expect, and yet. . .if you are willing to join me, I will count it the greatest honor of my life, apart from the grace of God.

I await your reply.

Yours,
Oliver

If I left my world, my position, all I'd ever known and joined him, only to have him gone for years or even die, what would happen then? In a place of strangers, could I make a way? Find a way, as he fought in a distant land?

I could stay here. Release him to the war and even continue to write to him as he fought for his country, but he offered me something beautiful. The chance to be his. Even if war separated us soon after, I could belong to him in every way for whatever time God allowed.

I closed my eyes, a prayer pulling up from my soul. Did love make me brave enough? An answer pooled through me before I finished my wordless pleas. I knew my answer.

```
Western Union:
December 20, 1915
Oliver,
When you send for me, I will come.
Sadie
```

Chapter 14

The long front attic room on the second floor of Camden House had a window on either side, but Clara would never have known it at first because of the massive amount of boxes and furniture packed in every nook imaginable. Plus, there was no ventilation, so despite the wintry chill outside, the room held the stuffy combination of stale air, old furniture, and lots of dust. She did happen to uncover an excellent vase, two pristine and antique Chippendale chairs, and the most extraordinary ceramic bowl with hand-painted scenes from an Asian-esque landscape.

None of the items had any obvious connection to the Camdens, but for some reason, even in the short time she'd known Gillie Weston, Clara had a feeling they'd matter to her.

After four solid hours of rummaging through the first third of the room, Clara emerged into the second-floor hallway and breathed in the scent of fresh baked bread wafting up the open stairwell from the kitchen. Her stomach growled in response and she laughed. How on earth could she be hungry after eating the massive breakfast Camden House offered? Bacon, or as Gillie called them "rashers," eggs, toast, pastries, jam, fruit.

But even at the thought, Clara's stomach gave another groan. She slipped to her corner room, washed up, and changed into a fresh outfit, one of her favorites for winter because it afforded her the opportunity to wear her burgundy cloche hat. Of course, she adored winter hats of all sorts, but her dad had bought her this one, so it came with its own special magic.

Clara cast a glance over the gray countryside out of her double-dormer window. The morning rain brought out the green tints in the hills all the more and gave the lake a mysterious stormy hue. Perhaps she could go for a walk before delving back into her dusty exploration.

She took the stairs toward the buttery aroma, slipped by the grand Christmas tree decorating the corner of the massive dining room, and passed a beautiful sitting room and an elegant breakfast room which had been turned into a tearoom. The scent led her to the back of the house, where an indecorous kitchen enveloped Clara in its delicious warmth. A small table stood to the far side of the room with four simple wooden chairs surrounding it, the place where Clara shared meals with Gillie, Dora—the cook—and any other staff.

Gillie and Dora stood with their backs to the door, their merry laughter bringing Clara fully into the room. The whole inn exuded a sense of joy comparable to the glow of the season, kind of like the way Clara hoped Blackwell's shone in its little corner of Asheville.

"It smells delicious in here."

"Well, here you are." Gillie turned and stepped forward, an apron wrapped around her thin frame. "I wondered if you'd find your way out of the cluttered tower."

"I can't believe no one's gone through it in over fifty years." Clara sat down on a stool by the counter. "I found some things I thought you might enjoy seeing. A few chairs, a vase, and this exquisite bowl."

"You're to be searching for your own treasures, not mine." Gillie placed bottled water in front of Clara and shook her head. "But I see how you are. I recognized it from the start. You're a caretaker. And your mother confirms it, which is why I've been tasked with ensuring that you have a little fun while you search for that deed."

"I suppose my mother sent specific instructions?" Clara took a drink of the water. How much did Mom share? Did she tell Gillie that Clara hadn't traveled in years? That her last "girls' night" was during college? That she preferred quiet evenings with a good book and chocolate? That her last date was—Clara cringed. Who could remember?

"Enough for me to sort you out a bit." Gillie's grin twitched and she gave a lengthy study of Clara from head to toe. "And, of course, there is your excellent style."

Clara looked down at her wool plaid skirt, white button-up, and cinched burgundy vest, complete with a pair of lace-up ankle boots, and chuckled. "Old-fashioned, you mean."

"There's nothing wrong with enjoying old-fashioned style or old-fashioned ways. Taking good care of your parents never goes out of fashion either, dear girl." She patted Clara's cheek, holding her gaze as if she understood something she didn't voice. She stepped back with another appreciative glance. "If I could wear vintage as wonderfully as you, I'd do it every day. As it is, the only vintage I don on a regular basis is jewelry. And my husband had excellent taste, so I can don it quite often."

The usual uncertainty in meeting new people held no power in the presence of Gillie Weston. Her personality fit "hostess" perfectly, from the glitter in her warm eyes to the curl of her ready smile. And even though she wore elegant slacks with a ruffled blouse covered by an apron, her vintage jewelry worked with her hostess ensemble.

"You make it so easy to feel comfortable here. And I'm looking forward to whatever you have cooking in that pot."

"Soup and fresh bread." Dora turned, her round face wreathed in dimples. "The perfect combination for a chilly afternoon. We'll have it done in a trite."

Trite?

"The sky has cleared for now." Gillie waved toward the back door with her spoon. "After being cooped up in the attic the entire morning, I shouldn't wonder if a bit of fresh air would do you good. You could take a stroll in the garden."

The plants just outside the nearest window glistened with fresh rain, and the winding, gray walls hiding some of the foliage teased Clara's curiosity. An English garden?

As she stepped from the house, a cool breeze dampened her cheeks and awakened her senses to an onslaught of scents. Flowers. Plants. Earth. Clara followed the stone path from the back door as it wound through a matching archway into a world of brilliant colors and winter birdsong.

She felt as though she'd stepped from black-and-white to color in Oz. Purples and shades of pinks, reds, and blues. Tall draping trees and rainbowlike ground cover with a stone walkway snaked through the center. With rain still clinging to the plants, the entire space carried an added vibrancy, shimmering as if dusted with diamonds.

Her smile stretched wide, a childlike wonder teasing her forward. As she rounded an inactive fountain in the center of the garden, she nearly stumbled over someone kneeling there.

"Oh, I'm sorry."

Max paused before standing, turning his body so that his right side was more visible than his left. Her smile fell. Did he always feel he had to adjust to his audience?

Free of his cap, his curls flew in all directions, thick and full, the blond color highlighting the gold rim around his eyes.

There was an earthiness about him, from the loose flap of his brown jacket to the smudge of dirt on his cheek just above his red scarf. They made quite the pair. For an instant, Clara wondered if a passing onlooker would think a grown-up Mary Lennox and Dickon had stepped from their book and reclaimed their secret garden.

"Your mother suggested I take a walk around the gardens before lunch." His unsettling quiet forced her into unnecessary explanations that she couldn't seem to stop. "Soup and fresh bread certainly sound good for a brisk day like today."

He glanced back at the house as he dusted his gloves against his brown pants.

"I've always wanted to visit a walled garden, and yours is stunning."

His gaze met hers again before his attention rose to her hat. He stared at it long enough that heat began creeping into her face.

She raised a hand to her head. "My uncle says I dress like an old woman."

He cleared his throat and reached to pick up his spade from the planter at his feet. "It suits you."

Was that a compliment or. . .did she really *look* like an old woman? Robbie wouldn't have let the opportunity pass. She wrestled with her smile and finally lost the battle. Max must have caught her expression, because he shook his head and gestured toward her with his gloves. "Not that you look like an old woman by any stretch of the imagination."

"Well, that's a relief, though my dad used to say that I stayed cold like one."

He squinted up at the sky and then leveled his creamy gaze back on her, his mouth pinched tight as if reining in a smile. "Then you should have a good week for your visit, because we're experiencing unseasonably warm weather."

Clara bit her bottom lip to tame her smile and tucked her coat more tightly around her body. "Unseasonably warm?"

He held her gaze for a moment longer and then dipped his head before returning to the planter. "Milder weather is expected the rest of the week. Good for exploring the area."

She studied his profile, waiting to see if he might say anything else, but he remained quietly working in the soil. Where his mother oozed immediate welcome, Max made her feel. . .well, she wasn't quite sure, but at any rate, she'd have to hold her conversations for the ladies of the house, because Mr. Maxwell Weston didn't seem to be the chatty sort.

And why did she care, anyway? She would be gone in a little over a week. But something about him piqued her curiosity, and she couldn't explain it. Was it the "caregiver" part of her, seeking to touch a wounded life? Or the realization that she and Max were both a little more on the "old soul" side of their midtwenties than most of their peers?

Clara sighed and laced her hands behind her back, taking a few steps toward a wall of vining yellow roses. Hints of their sweetness greeted her greedy nose and she drew the fragrance deep into her lungs. What an amazing discovery in December! "I didn't realize how many flowers still bloomed in winter." She reached out and smoothed her fingers over one of the petals. "It's all so beautiful."

"Aye, with the proper care the flowers should stay magnificent for a while yet."

"It certainly looks as though you give this place the proper care."

He paused in his digging. "It's a way to pass the time, I suppose."

"What a wonderful activity for passing the time." She sighed and glanced around the rainbowlike pallet of color. "Like creating a story through flowers."

He still knelt by his plants, but had stopped digging. In fact, he seemed to be studying her from his periphery. Perhaps he didn't want company. The air suddenly grew a few degrees cooler and she slipped back another step. Maybe his reticence to talk had been a clue all along.

"I didn't mean to intrude on your work." Of course he wanted to work alone. Didn't most gardeners? She took another step away from him. Well, she didn't really know any gardeners, but it seemed like a solitary job. "I'll just leave—"

"This here is heather." He gestured toward a large stone pot filled with thin stalks of pink and purple blooms. "It's often thought of as a flower of good luck or protection."

She blinked at his sudden comment and looked around, allowing his words to sink into comprehension. An ornate stone planter filled with heather stood on either side of each entryway into the garden. Air burst from her in a laugh. "For wishing luck and protection as you go and as you come."

His gaze flickered to hers, a smile wavering over his lips. "That's the idea."

"It's a good idea."

His attention held hers, as if weighing her sincerity, and then he pointed to a bush with small flowering white-and-purplish blooms beside the heather. "These are daphnes. Temperamental, but worth their unpredictable natures in the long run."

She stepped closer, breathing in the strong perfume. "Are they the ones with the lovely smell?"

He nodded. "Though there are a few others with complementary scents to that one."

"And what are daphnes thought to mean?"

He hesitated, reaching to rub a petal between his gloved fingers. "Authentic beauty or love." His gaze flipped back to hers. "An acceptance as one is."

"Truly?" Clara stared down at the modest, unobtrusive blossom. How peculiar that such a simple flowering bush meant something so beautiful. She reached to breathe in the scent again. "These may be my favorites then."

She stepped back, a sudden lightness in her chest. How long had it been since she'd just. . .breathed in the flowers? She stifled the desire to twirl like a little girl, though her plaid skirt would have provided a definite princess swirl. As she turned, the large tree in the center of the garden regained her attention, its massive branches draping blossoms over the garden like a pale pink umbrella.

"Oh, that is remarkable." Among the other pale colors scattered throughout the rock-framed space, the tree added the final touch of magic.

When Max didn't reply, she looked over at him leaning against the planter. He was staring at her with a strange, bemused curiosity, his expression almost a smile. And, for some reason, with the same urgency she felt to discover the end of a beloved book, she really wanted to know what his laugh sounded like.

Heat branched up her neck into her cheeks and she looked back at the tree, welcoming the cool December air against her skin. "Is that a cherry tree?"

"It is."

"I didn't know they bloomed in winter."

Her stomach tensed in awareness of his stare, but she refused to look his way. She barely knew him and yet, something prodded her to age the newness of their relationship into something more comfortable.

"Does it have a meaning too?"

He didn't answer right away, but then his deep voice warmed the distance like the purr of a waking Keurig. "Cherry blossoms give the sense of living in the moment. Not wasting the time given us."

Live all the days of your life, as her mother said. "My mother often says that people tend to struggle between living too much in the past or living too much for the future, so they miss out on today."

"Hmm. . ." He took a handkerchief from his pocket to wipe his brow. "Words to ponder, for certain."

"But not so easy to live by." She ran her palm over the damp blooms of heather. "I'm afraid I spend way too much time in the future with all the what-ifs."

His gaze skimmed down her Victorian-style overcoat, and he raised a brow.

"Just because I dress in vintage doesn't mean I don't have very real future issues to keep my mind busy."

"A balance then?"

If she didn't know better, she'd say he dipped his head back toward the planter to hide his smile.

Who was this? He gave off the distinct aura of someone who hovered in the past much more than the future. His eyes had held a haunted look when she'd first met him. Did it have to do with his scars?

Clara approached the cherry tree, and the branches draped around her like a jeweled umbrella. The scents mingled together, filling her lungs with candied fragrance and inspiring a quiet laugh despite herself. Wouldn't this be the perfect garden to describe in a book?

"I think you may dabble in magic, Mr. Weston." She hadn't meant to speak the words aloud, but his response confirmed her gaff.

"Magic, is it?"

She turned to accept the fate of her overactive imagination. "To create something so beautiful and purposeful." Her hand gestured to the vivid landscape. "Not just in looks but there's. . .well, it may sound strange, but there's a certain feeling about this place. Maybe that's why gardens have a tendency toward enchantment in books."

"I think it has more to do with hard work than magic." Even as he spoke, the glint in his eyes teased a flickering kinship. "But there is a distinctive something about a well-tended garden."

"It's like a fairyland even in the middle of winter." She dipped her head so her hat helped hide her face, her voice dropping lower as her imagination delved into more fiction. "Or perhaps the secret is that good gardeners are really wizards in disguise."

"Wizards?"

She turned toward him, realizing he stood much closer than she'd anticipated. "Well, good magical stories usually need at least a wizard, a princess, or a dragon."

"I can assure you, this garden hasn't housed a princess in a very long time." The other edge of his lip tipped almost enough to consider it a full smile. "But as to whether I'm a dragon or a wizard, Miss Blackwell, I shall leave it to you to decide."

Clara's next morning search provided nothing eventful except a lovely landscape painting which would look excellent on the walls of Clara's guest room, which Gillie thought a splendid idea.

On her way to the garden for another walk—maybe another interesting conversation with the gardener—Clara took a detour through Camden's library. The immediate sense of welcome and the scent of books swaddled her like a hug. Rows and rows lined the walls, with a massive window, a fireplace, and two doorways as the only breaks in the columns of hardbound spines.

What a shame to have all these dormant stories. Clara slid her fingers along the nearest row. Books without readers were like homes without people.

The sun shone as she stepped from the doorway onto the back patio, and, as Max had predicted, the early afternoon air held less bite than the day before. Everything glowed awake in the path of the sun's touch, adding even more of a storybook feel to the wintry view. A gentle breeze permeated the air with a plethora of scents she'd experienced the day before, and she took off her newsboy hat to enjoy the gentle gusts.

She'd barely passed the threshold of the garden when she caught sight of Max. He stood on a ladder in the latticed gazebo, apparently working on installing some sort of lighting, but as he raised his gaze to hers, his ladder quaked. He grappled for the additional lantern resting on top of the ladder while trying to keep the half-installed one from crashing to the gazebo floor.

"Oh, let me help." Clara ran forward.

Max nearly swiveled off the ladder as he turned, but Clara caught the ladder just in time for him to keep both lanterns from crashing to the floor.

"Thank you." He steadied the lantern back onto the hook and continued to screw it in place.

"I'm just glad I came along at the right time." Clara studied the few lanterns he'd already installed, visualizing the plan. "This will be a perfect place to sit in the evenings to enjoy the garden and the view."

"Just putting my magic to work."

Her smile split wide at his reference to their earlier conversation. Maybe he was warming up to dialogue after all. "Clever of you to disguise it with lanterns and a wobbly ladder to throw me off your trail."

He leaned forward, staring down at her, his elbows leaning on the top of the ladder. "I'm afraid I must pull out all the stops when the experts are about. Mum's wanted an outdoor dining area for several months now and finally decided on her lanterns of choice."

The iron lanterns curved with old-fashioned detail, similar to an ornament she'd seen hanging from a historic carriage during a museum tour once.

"She could easily fit three or four small tables in here. And wouldn't this be the most enchanting wedding venue!"

"Enchanting." He opened his palm for the lantern she held, his lips pressed too tight to hide his amusement.

"You think I'm silly." She pressed it into his palm.

"Quite the contrary." He began attaching the lantern to the hooks he'd already put into place. "Few people possess the perseverance to pester me into talking."

She folded her arms across her chest and waited for him to look at her. "So I'm a nuisance."

His smile nearly unleashed. "How was your plundering of the attic today?"

Nice avoidance, but he'd asked her a personal question so, she'd forgive him. "The spiders were extra friendly." She rubbed at her stiff shoulders. "But I'm glad to take a break and stretch my legs a little."

He skimmed her from toe to head before turning his attention to something in the distance beyond her. "Out the east door of the garden, there's a path that leads to something you may find interesting. About a mile out."

"Trying to get rid of the nuisance already?"

He held her gaze for a moment before turning back to the lantern. "Perhaps it's a magical path and I'm sending you on an adventure?"

She shoved her hat back on her head and chuckled. "I'm not sure whether to be terrified or intrigued." And with that, she set off on whatever adventure or misadventure Max Weston introduced.

The gentle, relaxed rhythm of this quiet, idyllic life suited Clara. The earth and sky. Tea, books, and gardens. A vastness of rolling hills and lush countryside. Of birdsong and rain-scented air. How strange to feel a sense of belonging in a place she'd never been before.

The scenery ushered her toward the lake Gillie referred to as Derwentwater. The mountains surrounding the lake were called things like Great Gable and Scafell Pike. She grinned. Definitely magical.

A gray stone steeple rose above the tree line on a hill ahead. A chapel, barely half the size of All Souls in Biltmore Village back home, but beautifully fitting to its surroundings. Two massive oaks rose into the blue afternoon sky, towering on either side of the steeple. Gravestones littered the grassy hill as if tossed in haphazard fashion.

She skimmed over the legible names on the smaller stones as she climbed the hill, some of the dates on the graves over four hundred years old. Nearest the church, stood three very different graves than the rest: two larger headstones, a decorative headstone featuring a Celtic cross, and in between them, a monument.

The towering memorial displayed one word. CAMDEN. With careful steps, Clara rounded the monument to view the front of the cross headstone. Two graves rested beneath it, both marked with the symbol of a World War I soldier.

Clara bent to read the first.

ROBERT LAWRENCE CAMDEN
5TH LANCERS
10 NOVEMBER, 1918
26 YEARS OLD

Was this Oliver's brother? Clara slid her attention to the neighboring grave, her breaths growing shallow, her heartbeat pounding in her ears. She knelt to brush loose leaves from the stone, and the name materialized.

OLIVER CHRISTOPHER CAMDEN
FIELD ARTILLERY, YORKSHIRE REGIMENT
25 MARCH, 1916
22 YEARS OLD

Here he was. The man so intricately connected with Sadie Blackwell, yet still such a mystery. How had they known one another? Had Sadie grieved his death?

Mrs. Carter's Biltmore letter was dated November 1915, so four months earlier, he'd been alive. Six months earlier, he'd been at Biltmore. She trailed her fingers over the lettering of his name, pushing back some of the dirt. Why did it feel as if she knew him?

Just letters on stone, but they stood for a person. A soul. A young man with a story, with hopes. Maybe even with someone who'd loved him.

Had Sadie been that someone? The realization emerged

like the solution to a mystery. Could Oliver Camden be Clara's great-grandfather?

A twig crunched to her left and she turned to find Max nearby. He stood, hands in the pockets of his brown jacket, his profile turned away from her. For some reason, she'd expected him. He didn't speak, almost as if he embraced the reverence of the discovery too.

She traced over the name again before breaking the silence. "I know it sounds strange, but do you think the lives of people in the past can reach through time and touch us in the future?"

He didn't answer right away. The wind rustled through the trees. A cow lowed in the distance.

"I think there are certain stories that leave a more timeless impression than others. Yes."

"Those men who fought." The reality of their plight, the utter loss pressing in on her. She waved toward their headstones. "Twenty-two years old. Twenty-six?"

She looked up at him, searching his expression and finding, no, more like *feeling* mutual understanding. "I wonder if we even understand what it's like to be brave nowadays." She brushed back a small branch from the headstone. "Oliver was brave." The bookshop came to mind. "Sadie was brave too."

Silence whispered between them again.

"Perhaps we have to look a little harder for the brave ones, for the courageous, in our time, but I believe they're still alive and well if we know how to search for them, how to see them." Max offered his hand, and something in his simple gesture solidified his statement about modern-day heroes. With a slight hesitation, she slid her fingers into his and he pulled her to a stand.

"You're right. We just have to look for them." She turned back to the graves and snapped a few photos with her phone.

"Perhaps, on our way back to the house, you can tell me this story of Sadie Blackwell?" He fell in step beside her as they weaved their way back to the path. "It sounds like a tale I ought to know."

Chapter 15

I hesitated before knocking on the door of the Oak Sitting Room. Walking through that door set in motion a chain of events that would change the course of my future forever. Not only would I forfeit this coveted position at Biltmore and leave the world I'd always known, but based on the letters and conversations I'd had with Oliver, Mrs. Camden wouldn't be particularly accepting of her son's choice of a wife. Yes, he was sacrificing his status in society to marry me, but I had a feeling he may be relinquishing even more. Both our dreams hung on a precipice.

I drew in a deep breath and closed my eyes, whispering one last prayer for strength. Courage wasn't courage without fear, and as my heart trembled from the uncertainty of the great unknown, I held to God's assurance. Whatever the future held, He was already there.

And whatever waited for me, I wanted Oliver to be a part of it.

My knock resounded with the finality of my choice.

At Mrs. Vanderbilt's invitation, I pushed open the heavy oak door and stepped forward. Her look of welcome began to dissolve as I approached. Perhaps it was the way I clutched the letter in my hand, as if a lifeline, or perhaps she read my intention well before I spoke, but whichever the case, she gestured toward the chair in front of her desk, ever gracious.

But my throat refused the words access.

"It's all right, Sadie. Whatever you have to say, it will be all right."

"Thank you, ma'am." Her gentle words nearly unlocked my waiting tears. "You cannot know how much I appreciate your kindness to me and my family all these years." I swallowed through the lump gathering in my throat. "And I've loved having the opportunity to step into my mother's position and enjoy the service and treasures of your library."

"Loved?"

I smoothed my hands over the letter and steadied my attention on the grand lady. "With heavy heart, I've come to resign my position at Biltmore."

The only reaction from Mrs. Vanderbilt was a barely audible intake of breath.

"I'm so sorry." My voice broke and I pinched my lips closed, lowering my eyes.

"What has brought about this decision? Has someone treated you unkindly?"

"No, ma'am." I looked back up at her. "Biltmore has been a wonderful place to work, but I find that my future lies elsewhere."

"I see. I'm sorry to hear you'll be leaving us." She folded her hands together, head slightly tilted as she studied me. "Are you in some sort of trouble, Sadie? You know I am willing to help you if I can."

My throat closed with tears. "You are all kindness, ma'am, but I. . . I am in no trouble." Or at least, not yet, but with an ocean to cross and a soldier to marry, the future hung with as much shadow as light. "I am leaving to take an. . .opportunity."

"An opportunity that keeps you nearby?"

I hesitated before answering. "No, ma'am."

Her gaze steadied on mine, as if reading every worry line on my brow. "An adventure far away then?"

"Yes, ma'am." There was no point avoiding the truth. She'd learn soon enough. "Very far away. Across an ocean, even."

Her gaze sharpened and then her attention dropped to the paper in my hand, comprehension dawning. "Oliver Camden."

It wasn't a question. I lowered my gaze. "Yes."

The silence dug into my confidence and I pinched the letter more tightly.

"How soon?"

"My ship leaves in a week, and, if I might be so bold, I feel as though Laura would be an excellent replacement for me. She has no idea of my plans, but she loves reading and has a quick mind."

She studied me, the tension in her expression thawing into a sad smile. "You've been planning this since he left?"

"Hoping for it more than planning, ma'am." I jolted pencil-straight in my chair. "But, please know, I didn't pursue anything with him. I give you my word. It all happened—"

She raised a palm to stop me. "Knowing Mr. Camden as I do, I have no doubt *he* set his cap at *you*. He's not one to stand with protocol or expectation that he deems unimportant." Her smile bloomed. "Oliver is a smart enough man to love with much more than his eyes or his purse, but with his mind and his heart. From the first time I saw the two of you engaged in conversation, I realized Miss Withersby didn't stand a chance."

My face must have reflected my surprise, because she chuckled. "I have eyes everywhere, Sadie. Haven't you learned that by now? Most of the time, they're my own."

My cheeks flamed hot. Did she have spies in the garden, particularly near a certain weeping willow?

"But your secret is safe with me until you choose to share your story. He is a good man. And Miss Withersby has happily found her match in the young and melancholic Mr. Dasher." She placed her palms on the desk and leaned forward. "I shall miss you. Like your mother before you, you have been an excellent member of my staff."

"Thank you, ma'am. It has been my honor."

"And before you leave, I wish to give you this." She brought out a little item wrapped in paper from a drawer in her desk. "I'd planned to give it to you at the Christmas party, but it felt too intimate for such a time." She placed it on the desk within my reach. "This was something I meant to give to your mother last Christmas, but she passed before I could. I'd like for you to have it."

The paper fell away to reveal an ornament. The intricate orb glowed with red-and-golden blown glass, and carved in the center lay an open book. One of the open pages held the scripted words *Read a story* and on the other open page, *Live a story.*

"It's beautiful," I whispered, brushing away a tear.

"You've spent years reading books and helping others fall in love with stories." Mrs. Vanderbilt's gaze softened with her smile. "Now it's time for you to live one of your own."

A bruise darkened Lark's cheekbone, even though she'd attempted to disguise it with powder. But with a turn and the way the lantern light hit, I saw. That paired with the dullness in her eyes and the way she diverted questions gave me all the information I needed.

"He's hitting you?"

Her body stiffened but she didn't look up from her tea. We'd chosen to meet at the bakery where Lark had worked, but it had taken her until my final day in Biltmore to schedule a time.

"You still haven't told me why you spent the money you've been saving to update your wardrobe. Is it because of this Oliver fellow?" Lark waved toward my simple but new green day suit. "Or are you just jealous of my excellent style?" She laughed a hollow sound.

I smoothed the sleeve of my jacket. Oliver had sent a ticket and transportation money to cover travel costs, but, as was likely the case for a man, he hadn't considered that the only clothes I possessed were hand-me-downs or servants' attire. And since I'd learned that Brick House had been recently purchased, I'd taken out my disappointment on shopping for my trousseau. Items I'd always wanted, but never dared buy. Nothing outrageous, but things I thought Oliver would like and items that would hopefully disguise my class difference.

"You didn't answer my question, which provides more confirmation than not."

"Does it really matter, Sadie?" An edge tinged her words, her gaze locked with mine. "I made my choice. I wasn't blind, but I chose to be. He gave off signs that I refused to see because the desire to live above the dust and bone-aching work we've come to know meant more to me than. . ." She raised her hand to her cheek. "Than this."

"A man should never strike his wife."

She stared at me for a long instant and then relaxed back into the chair. "He's only like this when he drinks too much. Otherwise, he's perfectly civil." She shrugged a shoulder. "Sweet, even."

"And with the way his business is going, do you think he's going to be inclined to drink less or more?"

Lark's face paled. She'd told me enough, and I'd read the papers enough, to know that Ralph's bank wasn't in the finest shape. She refused to answer.

"You cannot stay with him, Lark. It's not safe."

"Where else would I go, Sadie?" Her gaze quivered in mine. "Back to Aunt Elaine to live with nothing? A wife who left her husband because he secretly took out his anger on her? No one will believe me."

"Then I will send for you." I grabbed her gloved hand. "Once Oliver and I are settled, I'll send for you to come to me. Ralph won't chase you across an ocean."

"Come to you?" She shook her head. "An ocean? What are you talking about?"

"It's why I've been trying so desperately to meet with you." I steadied my gaze in hers. "He's sent for me and I'm going."

"What?" Her bottom lip dropped. "To England?"

"Yes. I would have told you sooner, but—"

"You're going to England?" The pitch in her voice rose with her volume. "Does Aunt Elaine know?"

"Yes, I told her last week." She'd kissed me and cried on my shoulder but wished me all the joy in the world, although I felt certain she thought I would die aboard ship. "You may justify Ralph's behavior all you want, but what will you do when there are children? And what if he becomes worse, Lark?"

A tinge of fear shimmied across her expression and my stomach sank. He'd already become worse. More than she'd imagined.

"If I send for you, will you come?" The words echoed with memory. Oliver. I almost smiled. He'd support my decision to invite Lark, to rescue her, whatever it took.

"To England?"

I nodded. "Oliver would agree with me. I know it." I squeezed her hand. "You must write to me, Lark. Keep me informed."

Her eyelids drifted closed, and when she opened them again, sadness dulled her eyes. "I will write to you. I promise to be a better sister, even as you leave to go thousands of miles away." She drew in a breath and squeezed my hand back. "But it's not your job to rescue me, Sadie."

"Lark—"

"No." She shook her head and pulled her hands away. "You're making your choice. I made mine. We both must live with the consequences of our decisions. Whatever those may be."

I waited for the seasickness, but, thankfully, it never came. For six days, as the steamship sped over the Atlantic, I mingled in a world almost as grand as Biltmore. The sea bathed me in salt air and crisp wind, beyond anything I'd ever read of, and yet, the descriptions in dozens of stories had, somehow, prepared me for the wild beauty and endless horizon. Waves spilled, one over the other, on some eternal race to the horizon, showcasing colors in every hue of gray, blue, and green.

The air tinged with promise, adventure, and, like the ornament Mrs. Vanderbilt had given me said, I embraced this moment of living my own story, even if I couldn't see over the aqua horizon. God was there. And here. And all the places in between. Couldn't I trust Him with the horizon as I trusted this ship to carry me to Oliver?

I'd researched the route and found several photo books showcasing steamships and Liverpool. I'd even sorted out how to transfer from the docks to the nearest train depot set for Fenwick, in the instance Oliver was delayed, but I shouldn't have worried. I'd barely reached the top of the gangway when I heard my name shouted from the dock below.

At first, the crowds blurred into one conglomeration of joyful outcries, but then, from the center of the spectators, he appeared, waving his hat in the air, his smile wide. Every doubt, every little worry that had dogged me across the ocean, faded away. Some dreams were meant for us to carry alone. Others were made to share.

I'd barely made it to the bottom of the gangway before he swept me into his arms and peppered me with kisses, his laughter blending in with my own.

"You're here." He paused, his hands on my shoulders as he examined my face. "And you look even more beautiful than I remember, which is quite the compliment."

I raised my hand to his cheek, touching him with the confidence and intimacy afforded an engaged woman. "I'm so glad to see you."

His smile gentled and he kissed me again, this time lingering a second longer than the ones before. "I'm tempted to take you to the church straightaway instead of waiting until tomorrow, but that wouldn't be very loving of me, would it?" He brushed back a loose strand of my hair and then braided his fingers through mine. "You deserve a good night's sleep and some time to prepare, as any bride should."

"I would marry you right away."

"Oooh." He narrowed his eyes and waved a finger at me. "Don't tempt me, my dear girl. I'm trying to be unselfish and the very embodiment of a gentleman, and no reputable clergy would go against the rules of the marriage banns. But for now I'll revel in having you within arms' reach." He laughed and pulled my arm through his. "First, we'll gather your things and then ride to the station, at which time we'll be able to happily converse during the long ride to Fenwick." He pressed his hand over mine against his arm. "Or you can fall asleep and I'll happily admire you resting beside me, even if you snore."

I gave him a playful jab, and somehow it was as if all those months apart disappeared. And now, I was free to be his, in front of the whole world.

"I'll escort you to Grandmama's for this evening—as we planned—and then tomorrow, she has promised me that she will get you to the church, posthaste." His smile faded from his profile as we walked along the dock. "But I must warn you, my beautiful dear, I have been unable to convince my mother to attend." He paused and turned to face me. "You know I hoped she'd have a change of heart, but she won't accept *you* apart from your class."

A heaviness sank through me, for his sake more than mine. "I'm sorry, Oliver."

"No matter." He shook his head, renewing the walk. "I've disappointed her most of my life, but I didn't want you to have to bear her disdain. What she misses from life due to her prejudice!"

"As long as I have your favor, I can bear whatever she launches at me."

"Till death us do part, my beautiful dear." His smile resurrected in full bloom and he leaned over and kissed my cheek. "You can do no wrong in Victoria's eyes, as well as my father's, though he keeps his admiration quiet for fear of Mother's wrath."

I squeezed in close to him, admiring his profile and wondering at how all these beautiful feelings could fit inside without rupturing my chest. Tomorrow, I would belong to him, with him, forever, and I couldn't imagine anything on earth so wonderful. Tears crept into my vision and my feet faltered.

He turned to me, his gaze sobering with concern, but I smiled. "I love you, Oliver Camden."

And with that admission, he laughed loud enough to garner attention from those nearby, grasped both my hands in his, and brought them to his lips. "I will not take it for granted, Sadie. We are in this together, my dear girl. Whether wars or fiercely unhappy mothers or time itself, we can weather them all."

Chapter 16

Nothing. Not one hint of Oliver Camden or a deed to Blackwell's. Anywhere.

Clara stared out the attic window on the opposite side from where she'd begun. Maybe one more day of searching the attic and she'd finish. Then what? Where else could she look?

She reached her hand into her skirt pocket and her fingers slid around a key ring. Maybe all hope wasn't gone.

Gillie had given her an old set of keys on her first morning at Camden House and suggested searching some of the outbuildings if the attic didn't prove successful, but was the effort really worth it? Just because Sadie had some connection to an Oliver Camden over one hundred years ago didn't mean any of this pillaging through decades of debris would provide any documentation to prove their connection. A century was a long time.

Clara dropped down on an antique rocking chair she'd uncovered and rubbed at her tired eyes. After her phone call with Mom last night, she really needed to return home. Uncle Julian had made an unwelcome visit, stirring up anxiety with his veiled threats and leaving Mom more rattled than she'd admit. Thankfully, Robbie had intervened, but the fact that Clara had been in England five days with nothing to show for it but a photo of a soldier's grave didn't bode well for Blackwell's future.

Lord, I know that You are in control of everything, even the dead-end roads, but I could really use Your help right now.

"You look as though you need a break."

Clara peered up to find Max standing in the doorway, his smile quirked with what she was beginning to recognize as his preferred expression. Bemused. He wasn't wearing his usual brown gardening attire, but instead sported a pair of jeans and red fitted sweater, both of which accentuated the sturdiness his large jacket had cloaked that first day at the airport.

Clara looked away, blinking at the turn of her thoughts. She wasn't currently searching for an Englishman. She stifled a groan. Well, to be honest, what American female avid reader didn't daydream about an Englishman now and again?

But right now, she needed to find a deed and get back home. Besides, Max probably wasn't even interested in some old-fashioned, daydreaming American woman who was very close to losing her source of income.

She breathed out a sigh and rocked back on her heels. "What did you have in mind?"

"A trip to Fenwick, perhaps?"

Clara pushed up from her crouched position and dusted off her skirt, casting him a grin. "Venturing away from the garden, Mr. Weston?"

"Only when absolutely necessary, you understand, and Fenwick isn't really venturing far." He patted the doorframe, scanning the room before his gaze returned to hers. "Besides, I'd be remiss in not introducing you to the village."

"Why do you say that?"

"I believe it's exactly your sort of place." His brows rose. "Magical, even." He stepped away from the threshold into the hallway as Clara met him. "Perchance, do you know how to ride a bicycle?"

She looked down at her plaid flared skirt and vintage-styled blue sweater. "A bicycle?"

He shot a grin over his shoulder before disappearing down the stairway. "You'll look like one of the ladies from *Call the Midwife*."

A laugh burst from her as she chased after him. "You watch *Call the Midwife*?"

"Only because I love my mother."

Okay, maybe crushing on her current Englishman wasn't such a waste of time after all.

A pair of old-fashioned-looking bikes waited at the front of the house. The one for Clara even had a little basket on the front. With the sky a gorgeous shade of blue and the backdrop of the evergreen hillsides, they took the mile driveway from the house, through the castle-like, if overgrown, gatehouse entrance, and down a winding road with stone fences framing either side.

"I can't believe it's December," she called to him as they coasted along the narrow road. "It feels like autumn."

He rode alongside on her left, the wind giving erratic tugs to his wild blond hair peeking from his derby. "I thought you might prefer this sort of outing rather than simply taking a car, and since the weather seemed to oblige. . ."

"I didn't realize how much I needed the break."

"Mum said you worked through supper last night."

Clara breathed in the cool air like a tonic to her fuzzy brain. "Do I smell heather?"

Max grinned and gestured with his chin toward a field on their left that shimmered with lavender hue. "You do."

"It's beautiful." She sighed, scanning the landscape ahead. "All of it."

"And you haven't even seen Fenwick yet." He raised a brow and turned his gaze back to the road. Clara followed.

As if unfolding from the inside of a fairy-tale pop-up book, the hills fell away to reveal a handful of stone and white-limestone houses tossed as if at random along the roadside. A steeple pierced the sky from the highest point in the village, its gray stone a marked contrast to the sapphire day. Shops, a restaurant, and—Clara laughed—a pub by the name of The Lady and the Magpie all cloistered in a little bundle along one main street, a few showcasing thatched roofs.

Christmas decor hung in various places along the street, culminating with the tree in the center of town. A three-story tan limestone structure displayed a decorative, hand-painted sign which read Fenwick Flats while massive trees grew up in various places around the buildings connected by hedgerows or rock fences. Max took her into a small shop called Roths, where he purchased some bottled waters and a couple of "baps," an English take on sandwiches, evidently.

"Let's put them in your basket and eat them by the lake, shall we?"

With an answering grin, she followed him down the street,

swerving around parked cars, and nearly tipped her bike over as she turned a curve where a whole pig hung in one window and a goose in the other. Clara's laugh exploded. Butcher shops in England and America were definitely different.

The buildings became less frequent and the trees parted to reveal the lake right before them. They crossed a picturesque rock bridge which led to an old church ruin perched on the edge of the lake, the mountains rising almost as if out of the water.

Max came to a stop at the rock fence surrounding the church's graveyard. "This is St. Peter's Chapel, or was." He left the bike and held hers as she dismounted. He took the baps from her basket. "Since you are fond of old things, I thought you might enjoy a walk about the town and a view from the oldest spot in Fenwick."

"It's remarkable." She fell in step beside him along the shoreline, the breeze ruffling her hair. She glanced back up at the church, its roof gone and walls crumbled in certain places. "That ruin just gives the whole setting more character."

Max led the way toward the church, weaving around a rock wall and some old headstones to where a stone bench waited, facing the lake. Another strange wave of awareness spilled through Clara, or perhaps it was just her imagination wandering in and out of this new world to which she'd been introduced. Had Oliver attended this church? Maybe before he'd traveled to the front lines?

"How old is this place?"

Max took a drink of his water and relaxed back against the bench. "Reverend Brigsby, one of the local clergy, said it's fairly new. Built in the mid-1700s on the spot of an older church."

Fairly new? Only the age of Clara's country. "And what happened to it?"

"A fire started one night in the spring of 1916, but no one ever discovered the cause. With the war taking so many young men from Fenwick, some speculate a troubled loved one ventured in to pray and accidentally set the fire."

Clara stared out over the tranquil scene, to a goose, wingspan broad, gliding to almost touch the water. "There was so much loss during that time."

He stared ahead and nodded.

"I suppose that's why we should appreciate this beauty all the more for what they died for. This peace and freedom. The ability to sit here on this bench and eat a bap." She raised the remainder of her sandwich. "With a new friend who has excellent taste in how to spend an afternoon."

His lips crooked. They sat in silence for a few minutes, finishing their lunch, and then Max stood, ushering them back along the shoreline.

"I've heard there are other ruins like this one all over England," Clara said.

"There are some particularly memorable ones in the highlands of Scotland." He took her empty wrapper and tossed it in a bin along their way. "Have you never been?"

"I haven't traveled very much, not with my dad's illness and then my mom's." Clara rolled the bottled water between her palms, casting another look over the lake to distract from the sudden emotion rising in her throat. "After Dad passed away, it just seemed easier to keep life simple."

"I understand that."

She offered him a smile. "Being so close, I suppose you travel to Scotland as often as you like."

"I visited when I was younger." He looked away. "But I don't travel much anymore."

"Why not?"

He leveled her with such a look her feet faltered to a stop. "Why not?"

"Yes. Why not?"

His countenance hardened and he glanced to the sky before marching toward the bicycles. "We should return to the house. Clouds are coming in."

She watched his retreating form, replaying the conversation in her head. Did he have something against Scotland? Shaking out of her stupor, she raced after him. "Wait, Max. What did I say? I don't underst—"

"What did you say?" He swung around, his amber eyes aflame. "Why don't you think I travel, Clara? Look at me!" He gestured toward the scarred side of his face. "Do you have any idea? People stare. They look away. I've even frightened children."

Having worked in a bookshop for years, she realized some children were easily frightened or shy, but could his face really scare them? His scars seemed almost invisible to her now. "I'm sorry, I didn't even think about that."

"How can you not think about it?" A humorless laugh burst out of him. "It's right in front of you every time you look at me."

"I don't see it."

He rolled his eyes and growled, then swung his leg over his bike.

Oh, how could she explain. "I mean, of course I *see* it, but I see you more."

He paused, hands on his handlebars, and stared at her with such intensity, she fumbled with mounting her bike to ignore his eyes. How could she explain? The burns were still on his face, still as evident as they'd been in the airport, and yet, they weren't.

They rode in silence, past the quaint town with its flower boxes and stone fences and the occasional person waving a hello to Max.

Her fists tightened on the handlebars and she released a sigh. What could she have done differently? Didn't he want her to see the man he was more than the scars on his face?

Another growl erupted, but this time it came from overhead as a swell of thunder burst out of nowhere. She'd read about the changefulness of England's weather, but witnessing how suddenly the day went from sunny to threatening forced her feet into faster motion. They'd barely made the turn toward Camden when the sky opened.

"We'll wait it out beneath the gatehouse archway," Max called, water running down his face.

She wiped at her eyes, her hair already dripping from the onslaught. The archway offered little protection as the wind blew the torrents toward them, the cold dampness seeping through her cardigan and blouse.

"I'm sorry I didn't bring my keys." Max raised his voice over the sound of the rain, looking up at the gatehouse. "We could have taken shelter inside."

Keys? Clara reached for her small purse slung around her neck. "Do you think the keys your mom gave me would work?"

She rested her bike against the side of the gatehouse and dug through her purse, her fingers slippery. Max came to stand close, holding his cap over her head in a vain attempt at shielding her from some of the rain. A sweet gesture, though, even if he was angry.

"These?"

He took the proffered key chain and raced to the gatehouse door, filtering through several keys before one turned the lock. The small space was crowded with myriad paraphernalia, mostly broken chairs and a few bent bicycles, which appeared shoved inside without much thought. Max reached back for Clara's arm and guided her through the jumble to a less cluttered area.

A potbelly stove stood almost directly across from them and a row of shelves and cabinets lined one window as if it had once been a...

"Kitchen?" Clara slipped a few steps forward, the dusty windows allowing in enough light to make out some of the items. She turned on the flashlight from her phone. "It looks like this was a kitchen."

Max flipped a switch on the wall, but nothing happened. "And wired for electricity at some point."

"And water." She turned the faucet and the faintest trickle dripped into the sink. "I never imagined gatehouses had kitchens." She chuckled. "Well, I don't suppose I've thought very much about gatehouses in general."

A small spiral staircase twisted up at the far end of the front room. Max circled the staircase, giving the banister a tug. "Want to explore a bit?" He gestured toward the window. "Since we're stuck here for the present."

"I *am* in England to investigate." Clara gave a helpless shrug and followed him up the winding stairs. At the top, she and Max added their phone lights to the faint glow coming through the massive windows on three sides of the room. The space gave off a hauntingly untouched look, very much like a sleeping castle.

"Is this some sort of sitting room?" Clara followed Max into a space the same shape as the one below, except lined with bookshelves. A set of chairs and a couch stood as if waiting for visitors, and a hallway disappeared beyond the room, over the archway of the guest house.

"It looks as if it was used as an apartment of sorts."

"You've never been here?"

He shook his head. "There's been no time to really explore or renovate any other buildings except the main house thus far."

Three books and a little decorative plate stood on one of the bookshelves. Unfortunately, whatever mild dampness that had gotten into the room over the years had damaged the more fragile things. . .like books. As Max walked down the hallway, Clara attempted to peel back some of the pages of the books, but most stuck together, words faded or beyond recognition.

"There's a bedroom on this side," Max called from down the hall. "The bed frame is still intact, but the mattress is rotted. There appear to be a few men's garments in the wardrobe as well."

Maybe from the gatekeeper? Clara peeled back the cover of the second book, a Shakespeare collection.

As the cover creaked open, a handwritten name on the inside inspired a gasp. *Oliver Camden.*

"What is it?" Max arrived at her side and she turned the book toward him.

"He was here."

Max looked from Clara to the book and back to the room. "What was he doing *here*?"

Clara shook her head and flipped through the stiff pages of the book, the light from the phone barely enough to make out the faded words on the pages.

"The rain's come to a stop. Let's take the books and come investigate in the morning, when we'll have better light." Max reached around her for the books.

"We?"

His gaze, so close, pleaded with her. "Forgive me, Clara."

The way his voice softened around her name stopped her in her turn. "I don't—"

He raised his palm to quiet her, his expression gentling. "I was wrong to be so angry. I've built expectations on a handful of experiences in my life and defined them as the rule for everyone's behavior. I've been putting people in a box." He lowered his gaze, pain creasing deeper grooves in his brow. "I put you in a box, and I'm sorry."

A wave of tenderness swept over me for this wounded man. "Of course I forgive you."

He rubbed the back of his neck before continuing. "What you

said, it humbled me."

Emotions warred across his face and she had the sudden urge to touch his cheek, to comfort him. "Which part?"

His lips twitched a sad smile before he lifted his gaze back to hers. "That you saw *me*."

"I do." She turned to pull the remaining book off the shelf to give her hands something to do in the wake of his focused attention. "And I'm glad."

She met his gaze then, and a sweet rush of warmth shot from her stomach up into her face. Then, with a grin to dispel his frown, he led the way out of the gatehouse.

Sunset glowed on the horizon over the lake when Clara finally made it to her room after helping with dinner. Finally a chance to investigate the books! For the most part, they were unsalvageable, but when carefully turning through the pages of an old copy of the fairy tale *Cinderella*, she uncovered an envelope.

When she broke the seal, the paper inside ripped, but not enough to dampen the discovery of a letter. The ink had faded over time, but the penmanship looked oddly familiar. . .and the greeting brought tears to Clara's eyes.

"Dearest Oliver, my own book goblin, I miss you more than I can say."

Clara skimmed over the paragraph. The author thanked Oliver for her Christmas present, a charm bracelet. She mentioned four particular charms: a fairy, a book, a weeping willow, and a teapot.

Those might not have meant much to anyone else, but Clara knew this author, this writing. With a little squeal, she grabbed her jacket and raced down the stairs to the patio door. The lanterns from the gazebo joined with the setting sun to give the garden a haloed benediction to the day, and a couple of guests sat at the tables enjoying an evening drink. Clara slipped around the hedgerows and ran toward a small cottage tucked at the end of the long garden.

She'd only seen Max's house from across the garden, but its red door and sloped roof reminded her of a hobbit hole for some reason. A stone hobbit hole, overgrown with ivy instead of grass. An absolutely perfect place to read a book!

She knocked on the door and then paused, a splash of awareness chilling over her.

What was she doing? Going to Max's house? Were they the "drop-in" kind of friends? She winced and took a step back. Probably not. Maybe he didn't hear the knock. She slipped back another step. If she ran really fast, she could disappear in the shadows and he'd never know she'd—

The door opened, partially. "Clara?"

Her heart thrummed up a beat at the way his bass tones brewed out her name. She offered an awkward wave and probably an equally graceless smile. "I'm sorry to disturb you."

"No, please." He stepped back and ushered her into a little entry that opened into a cozy sitting area complete with a rock fireplace, comfy chairs, a television on mute, and, of course, bookshelves.

"What a wonderfully charming house!"

"And well hidden from the world." He helped her with her jacket, his lips quirking into a grin. "I thought you would have seen enough of me for the day."

"I found something." She pulled her small journal from her skirt pocket. "In one of the books."

His brows rose and he led her around the corner to a little kitchen with a table and two chairs in the center. Clara pulled the letter from where she'd placed it safely within the pages of her journal and put it on the table. "Oliver and Sadie must have cared about each other romantically." She tapped the paper. "This bracelet she writes about here? Sadie gave it to my mom on Mom and Dad's tenth wedding anniversary."

He studied the page. "It certainly sounds more than friendly, especially with such an intimate gift."

"Right? And they must have met through books, somehow. Maybe the library at Biltmore? And she mentions a book charm, but Mom's bracelet doesn't have that."

"Which could have easily been lost over time," he offered.

"Exactly." Clara laughed, shaking her head at the wonder of it all. "But how did they get from a maid and an English gentleman, to. . ."

She waved toward the paper. "Whatever this was?"

"This letter must have been written in December 1915, which means the romance happened fast."

Her gaze met his. . .and caught. "And unexpected, clearly."

He tilted his head, searching her eyes, the air growing increasingly thick. "Clearly."

With something between a laugh and a sigh—heat scorching her cheeks—she looked down at the paper. "Maybe there's more about them in the gatehouse. Maybe even the deed somewhere."

He nodded, watching her with the same intensity as he had in the gatehouse, the temperature in the room zooming from cozy to sauna. "Thanks for coming to share it with me."

"Thanks for indulging me." His gaze snatched hers again, and she skimmed her teeth over her bottom lip with her smile. "Well, I figured you'd want to see." She cleared her throat and tucked the paper back into her journal. "I mean, you've been curious."

"I'm much more than curious, Clara." His voice swept low. "I'm invested."

Everything about his expression tugged her toward him, from the tender glow in his eyes to the crooked tilt of his lips. But they barely knew one another.

It's only a kiss, right? Not a lifetime commitment. The thought whispered through her, nudging her forward.

Only a kiss?

A kiss can carry the future on it. Her mother's quote slipped through her thoughts. She wanted what her parents had. Was it even possible to think Max could offer a love like that?

She pulled her gaze from his, taking in the room again. The television played some sort of historical show, maybe a crime one? "Thanks for letting me interrupt your movie with my. . .family mystery. I really appreciate it."

He drew in a breath, as if waking from a trance, and waved toward the television. "Want to watch? I've just brewed some tea." He gestured with his chin toward the stove, tossing an uncertain grin her way. "Mom sent over cake."

He wanted her to stay? She glanced back at the television and pressed a hand to her stomach to curb the sudden butterflies. "As long as the show isn't scary, then I'm all for tea, cake, and. . ." Her smile trembled into place. "A friend."

Clara whimpered as the credits rolled, and she pushed herself to the edge of the couch, pillow still pressed to her chest. "I can't believe you lied to me!"

Max turned in his chair, remote in hand, his eyes as wide as silver dollars. "Lied to you?"

" 'This show isn't scary. It's intense.' " She made air quotes as she mimicked his accent. " 'You'll love it.' "

"You thought it was scary?" He gave a very poor attempt at looking sorry, especially with his lips taking a crooked tilt.

"I didn't just think it. It *was*. That last scene had me trying to bury myself into your couch to get away."

"You were rather adorable, trying to hide your entire body behind that pillow."

She took the aforementioned pillow and slung it toward him. "You're. . .you're a stinker."

Some strangled sound came from him. "Stinker, is it?"

She wrestled with a growing urge to laugh. The way he said the word *stinker* sounded very unstinker-like. "Yes, royally."

"Royal stinker?" He chuckled and tucked the thrown pillow to his side. "I assure you, I bathe regularly and have no legitimate right to the throne."

"They hid the body in the walls! How can that not be scary?" She threw another pillow, and this time the most amazing thing happened.

The strangled sound erupted into. . .laughter. Deep and rich, rumbling like welcome thunder on a hot summer day, filling the room and almost making her future nightmares worth it. *Almost*. "You laugh, Mister It's-Excellent-Storytelling, but I'm the one who has to walk through that shadowed garden at night to get back to the big house, so you should at least feel a little sorry."

She stood and tossed one more pillow at him, hitting him squarely in the nose. . .and producing another bout of laughter.

He snatched the pillow as he stood and tossed it back on the couch. "That's enough pelting with pillows, Miss Blackwell."

Her face wasn't cooperating at all, because instead of the glare she *wanted* to send him, she had to bite back another smile. This gradual thawing of the reclusive Maxwell Weston came with some excellent side effects. His charm being one. His laughter, another.

"You deserved it, you know." She folded her arms across her chest. "Who knows what sorts of dreams I'll have tonight about stab wounds and home invasions."

"Fear not, fair maiden." He offered her his arm, his lips still twitching with the aftershocks of his amusement. "I shall escort you all the way to the main house."

She sent him her finest glare, which really wasn't particularly potent if she couldn't keep herself from smiling, and then pulled on her cardigan.

"And I didn't mean to frighten you." His expression sobered as he led the way to the door. "I only thought you'd enjoy it from a story perspective."

As they emerged into the darkness, his brow raised in silent entreaty, she linked her arm through his with an exaggerated sigh, and he tucked her warm by his side. The brisk night air breathed with the scent of pine and burning fire, and the sky twinkled with stars dotting the inky vastness. Cheerful lights emanated from the tall windows of Camden House, shining into the garden with such brilliance, Clara felt a little foolish in being afraid to walk alone.

"The story was very good," she admitted, raising her gaze back to his. "And wonderful character development."

"Even the villain?" One of his brows tipped with his grin.

"Even the villain." She shuddered. "Nasty as he was."

Lights from the library illuminated the vastness of the shelves packed with hundreds of neglected books. It seemed such a waste of good stories, with or without excellent villains.

"What are you thinking so far away?"

Max's voice pulled her smile and she slowed her pace. "All those stories waiting to be read."

He followed her gaze to the library windows, now towering above them as they neared the portico. "Yes, I've thought about that too. Mother's considered donating them to some university or other, but that hasn't felt right, if you know what I mean."

She drew in another breath of wintery night and cardamom. "Maybe we can think of something special together, since we both love books."

They came to stop at the house door, her feet reluctant to enter. Though watching a crime drama probably wasn't considered a date, it was easily the most enjoyable two hours she'd ever had with a man outside her family. Actually, almost all of her time with Max fit that description.

"Thank you for walking with me." She took the house key from her pocket. "Maybe being escorted by a wizard vanquishes nightmares."

A smile waited in his eyes as he edged closer. "I promise to banish all the shadows from your vicinity, Miss Blackwell." His brows gave a little shimmy. "After all, not everyone knows my secret."

"Well, Mr. Wizard. . ." She grinned and pressed a finger into his chest. "Next time, I get to pick the movie."

Heat fled her body as she realized she'd just invited herself to his place. "I mean—"

"Only if it's for dinner as well?"

She looked up. His gaze held hers, as uncertain as she felt, like they both were dangling hope in front of the other. Her voice refused to comply.

"Tomorrow, perhaps?"

The entreaty in his voice, his expression, spurred her into action. "Yes, I'd love that."

His smile burst free and her pulse responded with a sudden explosion. "Seven?"

She nodded, slipping the key in the door. "Thank you for. . .for tonight."

He pushed his hands into his pockets and stepped back. "My pleasure, Clara. Truly."

His simple burr of her name spilled all through her with definite magical qualities. "Good night, Max."

Chapter 17

M rs. Helen Camden cooed over me as if I were a doll being pre- pared as a Christmas gift. As much as I had worried about Oliver's family's acceptance, especially after hearing of his mother's disdain, I was completely ill-prepared for the reception by Oliver's grandmother.

She whisked me away from Oliver almost as soon as we arrived at her house and told him to "begone," as the bridegroom shouldn't see his bride on the eve before they wed. "It creates wonderful expecta- tion," she added with a twinkle in her pale blue eyes.

Clearly, Oliver had gotten his looks and his personality from the Camden side of the family.

After a delicious feast in the small dining room of Helen's cottage, we sat by the fire for dessert, where she pelted me with questions, and I asked a few of my own. It was after that evening that I under- stood with more clarity the power Oliver's mother, Caroline Camden, wielded among her family. So strong was her condescension, that poor Helen had chosen to move to this cottage on the far reaches of the Camden property instead of staying in the estate house.

The fact that Oliver had chosen to keep our temporary home at a distance from the estate house inspired more relief as the evening progressed. I'd lived a quiet life as long as I could remember, so soli- tude didn't frighten me. In fact, I slipped it on like a pair of well-loved shoes. To dwell within a battlefield at home, on constant watch for veiled threats and criticism? What had Oliver endured during his life to use whatever wealth he could manage to ensure my safety from his own mother?

As morning dawned, I glanced out the window to view the majestic English countryside. I'd never seen a world so green and lush, even if it was early February. The mountains comforted me with their presence, so much the same as those back home, yet different. If my new world included people like Helen Camden, little Victoria, and Oliver, then I could make Fenwick my home forever.

I'd barely finished breakfast in my room when a knock at the door welcomed Helen, along with one of her housemaids and. . .Victoria, all smiles. The housemaid held an armful of gowns and Helen carried a basket of ribbons and other paraphernalia.

"Sadie!" Victoria ran full force at me and wrapped her arms about my waist. "We're going to be sisters."

"Indeed we are." I laughed and lowered myself to hug her properly. "I believe you've grown since last I saw you."

Her smile bloomed into double dimples.

I looked from Victoria to Helen. "What are you all doing here?"

"Every bride deserves some bridesmaids to help her prepare for her wedding day." Helen chuckled and spilled the basket onto the bed.

I looked from one face to the other, her declaration taking much too long to comprehend. I'd anticipated a solitary endeavor, much like Jane Eyre on her ill-fated wedding day, but here I was, surrounded by laughter and more excitement than I'd ever garnered in my life.

"And, I brought a few gowns from which you may choose." Helen gestured for the maid, Aggie, to place the gowns across the bed. "I saw your travel clothes, and none of those will do for a wedding day, my dear. Your wedding day should be magical."

"Oh Mrs. Camden, I couldn't."

"No." She wagged a finger at me. "None of this 'Mrs. Camden' business. You are to be my family, dear girl, which means you shall call me Helen. We don't put on airs here, Sadie." She waved about the room. "One of the benefits of living away from the estate house."

The gowns, three in various shades and styles of white, drew me as if they held some sort of enchantment. Each with their own delicate and unique designs looked like something any woman at Biltmore would wear. Much too nice for me. I shook my head again.

"Appease an old woman. I've longed to pour my feminine delights on another female, but my daughter-in-law is not of a mind to take my hospitality unless it is in the form of money." She took one of my hands into hers. "Allow me this indulgence, to give you and my dear grandson a wedding day you will not quickly forget."

"You barely know me. Why are you so kind to me?"

"Dear girl, I can already tell from our conversation last night that you are the perfect match for our Oliver." Helen examined me, her smile softening. "He's always carried a gentle heart, and to know he broke with his mother and forfeited his inheritance to wed you, deserves a great deal of celebration. If you are special to him, you are special to me."

"And me," Victoria added, sitting down on the nearest chair with a bounce. "But I already liked you long before Ollie ever did."

I hoped I smiled at Victoria, but my mind was still processing what Helen said. "Oliver gave up his inheritance for me?"

"Ah, I see he hasn't told you. His brother, Robert, inherits most of the estate as firstborn, but Oliver's mother had some family money of her own she used as leverage against our dear boy. He would not be controlled."

Something akin to a whimper gurgled up from my throat, but Helen shook her head.

"Never you mind. He has an allowance from me, which remains until my death. He's never tended toward extravagance, so the amount should keep you humble, but comfortable." She patted my cheek, her face wreathed in smiles. "Now, let's choose that gown, shall we?"

I couldn't move. My eyes burned and my breath shivered out in an attempt to control my waiting tears. "He's the very best of men, I think."

"Yes, yes he is." She searched my face, her expression softening to a wobbly bottom lip. "And you will do quite well for him. I am sure."

My eyes filled so fast with tears I turned away to keep her from seeing them, but she seemed to understand. After collecting myself, I asked Victoria to help me choose a gown. We settled on a lovely Irish lace bodice overlaying a white silk underdress. The scalloped neckline highlighted more of my skin than I usually exposed with my collared servants' dresses, but Helen oohed over its delicate look and sashed waistline.

And then it happened, just like in *Cinderella*. The simple servant transformed into—I blinked at my reflection as Helen and her housemaid placed little white rosettes into my intricately designed hair—a lady.

A bride.

"You look like a princess," Victoria exclaimed, sliding her fingers over my skirt.

I'd never worn white and I'd certainly never dressed in anything as delicate and lovely as this gown, but with Oliver's love, Victoria's admiration, and Helen's confidence, I stepped completely into my new identity. Belonging. Hope.

"I barely recognize myself," I whispered.

"What?" Helen laughed. "Look at that smile on your face, the blush to your cheeks, and sparkle in your eyes. If I know anything at all, I'd say we've merely uncovered the beauty that was there all along."

Everything about the drive from Helen's to the church breathed with storybook air. The quaint town, the cobblestone streets and fences, and massive oaks with branches reaching out and up as if waiting for a celestial embrace.

And then there was the church. A masterpiece of stone and steeple, poised on a little knoll which led down to a beautiful lake, all framed in by those emerald mountains. Sunlight blinked through powdery clouds and glistened against the water like fairy lights. My own little fairy tale.

"St. Peter's Chapel," Helen offered as the carriage drew up to the door of the church. "I was married here years ago in a quiet ceremony like this, at my request. Charles, my Mr. Camden, didn't have a care for all the social fluff and gave me my way." She patted my hand. "Charles and Oliver were thick as thieves up until his death three years ago, and my dear grandson is so much like his grandfather, dove."

The endearment pooled warmth through me and I squeezed her hand back, unable to usher up a response. Helen exited the carriage first, assisted by the carriage driver, and I followed, careful to mind the dress.

"Come, let's adjust your veil." Helen's cheeks creased into dimples with her grin. "And then Victoria and I shall find our seats."

Victoria stood nearby with her hands clasped before her, her body nearly shaking with excitement, and I knew exactly what would make this wedding day even better.

"I'd like Victoria to be my flower girl, if she's willing?"

Victoria's eyes widened and her rosebud mouth dropped open.

Helen chuckled. "Well, dove, what's your answer?"

The little girl looked from her grandmother to me. "But I don't have any flowers."

I plucked several from the generous bouquet Helen's maid had compiled for me, a combination of seasonal crocuses, snowdrops, and irises, and pressed them into Victoria's hands. "Now you do."

Her giggle vaulted the distance to my heart.

The look Helen gave me when I turned back to her poured through every ounce of loneliness I'd known in my life and whispered belonging. What a makeshift family. A formerly wealthy gentleman who'd given up his inheritance for an orphaned servant, a prestigious grandmother who had been relegated to a small cottage, and a little girl who desperately longed for a loving mother.

I waited at the door as Helen went ahead and, at her entrance, a simple piano version of "Be Thou My Vision" floated to greet me. Victoria entered, tossing a grin over her shoulder before disappearing into the church, and then I followed. My gaze adjusted to the change in light and immediately found Oliver's. He stood beside his father, both in black morning coat, gray waistcoat, and pinstriped gray trousers. Oliver wore a purple iris on his lapel, matching the ones in my bouquet—a flower of faith, hope, and courage.

Courage. I smiled and took another step. Love gave me courage.

Oliver stayed by my side from the moment he took my hand in the church to the signing of our names in the church's registry—February 13, 1916—to the wonderfully simple reception at Helen's, until he tugged me away with a basket of sandwiches and we were finally alone.

Alone.

As the carriage pulled away from Helen's house, Oliver wasted no time in renewing the intimacy our few private moments had afforded so far. I didn't mind at all the way he cradled my face and caressed my mouth, my cheeks, my neck. In fact, his lips encouraged my own exploration. I chased his kiss as he pulled back, and his chuckle dissolved into a moan as he returned his lips to mine. I didn't know all the intricacies of being his wife, but I embraced this newfound freedom to express the vast emotions pouring through me for him. Kissing seemed an excellent way to show him what words failed to communicate sufficiently.

"Mrs. Camden, you appear to enjoy the benefits of married privacy a great deal. What would your husband think?"

I ran a palm down his cheek, still in awe of the liberties my new position not only allowed, but celebrated. "From the look on his face, I would make the assumption he rather enjoys my newfound freedom."

"You are rather astute in your observations."

He proved my assertions correct for another long period of appreciation as the carriage rolled along until he finally pulled away and tucked me in the curve of his side. "We are neither in the place nor the space for us to continue our mutual enjoyment, my dear, so before I lose my head and ravish you in the back of a carriage, I shall usher up all of my self-control and encourage you to think about gatehouses."

"Gatehouses?" Surprise burst from me in a laugh and I placed one of my palms against my heated cheek. "That's certainly a redirection from impassioned kisses, Mr. Camden."

He raised a brow, his grin slanted. "Not as redirected as you might think." His smile spread wide at my look of confusion. "Well, my darling Mrs. Camden, I know I wrote to you about it, but the actuality may prove a bit shocking. With our current circumstances, I wanted to afford you a private home during my time away while still giving you close access to Father and Grandmama. So my father gifted me one of the preexisting structures on the property as a wedding gift—without Mother knowing, of course."

I studied him. His caution would have inspired worry if I hadn't trusted him so much. "The gatehouse?"

"It's actually very castle-like, as I told you." He looked out the carriage window. "Only on a much smaller scale."

I had basically lived in a bedroom for the past two years as my only personal space, so the idea of living in a gatehouse, even a small one, with Oliver only encouraged my smile.

"Ah, you are not thwarted by my explanation, I see?"

"Not one bit. I'd happily spend time in a closet, let alone a gatehouse, as long as it was with you."

He rewarded my declaration with a rather thorough kiss. "You are absolutely wonderful, Sadie, and I love you."

I wasn't certain why his sweet comment garnered my tears, but his face suddenly blurred and I shook my head. "I can't believe you gave up your inheritance for *me*, Oliver."

"Why not? I wanted to be with you, and if something as ridiculous as my mother's penchant for social norms threatened to keep us apart, it seemed a fairly easy decision."

"But won't you miss the lifestyle? The money?"

He grimaced and brushed his fingers against my cheek. "Wealth is measured in more ways than money, my darling, and I feel rich as a king with you and our dreams."

"Our dreams?" The words barely rose above a whisper.

"You, me, and a cozy little bookshop. Perhaps with a little Camden or two." He squeezed my shoulder, tugging me closer. "It sounds rather perfect, if I do say so myself."

I laughed as I wiped away a rebel tear. Three weeks of these tender memories. Three, and then he'd leave for war. I forced the thoughts away and embraced the moment, the now, and this wonderful dreamlike reality of being with him. Being loved by him.

"And a rather obnoxious amount of kissing, I should think." He shrugged, feigning a look of pure innocence.

"Then perhaps you should increase the one or two little Camdens to a few more."

His laugh burst out and he pressed a kiss to my lips then gestured toward the window.

Clearly, my knowledge of gatehouses, which was extremely limited, failed to prepare me for the building appearing through the window. A two-story structure of stone with an archway down the center and a connection overhead with windows everywhere, bay windows on the second floor. Spires rose from the two separate towers on either side of the gateway, offering a castlelike-look, just as Oliver had said.

I leaned closer to the window and smiled. "It's perfect."

"I don't know why I doubted you." He took my hand and pulled me from the carriage, sweeping me up into his arms before I could take a step. "Let me take you to our castle, my lady."

Without another look back at the driver or the carriage, he marched forward and, with me helping from my perch in his arms, opened the door. We entered the coziest sitting room I could have imagined. A few simple chairs, a settee, and even—he flipped a switch—electric lights? "Oliver? How did you. . . ?

"Knowing my mother's fickleness, I've been saving my money for years." He set me down and closed the door behind us. "Besides, I need to properly prepare for my bride. You're used to Biltmore, and I wanted this place to be—"

I stopped his words with a kiss, my arms wrapped around his waist, holding him close. He was so good. So kind. How I ever managed to catch his eye, I do not know, but I thanked God for the providential fingerprints pasted all over this union, even with its uncertainties.

"It's perfect. Just being with you makes it perfect."

After a prolonged expression of my gratitude, which left my hair spilling over my shoulders and his coat in a heap on the floor, we made our way to a little winding staircase at the corner of the room. Across from the stairs, a small doorway led into a kitchen area.

"Sally, the daughter of Granny's maid, Eliza, is coming to be our cook and help with housekeeping until we can hire someone."

"Oliver, I can take care of—"

He halted my rebuttal with a kiss. "Well now, that works quite well for stopping arguments, doesn't it?" He kissed me again. "I've created a credit for you in all the shops in Fenwick which you may have need of. You'll want for nothing."

I followed him up the stairs, and the next room nearly brought me to tears all over again. Bookshelves, most empty, lined almost every wall, with a few small seating areas situated throughout. "Our library?"

"Our library," he answered. "Just waiting to be filled, but I already placed a few of my favorites on the shelves."

I turned to him, my heart so full I didn't know if I'd be able to speak. It was as if within a few hours, the meetings at Biltmore and the myriad of letters blended into this deeper bond between us. Two parts of the same heart. Two sides to the same dream.

"I wasn't looking for romance." I slipped my hand into his as we stared at the room. "That was never in my plans, but then you came, and I feel as though I've belonged with you from before our first conversation."

He gave my fingers a squeeze and walked with me across the room to a little hallway that led over the archway of the gatehouse. "You know how one can identify, most of the time, a good book by the end of the first chapter, and an excellent book by the end of the first page?"

I narrowed my eyes at him. "Yes."

"You are like an excellent book. I just knew. I didn't need to read the ending or even the next chapter. I didn't require all the answers or to have the future sorted. My heart knew I belonged with you, and that was enough."

And with that, he drew me into a bedroom filled with fading light from the tall windows, and an elegant four-poster bed situated against the far wall.

"I have something for you." He led me to the bed and gestured for me to sit, took an envelope from the side table, and placed it in my hand. "This is your wedding gift." He shrugged. "Our future."

I studied his face and then opened the envelope. A large iron key dropped into my lap as I drew out a piece of paper. "A key."

"A key," he repeated, sitting beside me on the bed, his grin twitching. "Now read the letter."

As I sorted out the first paragraph of a letter from Mr. Long about the Brick House, Oliver's intention became apparent. He'd purchased Brick House. . .for us. I blinked up at him. *For me.* "Oliver—" I didn't trust my voice for more, but his broad smile proved he understood.

"I've made sure to have him include your name on the deed because. . ." His brow darkened for an instant. "If something happens to me, I don't want anyone to take away our future. Once the war is over, we can start over together as ordinary bookshop owners with an extraordinary story of our own."

I cupped his cheek and pressed a soft kiss to his lips. "Thank you."

"Grandmama helped purchase it as well. She liked you before she even met you."

Because she loved him. What a remarkable feeling to be surrounded by love.

"I love you, Mrs. Sadie Camden."

I didn't answer with words, but I feel certain Oliver had no doubt of my appreciation, because he responded with similar enthusiasm, and that evening we showed each other the most beautiful expression of how two people from different worlds can become one in every way.

I would never be the same.

And I didn't wish to.

Chapter 18

Three hours and nothing else?" Clara rubbed her tired eyes and followed Max from the sitting room of the gatehouse into the little upstairs bedroom. They'd uncovered an old newspaper from February 1916, a woman's shoe, and two more books with Oliver's name written in them, but nothing related to Sadie or a deed.

"We still have this room and the storage room beneath." Max's hopeful response pulled at her smile.

They'd worked through the "rubbish" as Max called it, in the kitchen, which revealed some old china and an exquisite teapot.

The sitting room offered even less, just a bunch of empty bookshelves. "You'd think they were trying to build their own bookshop in here with all the bookshelves." Clara glanced behind her to the sitting room they'd just vacated and then nodded toward the other two bookshelves in the bedroom.

"Perhaps that was his plan." Max lobbed a grin over his shoulder as he pulled open the wardrobe.

"A bookshop?" But the thought stopped Clara in her approach. What a wonderfully unique place for a bookshop. Inside a gatehouse! Especially a castle-looking gatehouse. She gave the room a look with that new perspective in mind. Had Oliver wanted to start a bookshop like Sadie? Was that how their acquaintance began? "Well, Fenwick didn't have one from what I saw. Maybe he wanted to live more simply than an English gentleman?"

Max wrinkled his nose as he pushed through the sparse clothes in the wardrobe. Clara slipped around him to rummage through the dresser nearby. A hatpin and a woman's hairbrush hid in the very back of the top drawer, a few dark strands curling from the bristles. She pulled her fingers away, feeling as if she'd just intruded on something intimate. What would a woman's hairbrush be doing in Oliver's apartment? Could it have been Sadie's?

"Did you say the former owners never did anything with the gatehouse when they owned Camden?"

"No, it has been neglected since the early 1950s at least."

She stared back at the hairbrush and then turned to the next drawer. Empty.

"Clara, look at this."

She moved to Max's side, where he pushed back the clothes to reveal a vintage blouse.

"A woman's blouse?" His brows met.

"I found a woman's hairbrush too."

He didn't voice the question in his eyes, but pushed back another clothing item. A suit jacket? "This is an Oxford jacket."

"What does that mean?"

"It's a special jacket students were given when attending Oxford. See the emblem of the school, there." He gestured toward the right front of the jacket, which displayed a coat of arms. "Wait." His hand slid over the inside of the jacket. "There's something in this pocket."

Clara stepped back, her whole body cringing at what might have found its way into that jacket pocket after all these years. Carefully, Max slipped his fingers into the inner pocket and then—

"Ahh!" He screamed and pulled back, holding his hand.

"What? What happened?"

His grin spread and he winked. "Nothing, just trying to lighten your mood a little."

"Max Weston." She slapped his shoulder. Of all the things she'd expected him to do, that definitely hadn't been one of them. "Am I that easy to read?"

"Your face is rather expressive." He raised his hand and revealed what looked to be a photograph. His eyes widened. "Clara, she looks like—"

"Me," Clara whispered, staring at the woman not much younger than herself. She took the photo from Max and peered closer. Same dark hair, same nose and forehead. Her eye color wasn't as pale as

Clara's, but the shape looked similar. Clara had only seen photos of Granny Sadie when she'd been an older woman. Never any of her this young but, even faded with age, she knew the face. The smile. "It's… it's a tintype photo. Cheaper and more common in the early part of the nineteen hundreds."

"Is it Sadie?"

"I think so." She swallowed a gathering lump in her throat. "The cloth of the jacket must have protected the photograph, you think?"

"Perhaps." Max studied the photo, his shoulder pressed against hers. The welcome scent of earth and flowers and cologne edged closer. He stood at the perfect height for hugging. Her head could tuck just beneath his chin and then. . .

She blinked out of her stare to find him watching her.

"So, um, if he carried her photo, then they were definitely more than acquaintances."

"And more than friends, I'd say." His lips softened into that enigmatic crooked smile that said things her heart warmed to in response. "So, um, we can feel pretty certain that Oliver lived here, but a woman must have lived here too. At some point."

She showed him the brush and the hatpin. Along with the blouse in the wardrobe, the existence of such a delicate tea set gave a few more hints. Had Sadie been that woman? Had Oliver been the sort of man who would have entertained other women in his little gatehouse? Had Sadie been one of many penniless lovers?

"Was Sadie the kind of woman who would have traveled from America to England at such a time in history without a certainty of a man's affections?"

Max's question bit into her thoughts as if he'd read them. Clara stared down at the photo, studying the tilt of the woman's chin, the direct steadiness of her gaze. What little evidence they'd found paired with what she'd heard about Sadie her entire life offered a pretty solid guess. "I think that if she loved him, she was the exact kind of woman to leave everything for him."

They searched for another hour before Max said he had to get back to his house.

"I have dinner preparations to make." He stared ahead as he rode beside her, but she could hear the teasing in his voice.

"I hope you're not expecting a whole bunch from your dinner companion. It's been a long time since she's been on a date."

"The same could be said for her host."

Which could make this night even sweeter, since they could both be awkward together. "Is it a dress-up type dinner?"

"Dress-up?" His gaze skimmed her attire as her skirt flapped in the breeze. "Don't you always dress up?"

She exaggerated her eye roll for his benefit. "This is normal. I mean, nicer than normal."

"Hmm. . ." He looked up to the sky, deliberately lengthening his response. "I'm making chicken merlot with mushrooms, salad, bread, and dessert. Do you think we should dress that up a bit?"

The man could cook? Like that? Clara nearly whimpered at the pure pleasure in the thought. Her cooking abilities leaned more toward Duncan Hines than Martha Stewart, so anything that didn't come from a box or the freezer sounded positively candlelight-dining-worthy.

"That sounds pretty fancy to me."

"Fancy?" His brow rose with the turn of his lips. "Then dress-up it is."

Clara smoothed her hair back from her face before knocking on Max's door. She'd brought her favorite dress with her to England, just in case she needed something a little formal, and her mother always said the deep red, retro mermaid-style dress had a "glamorous" feel to it. Clara had even put a wave in her hair to get it to curl the right way so she could wear it down.

But now that she stood at Max's door, she began to rethink her self-indulgence. It wasn't that she didn't enjoy looking like a 1950s spy, but some people had a difficult time dealing with her adoration for all things vintage.

The door latch clicked from the other side.

Oh well, there was no going back now.

The first thing she noticed was Max's surprised expression, then the spatula he held in the air like the Tin Man's oil can, and then her focus zeroed in on a paisley-print bow tie and a pair of black suspenders overtop his white button-up.

He wore bow ties? And suspenders?

There was a distinct possibility she was looking into the face of her future husband.

Neither moved, until the tension burst from Clara in an awkward laugh. "I love your bow tie."

He absently reached up to touch his tie and then seemed to blink out of his frozen stance. "You. . .you look beautiful."

And still he stood, spatula in hand.

She tucked her head with a smile, heat coursing from her neck to her forehead.

He blinked and then seemed to rally. "Oh, come in." His gaze moved over her again and Clara barely kept her smile from taking over her entire face.

Maybe she should invest in spy clothes more often.

"Please, come in," he repeated. He cleared his throat and gave his head another shake as if reorienting himself before leading the way into his kitchen.

The rich aroma—a mixture of savory and sweet—paired with a bow-tie-wearing man in the kitchen of an English cottage might have been one of the best experiences Clara had known up to this point in her life.

"It smells delicious in here." She paused at the counter near him as he stirred something in the pot on the stove.

"Hopefully, it will be." He grinned, his gaze catching in Clara's again before he returned to his work. "If you'll take this to the table, I'll bring the plates."

He placed a basket of warm bread in her hands and gestured toward the table he'd moved to the back of the cottage, where a set of French doors framed it.

And with that, they settled into their usual conversation, with a little bit of something else, like fairy dust, sprinkled in that shifted the relationship to something different. They spoke of their childhoods and educations—his in accounting and Clara's in business—their mutual love for fantasy books, and Clara's adoration of bookshops, in general.

"Accounting has worked out well to help Mum with the inn," Max said, bringing small dishes of some chocolate confection to the table. "And it allowed me the freedom to indulge my hobbies of gardening and reading."

"Gardening seems to be pretty relaxing for you."

He took his seat and cast her a mischievous grin. "And all three, accounting, gardening, and reading, are excellent solitary activities."

"Solitude is a beautiful thing in moderation. At present. . ." She raised a brow as she brought her chocolate-laden fork to her lips. "I'm very glad you are not interested in solitude."

"So am I."

He lifted his gaze to hers, allowing their mutual admissions to pearl over the space between them.

So much had changed since the first day they'd met. Unexpectedly, and fast. Somehow, from their conversations and budding friendship, he'd found a place in her life and. . .her heart? She kept being reminded of the C. S. Lewis quote, *Friendship is born in that moment when one person says to another, 'What! You too?'*"

"I know you're disappointed we didn't locate the deed today, so perhaps it would help to recount what you know about Oliver and Sadie so far to give us a fresh perspective on other possible places to search," Max said.

"I think Oliver must have been in love with Sadie. They met at Biltmore through books?"

"An excellent way to meet." Max saluted with his cup.

"True." Clara nodded her agreement. "And then he bought her Blackwell's but was waiting for the deed to be finalized, so all we have is a letter about the purchase. Do you think he died before the deed arrived? Did the deed come here, or to Biltmore?"

"And did Sadie travel here, which seems quite possible? Marry Oliver?"

A question that had bothered Clara too. "If they were married, why did she keep her last name?"

He took a drink, his focus down. "I think we'll learn something helpful tomorrow."

Clara's gaze rose to his. "What do you know?"

"It's a surprise. After church tomorrow."

The flutter in her stomach stilled. "Surprise, is it?"

"Do you trust me?" He held her gaze.

She narrowed her eyes, allowing enough pause to dissolve his humor before answering. "Yes." Her grin flared. "But I have to be back by tomorrow evening because your mom is going to teach me how to make her famous red velvet cake."

"She's truly enjoyed getting to know you." He stood, reaching for Clara's dessert plate, so Clara followed suit by carrying her cup to the kitchen. "Now, teaching you her famous cake? That's a definite sign you're one of her favorites."

"She's easy to like and so happy here."

"She's happy now." He leaned against the counter, folding his arms across his chest. "But it took several years after the accident to get her back."

Clara slid a step closer, waiting for him to divulge more.

"She hasn't told you?"

"Only that your dad died in a car accident."

He rinsed off the dishes and Clara moved beside him to help with the drying, waiting. "We were coming home from visiting some friends. My older sister, Angelica, had recently left for her first mission trip to Africa, so it was only me and my parents. A truck came out of nowhere and slammed into us on the driver's side."

Clara's hands froze on the plate she was drying, her stomach clenched in anticipation.

"I pulled Mum from the car. She was unconscious. When I opened my father's door, an explosion knocked me back. I was able to turn my head, but I couldn't get away in time."

Her attention slid over his scars. Burns.

"I never lost consciousness and was left standing by a burning car with a mother who was unconscious and the knowledge that my father was dead. Then I was separated from Mum while doctors attempted to salvage what they could of the left side of my face, and I didn't know if she survived or not." He shook his head and handed her another dish. "I've never felt so alone, so helpless."

Clara took the plate from him, hoping her expression shone with the understanding she felt. Standing by her father's deathbed and trying to keep her mother from becoming physically distraught had been the most difficult moments of her life.

"I understood God's presence then, as I never had before." He chose one of their teacups to clean next. "There was this indescribable and overwhelming sense of—"

"Comfort," she whispered.

His gaze lingered in hers. "Yes."

How was it possible to care so deeply for—to understand—someone she hadn't even known a week? It was all well and good in fairy tales, those were *fairy tales*, but here? In the real world?

He tilted his head closer and for an instant, she thought he meant to kiss her. And she, in that same instant, hoped he would. Time crawled to a stop. The air grew thick. Her attention flickered from his lips to his amber eyes.

"Would you care to dance?"

She tugged her thoughts from the idea of his lips on hers and coughed. "What?"

A rush of red darkened his face and he looked away. "W–would you care to dance. . .with me?"

Clara snapped her lips closed and worked words through her throat. "Without music?"

His smile resurrected and his eyes took on an added twinkle. "That, I can fix."

And he did, choosing none other than Tony Bennett to croon through the living room. Clara swooned from the knees upward. A dashing man in a bow tie who loved his family, books, gardening, and Bennett. . .and he was slipping his arm around her waist to dance with her? How was she supposed to come up with a coherent sentence for the next ten minutes or possibly hours?

His hand closed around hers and they moved in synchrony, his fresh scent of cardamom and firewood teasing her closer. His palm moved more securely against her back. His gentleness, his touch, sweetly intoxicating.

"I haven't danced with someone in a while," she murmured, closing her eyes to enjoy the warmth of his touch.

"Do you usually dance alone?"

His teasing words, so near her ear, pearled tingles in their wake. "Almost daily."

She felt his chuckle more than heard it.

"But. . .but I prefer this to dancing alone." Had she spoken her thoughts aloud?

Her body tensed, but he quickly adjusted and tugged her a little closer. "I prefer this to you dancing alone too."

Like the slow hand of a pendulum rocking forward, each step drew them closer, until she rested her chin against his shoulder, and everything clicked into place. Here. With him.

"Clara."

"Mmhmm," she murmured into the comfort of his shoulder.

His silence pulled her attention up.

"What you said at the lake, about seeing me?"

"Yes?"

"Thank you," he whispered.

Her chest deflated. This strong, quiet man struggled every day against the lies of his own mind, the searing voices that thrust him further into reclusion, away from a world his kindness could touch.

"Well, I really like what I see." Her breaths slipped into a shallower rhythm at the unexpected admission. His gaze met hers, searching, beckoning for her to clarify. "But even more than that, I. . .like who you are."

Air shocked from his parted lips as he continued to stare, his attention riveted to hers as if he didn't believe her words. How could she convince him?

Her pulse took an upswing as an idea surfaced to perfection in her mind. She brought her free palm up to cradle his face, watching the confusion in his eyes shift to shock as she closed in. Her breath shivered between them as her mouth touched his so gently, she felt the ridges of his lips slip across hers. She had very little experience with romance, and even less with kissing, but something in her heart responded to him, and even if she fumbled through, he needed to know she cared in this very tangible sort of way.

She pulled back an inch, her palm still on his cheek. Those golden eyes probed hers, disbelief giving way to a gloriously crooked smile. His fingers slid down a loose strand of her hair, his gaze caressing more tenderly than any touch she'd known. His lips flinched wider. She'd reached him. Shown him the truth. And suddenly it didn't matter whether she blundered through romance or kissing, because that grin quelled all her doubts into smithereens.

Without another hesitation, he breached the distance between them, taking over the kiss, and for all the words he failed to say, he made up for in a very nonverbal kind of way.

Chapter 19

I lived in a world of dreams.

For the first two days of our married life, we stayed in and around our little castle, enjoying the felicity and discovery of each other, the joy of getting as close as two souls ever could on earth. We read to each other, took long walks, and spoke of bookshops and babies and life after the war. Each evening, Helen welcomed us to her cottage for supper, and this little dream of mine swelled into a sense of family.

Our third day, Oliver took me on a proper tour of Fenwick, introducing me to all of the adoring shopkeepers, clerks, and his working-class friends. They welcomed me with shy smiles and loud laughter and, in some instances, embraces.

When we approached a particular building, near the end of our tour, Oliver wiggled his brows in dramatic flair and flourished a bow. "Madam, this will be your favorite stop, I do believe."

I looked up to the wooden sign dangling from a chain above and grinned. ENOCH'S BOOK BINDINGS.

"People rarely take note of this place, unfortunately. It's the only bookshop in Fenwick and rarely includes new books because Enoch is determined to rescue the castaways."

"What do you mean?"

Oliver reached for the door. "I'll show you."

And so it was. Enoch Everly saved books. People from all around brought their broken or old books to him, and with his wrinkled and gnarled hands, he'd piece them back together and rebind them so they had a second chance.

His gray hair flew in all sorts of directions, thin and wispy, and a set of round, wire-rimmed glasses tipped to the edge of a hawklike nose.

A young woman slipped among the shelves lining the small shop, her tattered gray dress and pale face giving more of a ghostly quality than human. She raised dark eyes to me, her bottom lip puckering into a frown, and then she skittered out of sight.

"That be my grandniece, Anna." Enoch raised his pale eyes to me, nodding in the direction she disappeared. "You might see her sneakin' out to get another book. That's what she does. Cooks and reads, if she has the chance, when she's not bindin' books or hidin'."

"Hiding?" I glanced back at the doorway through which Anna had disappeared.

"Mr. Oliver can tell you more about her, if ye wish to know, but don't expect her to talk to you none. She's done with most folks after all the trouble they've caused. Stuffed shirts."

Enoch turned to talk with another patron, and Oliver leaned close. "She's been cast out by all good society, I'm afraid to say. Even in our little hamlet. But Enoch has weathered the stuffed shirts before and took her in despite them."

"What has she done?"

"She fell into some bad company a few years ago and disappeared from town." He lowered his voice, tugging me farther away from the curious onlookers. "Returned carrying some man's child and destitute for food and shelter."

"Her parents?"

He shook his head. "They're rather well situated in Fenwick society, so they'd have nothing to do with her." Oliver nodded toward Enoch. "His daughter suffered a similar fate and was too ill to be saved by the time she came home, so Enoch took Anna in to ensure the same end didn't come to her."

I stared back at the doorway. "And the child?"

"Given up to a local family who'd recently lost their son."

I pressed my palm to my stomach, a hollowness aching through my middle. Giving up one's child? "How horrible."

"I can't imagine making that choice." He ran a palm down my arm and offered a sad smile. "But the child is in a very good place. Loved immensely and well cared for."

I took his arm as we bid our farewells to Enoch and walked out of the shop. "I wanted you to know the place because I have a feeling you'll need more to do than twiddle your thumbs at the gatehouse."

I stopped walking and looked up at him. "So you're offering my services, are you?"

"It *is* a bookshop, of sorts." He tipped his head toward her, a smile dancing in his eyes. "And you are known for being a bit bookish."

"A bit." My smile slipped free.

"And Enoch could use some help, which would also give you ample opportunity to research how to tend such a shop for. . ." His brows wiggled playfully. "A certain brilliant couple's future."

"You are a very smart man." We resumed our walk, my grin brimming wider with each step.

"Smarter now." He placed his hand over mine resting on his arm, and breathed out a sigh. "How I wish I could slow the hours to days."

It was the first time he'd mentioned leaving since I'd arrived. The first glimpse of regret in his voice. My heart lurched against the reality. "We shall live off of every hour. Each one. Scenes in our own story that we can revisit when we're apart."

He bathed me in such a tender smile my eyes stung. "My favorite story."

"And mine."

We toured a few more shops, Oliver instructing me on which ones had credit in place for me and which to avoid. He took me on a walk over a lovely stone bridge back to the church where we'd been married, and we sat on a bench by the lake and talked and laughed and created yet another scene for our story.

Dinner with Helen brought its usual delights, with her ready wit and pleasantness. She informed us that the cook she'd recommended to us was to be married within the month, so Oliver and I had an assignment of locating a new cook before he left, if possible. Helen offered a few options for us to pursue.

We walked back to our little castle, hand in hand, the night sky rife with millions of stars. Silence accompanied our steps, perhaps brought on by his earlier acknowledgement. We'd barely made it into the door of the gatehouse when he turned to me and pulled me into his arms, cocooning me within his embrace. I buried close, eyes closed, memorizing every touch and scent. His heartbeat thrummed against my ear, steady and strong. I turned ever so slightly so my lips rested against the skin of his neck just above his collar. He smelled of vanilla, fresh air, and the leather lining the inside of his jacket collar. I refused to cry. Tears weren't meant for now. Not when he was here, holding me, brushing kisses against my head and face.

I had never looked for romance, but God brought me Oliver. . .and more love than I ever imagined a heart could hold. His fingers worked their way up into my hair, his careful practice from the last few days removing pins, releasing locks to fall around my face. I pushed his jacket from his shoulders and then cradled his cheeks with my palms, speaking without words.

With a gentle smile, he led me up the stairs and through our library to our bedroom, and we wrote another beautiful scene in the story of our lives. A scene only meant for us.

While Oliver discussed a few matters with Mr. Chase, the banker, I made my way across the street to Enoch's to inquire if he would be willing to allow me to learn his trade once Oliver went to the front. The man offered a sly grin, studying my lovely navy walking suit. "You're too much of a lady to work here, Mrs. Camden."

I teased the older man with a crooked brow and placed one hand to my hip. "What would you say if I told you I have plenty of practice not only working, but working with books."

His white brows tipped skyward. "So it's true, is it? Mr. Oliver married a—" He lowered his voice. "Were you really a housemaid, then?"

My grin grew and I nodded.

"I say. . ." He pushed a hand through his snowy hair, causing it to rise to new heights. "And you'd want to be here? Working in a shop?"

"I'd like to volunteer my time at first, to learn how the shop works, but then, if you think I'm worthy of pay, I'll take that too."

He chuckled and rubbed his chin. "Aye, that sounds like a plan then. Won't I be the talk of Fenwick with the new Mrs. Camden in my shop." His expression sobered and he cast a glance over his shoulder.

"Since you was who you was and all, maybe you could. . ." He cleared his throat and stepped closer. "I heard tell from Mrs. Helen that you and Mr. Oliver are looking for a cook."

I searched his face. "We are."

"My Anna, here. She's a hard worker, and if anyone's learned from their mistakes, it's her." His voice rasped with emotion and he blinked more rapidly, clearing his throat again. "Do you think the two of you would consider her?"

I can't explain it, but my heart squeezed at the way this uncle cared for his fallen niece, his gentle entreaty to offer her something more.

"Do you think she could come to the Camden gatehouse for an interview Monday morning at ten?"

The man's smile stretched into a dozen wrinkles. "I'd say she would be there at sunrise if you let her have the chance."

"Then I look forward to seeing her Monday, bright and early." I put out my hand and he took it. "And keep in mind my request, Mr. Enoch. I plan to spend my time with Oliver before he leaves for the front, but once he's gone, you can be sure I'll become a fixture here, if you let me."

Chapter 20

Grace Chapel, a remodeled church braced on the edge of the mountain and overlooking Lake Derwentwater, offered a wonderful combination of charming townsfolk, beautiful atmosphere, and excellent preaching. Clara didn't know the melodies to some of the hymns they sang, but a few praise songs were familiar. The church fit within the quaint town of Fenwick as perfectly as stone walls and sheep pastures, and with Max to one side—in another bow tie— and Gillie on the other, Clara felt as if she'd belonged to this little world for much longer than almost a week.

How could that be?

What a wonderful thought that God dwelt as much here as He did back at her church in the States, and that she could feel so at home herself. She'd stayed so close to home for so long, her world had grown small, somewhat stifled. Was it possible for her dreams to grow beyond what she'd thought them to be?

The notion lingered for a moment, during the final hymn, as the voices rose around her in myriad harmony and skill. When the service ended, friendly folks stalled their exit to meet Clara or chat with Gillie about whatever local news happened to be the flavor of the day. Max kept close, responding in his quiet way, his smile at the ready among the folks of Fenwick. He easily welcomed her into conversations and, as they left the church, he wrapped her hand in his for a subtle embrace before opening the car door for her.

Clara sat in the back of the car basking in Max's affection, in the sweetness of his world, and trying very hard to keep the future at bay for another day. The idea of returning home after such a glorious introduction to romance and friendship left her quivering on the inside, so she turned her mind to the countryside and searched for more descriptions to add to the growing children's book in her mind.

"Max mentioned that you two have a special afternoon planned." Gillie grinned at Clara from the passenger's seat. "But don't let the time get away from you, dear. We have a cake to make."

"Make sure that son of yours is listening." Clara met Max's gaze in the rearview mirror, his eyes creasing with unleashed laughter. "He's the one who's set up this surprise, so I know nothing about it."

"Ah, well, you're going to be bowled over, luv." Gillie chuckled and patted Max on the shoulder. "I nearly thought Christmas had come and gone at Max's excitement in finding—"

"Mum." He shot her a warning look. "Surprise and all."

"Yes, yes." Gillie sighed and turned back to Clara. "I'm horrible at surprises, Clara. I become so thrilled with the prospect of the receiver's excitement, I'm positively hinged to tell all as soon as possible, but Max is excellent at surprises. And loves granting them." She patted his shoulder again. "Like his father."

He glanced over at his mom, and Clara felt as if she'd peeked in on a private conversation. A sweet one, between two people who understood each another. Clara knew that connection with both her parents, a blessing too few children experienced.

"Have you made any more headway on finding what you needed, Clara dear?"

Clara couldn't tame her smile at Gillie's endearment. She'd drawn Clara into the community of her inn as if she were part of the family. "Not what I need to find, but I'm still hopeful something will turn up."

"And the email you received last night from the Biltmore archivist," Max added, meeting her gaze through the mirror again. "It sounded interesting."

"She didn't give details, only that she'd uncovered a letter Sadie wrote to Mrs. Vanderbilt in 1917 regarding some sort of project Sadie was working on. But at this point any information could be helpful, so I hope to meet with her as soon as I get back home."

"Well, I hope it won't take a family mystery to have you return to us in the future, Clara." Gillie sent a look to Max before returning her gaze forward. "You'll always find a place to stay."

After lunch at a two-hundred-year-old inn called The Copper Pot, they took a stroll down main street Fenwick, and Clara appreciated again the conglomeration of buildings lining the narrow lane. Some thatched-roofed limestone, others tan with slated roofs, a few stone ones, and all patched together in the most idyllic line with an occasional tree or lamppost or sign breaking the row. Yet, among the restaurants, inns, shops, two banks, and churches, there wasn't a bookshop in sight.

As Max and Clara took a narrow road away from Camden House and their conversation moved from admiration for Fenwick, Gillie, and excellent sermons, the countryside continued its breathtaking unveiling. . .and the road seemed to grow narrower.

"I don't think I could ever drive on these roads." Clara straightened after she'd pressed up against the door as they passed a car. "How on earth do you keep from hitting every other vehicle on the road?"

He offered her his signature grin and returned his attention to the road. "You learn and practice, and use the laybys when necessary."

She looked over at one of the "laybys," an added space on the side of the road where one car could stop to let another pass.

"I promise to teach you when you return."

She turned to him, but he kept his face forward. Return. Right. She only had a few days left and then. . .back to everyday life. Her breath squeezed through her tightening throat. How was it possible to care about him so much already? To feel connected to him in an almost tangible way? And what would it be like to live thousands of miles apart, now that she'd experienced. . .whatever this was with him?

She'd find a way.

She placed her hand over his resting on the gear shift. "It's a deal."

He held her gaze for a moment, the gravity of her statement mirrored in his eyes. "Good," he whispered before turning his attention back to the road.

"Maybe when I come back, we can talk about how wonderful it would be to have a bookshop in Fenwick." Clara bit her bottom lip with her smile. "You know it could use one."

"An excellent conversation to ensure your speedy return."

His grin broadened and, as if he'd planned the moment, he gestured with his chin to the front window. With a raised brow, Clara followed his gaze and gasped. The coast appeared ahead, as if by magic. The car followed the beach along a narrow road perched on a cliff overlooking the vast expanse of cobalt ocean. "It's the sea!"

"Saltom Bay, to be precise." He beamed like a little boy who'd given out an early Christmas present. Clara curbed the desire to lean over and kiss him, especially since that could very well lead to their deaths off a cliff. But what a way to go!

"It's amazing. Cliffs and oceans! We don't have anything that looks like this off the coast of North Carolina."

"And your surprise happens to live in a house with a view of the sea."

She stared at his profile as he turned through a set of gates onto what appeared to be a driveway. Her surprise was a person? Who in the world could he possibly want her to meet? Her smile softened. Maybe one of his grandparents? Or a friend?

Max pulled the car to a stop in front of a beautiful two-story, whitewashed limestone house with a massive yew on either side, their knotted trunks twisting up to create an archway over the front of the house.

"What a wonderful place!" Clara leaned forward, taking in the tall windows on either side of the simple wooden door, a wreath hanging on display. "Is every spot in England like stepping into a book?"

"I'm only showing you the best," Max answered. He exited the car and met her on the other side. "To give you every incentive to return."

She tugged on his jacket lapel. "I have pretty good incentive already."

The look he gave her, so tender, drew her forward, and he captured her lips with his. Maybe Clara was dreaming, lost inside of a storybook in her head, because this little taste of romance captured almost every daydream she'd ever imagined.

"I never expected you," he whispered, searching her eyes.

"Nor I you." She gave his lapel another tug, her lips tingling from the touch of his. "I think a higher hand certainly worked some heavenly magic into this meeting."

His smile softened and he slid a strand of her hair through his fingers before stepping back. "I'll stay in the car." He gestured toward the door. "She's expecting you."

The sudden warmth of his closeness vanished. "Wait, you're not going with me?"

"You don't need me for this, Clara."

He nudged her toward the door and she shuffled forward, looking back at him as if he'd lost his mind. How could he up and leave her at a stranger's door, especially right after they'd engaged in such wonderful displays of affection?

She paused, but he nodded, his grin barely held in check. Oh, amused was he? She narrowed her eyes at him, drew in a deep breath, and marched toward the door. The doorbell resounded deep inside the house and Clara cast a look back at Max, who only winked and returned to the driver's side of the car.

With the sound of turning locks and then a click, the door opened to reveal an older woman with beautiful mocha-colored eyes and a head haloed in white hair. Her little round mouth opened into an O and she pressed a palm to her chest. "Oh heavens, you look just like her."

Clara blinked, sent another look over her shoulder to Max, and forced words into the silence between them. "Like who?"

"Who?" The woman shook her head, her smile growing. "Why, your great-grandmother, Sadie Camden, Blackwell, as was."

It was Clara's turn to stare, speechless. Had she heard correctly?

"Camden? You mean, she and Oliver were married?"

"You didn't know?"

Clara wasn't sure whether she shook her head or not, but the woman laughed. "Well now, my name is Mrs. Margaret Sadie Rivers Wilson, and I was named after your great-grandmother."

Clara grabbed the doorframe, her knees growing weak. "You were named after Granny Sadie? How. . .how can that be?"

With a gentle touch to Clara's arm, Mrs. Wilson guided Clara forward through the entry. "Well now, that's exactly why your friend, Mr. Weston, found me." Her dark eyes brightened with a smile. "I have a wonderful story to tell you, and you have an ending to tell me."

"Your great-grandmother is quite the fable in our family." Mrs. Wilson led Clara into a sitting room with more modern furniture than the old-fashioned exterior of the house presented. A brown leather couch with two blue Heywood chairs and matching ottomans made up the sitting spaces, and a coffee table stood in the center covered with photos.

"I. . .is she?" Everything about this series of events was unbelievable. Clara's mind failed to keep up. She nodded to another woman in the room, a younger version of Mrs. Wilson, and took the proffered chair.

"This is my middle daughter, Esme Jenkins. She lives here with me." Mrs. Wilson sat across from Clara and gestured toward the photos. "I've a suspicion, from your initial surprise, that you don't know much about Oliver Camden?"

Clara shook her head, glancing down at the photos. "No, not much at all. I know he met Sadie at Biltmore, his family used to live in Camden House, and he died in World War I."

"Then I suppose you don't know much about Victoria, Oliver's sister?"

Clara scratched her memory for an answer. "Was she the sister Sadie saved?"

Mrs. Wilson's smile brimmed and she rocked back in her chair. "Yes, exactly. Victoria Camden Rivers was my mother."

"Your. . .your mother?"

"Yes, and the only surviving child of Heathcliff and Caroline Camden, since both of their sons died in the Great War."

Clara looked from the photo-laden table back to Mrs. Wilson. "Is that how you learned about Sadie?"

"An excellent question." She raised a finger. "But first, let us clarify a few things. How many children did your great-grandmother, Sadie, have?"

"Only one. A son. She never told us who the father was."

"Oh Mother, it must be! Look at her eyes." Esme Jenkins reentered the room with a tray of tea. "After all this time?"

My eyes?

Mrs. Wilson moved to the edge of the couch, a magnetizing light in her eyes. "Do you know the date of your grandfather's birth? Sadie's son?"

Clara looked from Mrs. Wilson to Esme and back. "Yes. He was born November 12, 1916. John Oliver Blackwell."

Air burst from Mrs. Wilson's nose and she brought her hands together. "We didn't know for sure if Sadie bore a child or not, but the date concurs with her time here. Her marriage with Oliver." Her gaze explored my face. "You are family, Clara Blackwell. Our family." A light laugh burst from her. "Oh, my mother would have loved to have known about you."

Clara had an entire family in England she'd never known about. Cousins, aunts, uncles. . .her small world as an only child of two practically only children swelled astronomically. Uncle Julian and Robbie had been the only family Clara had ever known. Now she waited on the brink of discovering the answers to a century of unanswered questions.

"What do you know of Oliver and Sadie?"

"Not much." Clara shrugged. "Oliver and Sadie met at Biltmore in late summer 1915 and developed some sort of romantic attachment." She waved toward Mrs. Wilson. "Marriage sometime in early 1916. But Olivier died in March 1916, and Granny Sadie moved back to the States soon after."

"Your deduction about Sadie and Oliver meeting at Biltmore is true. It appears Oliver tended toward stepping outside of protocol." Mrs. Wilson's smile deepened the wrinkles on her face. "Making friends with the servants, joining in town parties, having dreams of keeping a quiet life in the country tending his own chickens, and nursing a dream of a simple life."

"And all this time, your mother knew their story, Mrs. Wilson?"

"No Mrs. Wilson among family, my dear. You must call me Maggie." She tsked. "And, yes, my mother divulged the story when I became interested in genealogy about twenty years ago. She'd never mentioned Sadie before, because, you see, her mother, Caroline Camden, fell into a disabling depression after both Oliver and Robert died in the war. Not that she'd impacted my mother's life a great deal. She'd been mostly involved in her social world and the like. Three years after her death, Grandfather remarried a woman who had as generous a nature as one could ever possess. Sadie's story disappeared beneath the joy and expectations of Mother's new family, for soon she had another brother and sister."

Clara smiled even as her eyes stung. "I'm glad she healed."

"Yes, but she didn't forget. When I began asking her questions, she unfolded the story of her dearest brother's life, and since she had kept a diary almost religiously from the time she was seven, she had a record of her memories."

"Sadie was in her diary?" Clara barely realized that Esme left a cup of tea on the table beside her, her focus was so much on her. . .cousin Maggie.

"Oh yes, we know the story up until Sadie left her life in England, which is where you'll help finish the story. My mother, Vicky, loved your great-grandmother. Even as a young child who didn't fully understand the ways of the world, she knew something was special about Sadie, something Oliver seemed to see as well."

Clara sniffled and took the cup into hand, the contents warming her cold palms. Her mind swirled with too many thoughts to even catch one.

"It seems that Oliver fell in love with your grandmother almost instantly. Evidently, he pursued Sadie until she surrendered to his charms. Mother said he was always devastatingly charming."

Clara grinned despite her blurry vision. "Of the few notes I've seen from him, I'd agree."

"After he returned to England, they exchanged letters until he sent for her, at which time they married."

Married. The answer after all this time. But why didn't she take Oliver's name? Why leave the parentage of her son a mystery?

"Oh, but I've run ahead. Let me introduce you to a few people you may have never seen." Maggie reached for a few photos on the table. "This is Victoria and Oliver on the ship to America, where they stayed at Biltmore."

Clara blinked away the tears and took the proffered photograph. Her attention immediately moved to the young man in the photo. Tall and lean with a brilliant smile. The pair both had light hair and pale eyes. Could they have been pale blue? Like hers? Her lips responded to his smile as if he looked through the years and saw her. What a strange feeling!

"He's so handsome."

"Isn't he?" She nodded at the photo. "Dashing, I'd say, and from

Mother's accounts, he was the light of her life. Read to her, danced with her, spent time with her when it wasn't a usual expectation of older brothers of their social status."

Clara could almost feel his smile through the photo, so vibrant. She moved her attention to the little girl with pale curls spilling around her shoulders. She had her face upturned, grinning up at her brother with clear adoration on her young face. This man was Clara's great-grandfather?

Clara raised her gaze to Maggie, searching her face. "What happened?"

"Here are my grandparents, Heathcliff and Caroline." She pushed another photo forward. "They play an integral role in the story."

Oliver looked a lot like his father. Same build, eyes, and smile, though Mr. Camden's shone with more subtlety. Mrs. Camden stared at the camera, emotionless. Her darker hair disappeared beneath a magnificent hat, and her tall figure was accentuated by the fit of her gown.

"Sadie and Oliver lived in the gatehouse after they married. He'd taken on the expense to have it refurbished to offer to his young bride so that they could live separate from his mother. He planned to find them a more suitable home once he returned from war. He thought this would keep Sadie close enough to assistance, if she needed it, but not too close to Grandmother Camden."

"How long were they together before he left for war?" Clara brought her cup to her lips.

"According to Mother's diary, about three weeks passed from the time of their wedding to Oliver's departure."

"Only three weeks?" Clara whispered, glancing back at Oliver's photo. Others of him littered the table. Some with his parents or Victoria, a few by himself with a large hound or on horseback, but in almost every one, he wore a smile Clara felt.

"Yes, such a short time. So many young couples of the era lived with death all around them." Maggie glanced over the photos as if lost in thought. "And I hope the ending to Sadie's story is much happier than a young widow who was forced to leave by an angry mother-in-law."

"What do you mean?"

"Mother didn't know all the details. All she knew was a week or two after the report of Oliver's death, she overheard parts of a conversation between Grandmother and Sadie. It appears Grandmother gave some sort of ultimatum to force Sadie to return to America. It wasn't until decades later, when Mother was going through her parents' belongings, that she came upon two unopened letters from Sadie addressed to my mother."

Clara stared at her. "Mrs. Camden had kept them from her?"

"Indeed." Maggie gave a sad nod. "Once Mother opened them, they didn't give any revelation to Sadie's life back in America, but Mother said how much it would have meant to her to know Sadie had attempted to correspond, as she'd promised."

"Of course. From all I've heard of Granny Sadie, she would have wanted that too."

Maggie studied Clara a moment. "And what became of her when she left? How did her story end?"

Clara placed her cup on the table. "She returned to Asheville, opened a bookshop, and raised her son, John. When John died in World War II, his wife gave their young son to Granny Sadie and returned to her family in the south. So Granny raised her grandson, who was my father, and passed the bookshop on to him."

"A bookshop. How appropriate." Maggie chuckled. "Oliver would have loved it."

"I think. . .I think he purchased the bookshop for her, for them, as a plan for their future."

"Ah, yes." Maggie turned to Esme. "Did you ask Allison to take those papers to Camden House tomorrow?"

"I did, Mum."

Margaret turned back to Clara. "Allison is my oldest daughter. I can't remember if the deed is in those papers or not, but the marriage certificate is, as well as some of Sadie's letters that have survived time."

"The marriage certificate?"

"Indeed. We don't know how my grandmother ended up with it or why she kept it, but my mother found it with her mother's papers."

"And…" Clara pressed her palm against her chest. "Her letters?"

"Yes, the ones she wrote to Oliver while they were apart. If I recall correctly, they hold lovely insights into both your granny's character and her and Oliver's relationship." She took a bite of a scone and then returned her dish to the table. "There's also a very special photo. Mother said it was taken on their wedding day."

Clara would get to see Oliver and Sadie together? She'd been imagining them as a couple during the entire conversation, but to see them? She grinned. "I can't wait."

"And a few other items, which I can't recall. But take as many photos or copies of the papers that you need, and if the deed is in those documents, you are welcome to take the original with you to ensure you can stop whatever nonsense is happening to the bookshop."

Their conversation continued for another hour, as Clara asked questions and took photos of the many black-and-whites scattered across the table. She even convinced Maggie and Esme to join her for a selfie. Before Clara left the country house, she hugged both of them and promised to return. After all, they were family, and she had years of catching up to do.

She bid them farewell, and Max met her on the passenger side of the car, his grin a welcome sight not only because she'd come to care about him, but also because of the gift he'd given her that afternoon. Something no one else would have thought to offer.

As soon as he closed the driver's side door and turned toward her, she grabbed his face between her palms and kissed him long enough to have him thoroughly reciprocate. "You are just the most wonderful man in the whole world."

"I will gladly offer my services on a regular basis if similar kisses are my reward."

Clara pressed a palm to her cheek, her face warming beneath his tender perusal. "I'm pretty sure we both benefit from that kind of reward."

"An excellent pastime, then?" He put the car in gear and began the drive back to Camden House as if what he'd done hadn't changed *everything*.

"How did you find them?"

He raised a brow and kept his focus on the road. "After you told me Oliver and Sadie's story, I did some research and tracked down Mrs. Wilson through the previous owners of Camden House. It took a little time, but it appears to have been worth it."

"Worth it?" She waved back toward the way they'd come. "They're my family, Max. Oliver and Sadie were married, and my grandfather was their son."

He tossed her a narrow-eyed glance. "It's what we thought all along, isn't it? You've got some solid English blood in you." He glanced back toward the house. "Did you locate the deed to Blackwell's?"

"Not yet, but I'm hopeful. Maggie's daughter is bringing some old documents to Camden House tomorrow for me to look through. She seems to think the deed may be included in them."

He offered his signature smile in answer, his expression encouraging her to continue.

"I took pictures of the family photos she had. Oliver and Victoria. And their father. And Camden House at the turn of the century. And among the old papers we're getting tomorrow are some of Sadie's love letters to Oliver." She sighed back into the seat. "I just can't believe it. There was so much to Sadie's life no one knew. Not even my dad." She turned her head, as it rested against the back of the car's seat, and studied Max's profile. Even his scarred side appeared less intense than when she'd first met him. All she noticed was a gentle man with a quiet sarcasm and a tender heart, who kissed like he'd waited all his life to do so.

"Thank you, Max."

He turned at her whispered words, his smile slanted in acceptance of her gratitude.

"There is this wonderful photo of Oliver." She pulled out her phone from where she'd stashed it in her purse during the last half hour of her conversation with Maggie. "He was laughing and seemed so happy. I thought you'd like to—" A line of missed calls rolled down her phone. All from Robbie.

All heat fled her face.

"What is it?"

She flinched at the suddenness of Max's voice in her thoughts. "Robbie's called at least five times over the past half hour. He didn't leave a message."

Max's expression sobered and the car jolted forward into a faster speed. "There's a restaurant about five miles ahead which should have Wi-Fi."

Clara nodded, afraid to allow her mind to wander too far into the what-ifs. Was Mother all right? Had Julian done something to jeopardize the bookshop? Had the law discovered they didn't have a deed and given the shop back to Mr. Long without giving Clara time to save it?

Before the car came to a full stop, Clara slipped out and rushed inside. The phone rang only once before Robbie answered.

"What is it? Is Mom okay? Are you?"

Silence met her questions and then Robbie responded, soft, slow. "Your mom's had a massive heart attack, Clara. We just arrived at the hospital, but it doesn't look good."

Chapter 21

Though I'd lived in England and been Oliver's wife for two weeks, I hadn't stepped one foot into Camden House. In part, it was Oliver's desire to protect me from the disdain of his mother, but also, I learned as we walked toward the grand house for dinner, she would not see me. To which, Oliver had said, she would not see him either.

With his departure only a few days away, Mrs. Camden acquiesced. Oliver left the final decision to me, ever protective, but I longed to be an agent of reconciliation between him and his mother, if I had the ability within me to do so.

The house rose before us. We'd taken the carriage instead of walking, since the weather looked uncertain, but even from the carriage window, the house made an impressive introduction. Emerald mountains rose behind it, in sharp contrast to the pale cream exterior, and the windows. . .so many windows. With the beauty of the countryside, every house should be cloaked in windows, if possible.

Oliver assisted me from the carriage and held my hand until we reached the door, his smile tight. We'd spoken about this scenario on several occasions, talking through how to react, the best way to ease the transition of her hostility to, at the very least, indifference. Kindness. Patience.

Oliver gave my hand another squeeze and leaned to kiss my cheek before ringing the bell.

A rather somber-looking man greeted us, his attention keeping to the ground as he ushered us forward through an entryway of stone and hardwood floors. A lovely stone fireplace stood to the left, its fire glowing brightly against the dark furniture nearby. Down a long hallway to the left, I caught sight of bookshelves.

"The library," Oliver whispered, his grin perched crooked. "I'll see if we can relocate a few books from there to our little castle later."

My smile burst free and I shook my head as we passed a set of closed double doors to our right. Oliver looked from the doors to the butler, his brow wrinkling with a frown. I had little time to sort out his sudden shift in mood, for as we turned the next corner, we came to an intimate, yet beautifully decorated dining area, though nothing like the expansive dining room Oliver had described.

Mr. Camden walked forward, hand extended and smile as welcoming as ever. "So good to have you visit, Sadie." He bowed over my hand and patted Oliver on the back. "I saw you two walking in town together a few days ago, laughing. Seems marriage is agreeing with you."

Oliver's grin returned and he placed a palm to my back. "Indeed, Father. Not only agreeing but delightful and contented and enjoyable—"

"Please, Oliver, don't make a spectacle of yourself." A woman stepped from behind Mr. Camden, her soft brown hair twisted back and her dark gaze slipping from the hem of my burgundy gown to the top of my pinned head. "You'll embarrass Sadie."

It took all my willpower to hold onto my smile when I desperately wanted to confirm every adjective Oliver had used and add a few more of my own. "Mrs. Camden." I offered a slight curtsy, which seemed to please her enough to perpetuate her smile.

"I hope you enjoy roasted chicken, Sadie," Mr. Camden said, bringing his palms together, either oblivious to the tension in the room or ignoring it. "Our cook is truly excellent at her craft."

"Oliver spoke very highly of Mrs. Long. I look forward to trying whatever she's made for us."

"Of course you do." Mrs. Camden's brows rose in mock innocence as she gestured toward the table. "Shall we?"

Oliver's attention focused on his mother as he took the seat beside me. "I don't recall us using the breakfast room for dinner in the past. Is this a special occasion?"

"It is." The lack of movement in Mrs. Camden's composed expression left an unsettling twinge in my stomach. "We thought Sadie would be more accustomed to smaller spaces. No use in overwhelming her on her first visit, especially given her upbringing."

I grabbed Oliver's hand to silence him before the rising color in his face turned into unhelpful words. If I was going to be near enough to Camden House to possibly come in contact with Mrs. Camden, and Oliver planned to go to war, I had to attempt to maintain civility, if nothing else.

"I appreciate your concern for my comfort, Mrs. Camden."

Her eyes narrowed almost imperceptibly.

"Though you may underestimate Sadie's experience in a house nearly three times this size, Mother."

"Yes, dear." Mrs. Camden's unswerving gaze bore into Sadie's. "But I doubt she dined with the family, given her position."

I squeezed Oliver's hand again underneath the table and he turned his face my way, brows rising with his increased frustration. I donned my sweetest smile, or at least I hoped I did, and the tension in those familiar lips of his softened, but not the resolution in his eyes. He wouldn't allow his mother many more liberties.

"Where is Vicky this evening?"

My question brought Mrs. Camden's attention back to me. Cold. Dark. Frightfully emotionless. "It is much too late for her to join us."

Much too late? The evening barely shadowed the sky outside, but perhaps it was Mrs. Camden's further attempt to keep me from becoming closer to the family. How could I ever breach this chasm? I offered a silent prayer heavenward for strength and wisdom.

The dinner moved forward fairly painlessly except for a few subtle comments from Mrs. Camden about my social status or my inability to appreciate certain aspects of higher society. With each, the tautness in Oliver's spine tightened vertebrae by vertebrae, until one more statement would prove too much for his kind heart and protective nature to endure.

I attempted to refrain from speaking much at all, except to answer a direct question or to agree with something Oliver said, but as the evening progressed, Mrs. Camden grew increasingly more terse in her responses. Her expression failed to cloak her contempt as it had done in the beginning, and I knew the night boded ill.

"Have you found the gatehouse to your liking?" This from Mr. Camden, his smile too bright.

"Indeed, it provides everything we need, and since no one from the house uses that entrance any longer, we are content in our solitude." Oliver grinned at me, an invitation to respond.

"It's so close to town, which will be nice once Oliver is away." I nodded my thanks to the footman who placed dessert before me. "And wonderfully near Helen's."

"Helen's?" The name hissed from Mrs. Camden's lips. "Ah, I see how you've survived in your chosen poverty, Oliver. You've fallen into the good graces of that woman."

"Good graces?" Oliver lowered his napkin and steadied his attention on his mother. "And poverty? Mother, I have consistently saved money. I have not only the ability to purchase the gatehouse and the five acres surrounding it, but also to provide for my wife for the foreseeable future."

"When it's all gone, don't expect me to offer your inheritance back. Not after this." She waved her hand toward me. "I will not have some servant as a legitimate member—"

"It is convenient, then, that I have no wish to subject my bride to legitimacy in this family." Oliver tossed his napkin on the table and stood, dipping his chin to his mother. "Father, I believe we've reached our fill." He turned to me and offered his hand. "My dear?"

"You ungrateful child!" Mrs. Camden shot to her feet, turning the full fury of her glare on me. "And you. Are you happy with how you've ruined my son's life? Stolen his inheritance from him? Stripped him of the dignity of his position?"

"Caroline," Mr. Camden said, but to no avail.

"I made my choice, Mother, and I would do it again, without a second thought." He brought me to his side and stepped back. "And, if my dignity is based on the status of my family, I lost it a long time ago."

His mother gasped.

"In fact, I feel as though the whole attitude of my life has been set right in finding Sadie. The important things in life." A laugh burst from him and his face fairly glowed. I couldn't help but stare. "She's the best person I know, and I am honored to be part of her life." He looked at me, blanketing me with his certainty. "Her heart."

I knew he loved me, but watching him stand before his mother, who despised me in every way—hearing his declaration spoken with such confidence and love! No fairy tale in all the world painted love as beautifully as this. No novel touched my heart with such an odd combination of visceral weightiness and sheer joy. Only in the pages of scripture had I found anything so beautiful, showcasing what it meant to be so loved for exactly who I was.

"I should have known long ago that you'd never amount to anything, with your wayward interests and rebellion. No wonder you'd stoop to the underbelly of society to find someone who would have you."

Heat shot from my stomach to my face. "I'm sorry for you, Mrs. Camden, that you are blind and your measuring stick so distorted. In God's economy, Oliver is the best of men. He is measured rightly through his kindness and his generosity and his joy. I hope to have just a portion of his strength of character and honor and goodness. You don't even know your own son!"

Her lips curled. "How dare you speak to me in such a manner."

"I have every right to defend him. He is mine, and his reputation, his heart, his future, is as important to me as it is to you. Even more so."

"You've ruined him," she growled out the blame. "He has no future now."

"I believe that's our cue to leave, my dear." Oliver turned to his father. "Good night, Father." He set his gaze on his mother, his jaw tight. "Goodbye, Mother."

"Goodbye?" She pushed back from the table as Oliver tucked my arm in his and walked from the room.

"Don't you walk away from me. You are not dismissed!" Mrs. Camden's scream echoed over the ornate walls around us as Oliver marched us down the hallway. "Oliver!"

He kept his pace, only pausing to let the carriage driver know to meet us on the road once he had the carriage ready.

"I'm sorry, Sadie. I had such hopes since my last conversation with her." The night enveloped us as we walked up the lane toward our castle, the sound of the carriage horse coming up behind us. "But she is determined and untouchable. I'm glad all the more that we live closer to Granny than Camden House, because that's where you'll find companionship and encouragement while I'm away." He tossed a look over his shoulder toward the house, his gaze examining the sight as if attempting to memorize it.

"I'm sorry, Oliver."

"No." He shook his head and brought my hand to his lips. "My home and my heart are right where they want to be." The carriage came to a stop and he helped me inside before joining me, drawing close, touching my face. "Promise me you won't let her words poison you. I made my choice with my eyes wide open. I love you, and I wouldn't change one moment."

I leaned into the warmth of his palm against my cheek. "I love you too."

Quiet swelled between us. My heart knotted with a thousand emotions, stealing my voice. Separation loomed on the horizon, distance, and an uncertain future.

I had lived nineteen years of my life without him and after nearly three weeks as his bride, he somehow took up my whole world. Every favorite memory involved him, even Biltmore held so much of him in my thoughts, that it was easy to imagine we'd known each other much longer than we actually had.

We did not speak until we'd made it inside our little castle. He helped me remove my cloak and I his coat, each action somehow more precious and tender than the day before. Then he sat beside me in our little sitting room, grasped both my hands, and drew them to his lips, pressing for seconds upon seconds. When he finally raised his gaze to mine, my heart nearly broke all over again at the sight of tears in his eyes. "How can I leave you, my darling Sadie?"

My entire body stiffened against the conversation we'd avoided for days. Whispers of it had been in our comments and actions, but speaking the words somehow gave power to the reality. I'd not been afraid until now. Our little world—our fairy tale—was supposed to stay as it was for ever after, but the cold world of war crept into the story, and we had to turn the page.

"Sadie." His whisper warmed my cheek, and I squeezed my eyes closed to stay the tears. "Promise me something."

My brow pinched from the strain to beg him to be silent. To not speak. Instead, I smoothed my cheek against his, breathing in vanilla and soap. "Anything, Oliver."

He framed my face with his palms and held my gaze, his eyes

glistening with unshed tears. "If the worst happens—"

"Oliver, I can't—"

"Promise me you'll keep our dream, if you can." He nodded, smiling through the tears. "We already have the shop. It just waits for the shopkeepers."

"Both of us."

He shook his head. "But it will be both of us, even if it is only you, because we're a part of one another. Like you said to my mother. No matter what happens, you can make this dream come true, my darling."

I shook my head and looked down at my lap, tears staining my gown like raindrops.

"Sadie, don't waste your grief."

My head came up. "How can my grief be wasted? I would grieve for you because I love you."

"But grief is a tricky thing. Don't let it steal your life." He wiped a tear from my cheek and smiled down at me with such tenderness, tears doubled their efforts. "You are made of amazing stuff, enough to make any dream come true, enough heart to change the world around you. You've certainly changed mine."

"Then come back to me when all this is over." I cupped his face, holding his gaze, begging for a promise he couldn't make. "Live this life with me. Join me in our future. Whatever happens, come back to me."

He pressed a gentle kiss to my lips but did not answer.

Long into the night, I clung to him, replaying his words, his touch, his pulse in my ear as I lay my head against his chest. I knew this moment had to come. The jarring reality within the fairy tale. I clung to the hope that God had many more chapters yet to write of our story . . .and prayed for the strength to dream beyond tomorrow.

Chapter 22

The consistent beep of the heart monitor pulsed through the quiet room, each beat a reminder that Clara's mom was alive for another day. In fact, the doctors had given both Clara and her mother the good news that Mom appeared to be improving. Clara rubbed her tired eyes and tried to focus on the email Maggie had just sent from England. Cousin Margaret. Clara almost grinned at the thought of the wiry woman and her passionate personality. . .and of the fact Clara had an entire family an ocean away still waiting to meet her.

Maggie's emails had been consistent, and sometimes funny, especially as she explained having to ask her daughter how to add attachments to emails, which eventually came through. . .upside down.

"It's good to see that smile."

Clara looked up from her phone to find her mother awake, the tender expression on her face nearly unraveling Clara's composure all over again. Robbie had been by a few times to check on them, but otherwise, Clara had spent way too much time alone with her anxious thoughts and her frail mother. Not the best combination for dry tear ducts.

"Yours too." Clara unwound her sore body from the chair and scooted closer to the bed. "I was just reading over an email Maggie sent to me."

Mom's cheeks creased with her widening grin. "Maggie, your new-found cousin, isn't it?"

Clara offered a tired chuckle. "Yes, along with who knows how many more I've never met." She returned her phone to her pocket and reached for her mom's hand. "Maggie said she contacted her solicitor and he has a few more things to deliver to Max and Gillie later this week that might be helpful with the bookshop."

"I have a feeling Max will get those items to you lickety-split."

Clara narrowed her eyes at her mother and tamed her smile. "Why do you say that?"

"Reading between the lines from the stories you've shared, I'd say you two hit it off pretty well."

Clara shrugged and sat back in her chair, trying to quell the sudden fluttering in her chest. Circumstances didn't bode well for an international romance between them. He had to stay with his mom. She had to stay with hers. How on earth could a relationship work like that? And despite their daily emails and almost daily phone calls, any immediate plans waited on Mom's prognosis and the bookshop's future. Romancing an Englishman didn't figure into those prospects very clearly.

Though she missed him. . .even after only three days apart. How ridiculous was that?

"I think he'll make an excellent friend."

One of Mom's eyebrows took a turn. "Friend?"

"Practically speaking, Mom, anything more than friendship at the moment isn't a great idea." Though memories of his kiss never drifted far from Clara's thoughts. A pleasant distraction in the middle of sleepless nights on an uncomfortable foldout chair and constant nurse visits.

"It's always the right time for the right romance, my girl." Mom's resident twinkle reemerged in her eyes after too many days' absence. "Finding someone who understands you like few ever could and who wants to spend days just *being* with you, it alters your world forever."

Clara stared at her mom as memories like photos flipped through her mind of her parents together, their beautiful friendship and camaraderie. Clara had always valued it, but since meeting Max, the recollections resurfaced with a different hue. . .a wistful longing full of questions like, Could Max be the match for me? Was love like her parents' even possible anymore?

She folded her hands together, her smile resurrecting the slightest bit. Perhaps with Max.

"Like you and Dad."

Mom nodded, her gaze taking on that distant expression she usually got when she thought about her dear husband. "I loved him from the first time he smiled at me."

On the local college campus. Like something from a movie. She'd bumped into him because she was absorbed in the book she was reading. They both spilled their books onto the ground, and when they'd looked up from trying to retrieve their scattered belongings, they'd both just. . .known. Dad said it was because Mom was reading *Le Mort d'Artur*, and he knew any woman reading medieval literature, not to mention fantasy-based medieval literature, had to be worth knowing.

And a part of Mom seemed to disappear when Dad died. Not enough that just anyone would notice, but Clara had.

"He sure had a great smile," Clara added, uncertain of how to navigate this fragile moment where time spilled over itself.

"You have his smile and his eyes. The Blackwell eyes."

Clara raised a brow. "Actually, they're Camden eyes. Dad had his grandfather's eyes."

"That's right." Mom nodded. "And I can't wait to see those photos when Max sends the scanned copies. They'll be so much clearer."

"Well, I don't expect he'll have time until after Christmas." Clara squeezed her mom's hand again. "And I'm hoping we can celebrate at home instead of here."

"That gives me a good five days to get my act together then, doesn't it?" Mom released a soft chuckle and pushed herself up to a better sitting position.

She looked better. Healthier. But anything was an improvement from seeing her pale and lifeless as she had been when Clara first arrived at the hospital directly from the airport.

"And you are keeping your promise to me, young lady." Mom pointed her finger at Clara, her voice edging with more strength.

"My promise?"

"That you will go home today and sleep in your own bed."

Clara crossed her arms, ready to do battle, but the fire in her mother's eyes challenged her. "You said once I ate two full meals you'd go. Remember that?"

Clara deflated into a begrudging frown.

"I ate my tasteless breakfast and my slightly better lunch, so I'm holding you to your promise." She wagged her finger, her countenance sobering. "I'll not have you get sick too. Traveling. Sleeping in a hospital for three nights. You need rest, Clara."

"Fine." She leaned forward, holding her mom's gaze. "But I'll be back first thing in the morning, and I may even send Robbie to check on you right before bed."

"You can't keep spinning like this, Clara. Always hovering around me, trying to make sure I'm taken care of." Mom squeezed Clara's fingers. "You've spent the past five years of your life taking care of your father and then me, walking around as if I was going to drop dead any minute."

"And you very well could." Clara waved toward the bed.

"As could you," Mom reprimanded softly. "You can't keep living this anxious life, this half-life, by keeping so close you don't even try to fly. I've lived my life and I've lived it well. Have you, Clara?"

Her words spilled like ice over Clara's skin. "I don't understa—"

"What do *you* want? What dreams do you have?" Her mom's gaze bore into Clara's, sending her back into the chair. "I know that one of them is love, marriage, a family of your own. When do you plan to start that?"

"I. . .I don't want to waste what time I have left with you."

"Waste?" She offered a sad laugh. "My girl, have you ever considered that I'd like to witness your dreams come true? I'd like to watch them happen, if God allows? That one of my biggest dreams is to see you fulfilling yours? So. . .what do *you* want?"

Clara sat riveted to the chair, her vision bleary from a sudden rush of tears. The question echoed through her from previous moments of solitude when she'd silently wondered the same thing. She'd watched life go by. England and Gillie and Max had given her a taste of living beyond the walls she'd built around herself. Her parents had never forced those expectations on her. She'd embraced them and defined them herself.

What did she want? The smiling faces of book-loving patrons blended in with scenes from Biltmore to England to. . .Max. At the core of her dreams settled a sweet hope of finding what her parents knew. Love.

But what did that look like? How could it happen? What would she have to do to truly embrace her future?

Her heart trembled as the question nudged her courage.

A knock at the door broke through the silence and a nurse peeked her head around the door. "Clara, there's a gentleman out here asking to see you. He said he needed to talk to you about some important documents?"

Clara's eyes fluttered closed in a quick prayer. Surely Uncle Julian hadn't shown up at the hospital.

"Clara?"

Clara met her mother's gaze and forced a smile, covering her mom's cool hand with her own. "I'm sure it's nothing serious, Mom. I'll take care of it."

Clara braced herself and rounded the door. The long, sterile hallway stretched before her. The only festive decor stood on the nurses' station desk in the form of a jolly-looking Santa Claus figurine. She closed her mother's door to keep Mom from hearing any unwelcome information from the upcoming conversation and stepped down the hallway toward the waiting area.

The large room, with massive windows allowing late afternoon light into the space, stood almost empty. A couple sat in the far corner, both looking at magazines. A woman sat near them, scrolling through her phone. Clara glanced over the potted plants and landscape paintings, searching for the reason she'd come, and froze. Standing near the wall, slightly concealed by one of the large treelike plants in the room, stood a familiar profile, but not Uncle Julian's.

"Max?" She blinked to clear her vision, but the figure moved at her call, clearing, proving her vision true. "You're here?"

He smiled in that nervous way she'd seen inside her head for the past three days. "I hope you don't mind."

"Mind?" Clara's laugh burst out, more air than noise. "No, of course not." She edged a step closer, still not trusting her vision.

"I brought everything Maggie sent, but it seems she has a few more things." He drew in a shaky breath and rubbed his palms against his jeans. "So perhaps I should have waited another day before coming."

"I can't believe you came at all."

His expression sobered and he stepped closer, his caramel gaze searching hers. "I. . .I didn't want you to be alone."

Those words broke some invisible barrier in her, a dam she'd used to hold back the endless emotions of the past few days. A sob shook through her and she stepped into cardamom and warmth. His strong arms wrapped around her, settling over her with a sudden sense of home. He'd come all this way—the man who rarely left his little village. She buried closer, the fibers of his knit sweater smoothing against her palms. Cardamom mingled with roasting firewood and the smell of Camden House.

"Thank you," she whispered, nestling her damp cheek against his shoulder. "I know how hard it must have been for you."

He shook his head and ran a hand over her hair, brushing it back from her damp cheek. "No. I realized it didn't matter what anybody thought." She felt the rumble of his reply more than heard it as it reverberated through his chest. "All that mattered was what *you* thought, and what you needed."

Another sob shook her shoulders and she squeezed closer to him. She shut her eyes, listening, understanding, and attempting to sort out how she could care so deeply for someone she'd known for such a short time. No, this wasn't some shallow whiff of heady romance that would dissipate in the light of time and distance and real life. Perhaps this was exactly what it appeared to be: a romance orchestrated to perfection by a heavenly hand.

The uncertainties of logistics and the future quelled beneath this unswerving confidence of being loved, and. . .of loving in return. She embraced him, this choice. . .this moment.

His mere presence seemed to shoulder some of her fear. Yes, she'd prayed, and God's comfort smoothed over the edges of her raw emotions, but He also provided a person to act as an agent of His comfort. Max.

"I. . .I hoped it wouldn't seem too forward, too presumptuous."

"No, not at all." She shook her head against his shoulder, holding on until the tears abated. "I'm so glad you came."

She pulled back and wiped at her eyes only to find him offering her a handkerchief. After blinking down at it for a solid five seconds, Clara snatched it with an added sniffle of gratitude. Bow ties, handkerchiefs, knit sweaters, and kisses. Did that fit her Christmas list or what?

"Maggie didn't find the deed, but she did locate the marriage certificate." He reached down at his side and tugged a duffel bag onto his shoulder.

"That. . .that will help." She fumbled through a response, still trying to wrap her mind around the fact that Max was there. "At least it proves their legal connection, and it will go along with the other things I have in the office. The other findings."

"I thought so as well." He paused to tug a piece of hair from in front of her eyes, and she nearly melted right back into his sweater again.

"And there are some other things that are worth seeing." He patted his bag. "Photos and letters. All tightening the connection between the two of them."

"And every thread of evidence will help my case with the bookshop."

He nodded. "Exactly."

She stared up at him, her eyes stinging afresh, and then she rocked up on tiptoe to press a kiss against his cheek. "You're simply wonderful, Max Weston."

He smiled and looked away, as if he wasn't sure what to do with such open affection, but he squeezed her hand. She couldn't stop grinning. Was one of her dreams coming true right before her eyes?

As she gave him another hug, her attention caught on a figure standing not too far away. Dark suit. Hideous mustache. She squinted. Uncle Julian? He was stepping backwards, as if slinking away, but he caught her gaze, and his expression froze, collapsed, and then. . . exploded into a strangled smile.

He closed the distance, his presence resurrecting all sorts of warning vibes in her stomach. He nodded at Max before addressing Clara. "I came to see how your mother was doing, but I hear things are better."

"Yes. She's much improved." Clara forced a smile, every impulse screaming for her to ignore the man, and then turned to Max. "Uncle Julian, this is my. . ."

What to call him? She hadn't thought about him as anything other than. . .Max. She looked up at him for help and, with a twinkle in his eyes and a half-shrug, he offered his hand to Julian. "Clara's boyfriend."

Her eyes drifted closed from the sheer delight coursing through her. Who needed ruby red slippers with such a man!

"Pleasure." Though Julian's intonation didn't hold one ounce of pleasure. He turned to Clara. "Well, since you have company I won't stay any longer, but I hope we can finish our conversation about the bookshop next week. After Christmas?"

Clara stood a little taller. "I feel certain we'll be able to bring this little misunderstanding to a close."

With that, he turned and slunk away. . .or at least that's what it looked like to Clara.

"I'm certainly glad he's not your only family member." Max grimaced, his attention on Julian's retreating form.

"Right?" Clara shook her head. "And his son is nothing like him. You'll love Robbie."

She ran a palm over her face and suddenly felt Max's hand on her back. "Is there anything I can do?"

"Being here is more than I could have imagined." She took his hand and then laughed as reality dawned. "You're here!"

"I'm here," he repeated, one brow arching.

"That means you can meet Mom!" She tugged him a step forward. "She's awake right now."

His attention swung back to her face. "I don't. . .don't want to intrude."

"You're not intruding. This will make her day." She pulled him forward another step. "Really, Max. You could make two ladies' days for the price of one. Besides, she'll definitely want to meet my *boyfriend*."

His grin inched wide, creasing the corners of his eyes. "Well then, let's go meet your mum."

"You came all this way?" Mom repeated for the third time, staring at Max with the same kind of awed expression Clara must have worn about fifteen minutes earlier. Mom looked over at Clara, her expression hiding nothing. "That says so much about you."

Clara rolled her eyes but couldn't tame her grin.

"I'm glad you're feeling better, Mrs. Blackwell." Max stepped forward, somewhat hesitantly, likely gauging how his appearance might impact Mom, but she only beamed up at him as if he wore a suit of armor.

"No Mrs. Blackwell." She waved away his formality. "You must call me Eleanor." Her gaze slipped to Clara again. "Because I think we're all bound to be good friends."

Heat clung to Clara's cheeks but she only smiled wider. Why had it taken her being forced to England and then her mom almost dying for her to figure out what living was all about? She shook her head and gestured toward the chair beside her for Max. It didn't matter. She was beginning to understand now. She looked over at her mom. There was still time.

"Max brought the marriage certificate and some photos to share."

"I've wanted to be a part of this adventure, and now you've brought the adventure to me." Mom adjusted the bedside table closer, her eyes twinkling. "Let's see what you have for us, dear boy."

The endearment paused Max's movements, and he flipped his attention to her a second before continuing. Yep, Mom was already halfway in love with Max. Join the club.

With careful hands, Max produced the marriage certificate. Yellow and curled at the edges, the inked names still shone clear. *Oliver Christopher and Sadie Clarice. 18 February 1916*. Married a little over a month before Oliver's death, living together for even less.

"Here's one of the special discoveries." Max shifted his gaze from Clara to Mom as he took a small plastic baggie from his duffel and placed it before them.

Clara leaned forward, her fingers slowly reaching toward the old photo.

"Is that. . ." Mom whispered.

"Oliver and Sadie on their wedding day," Clara answered, chuckling. "They look so happy."

"Uncommon for most photographs of that time period," Max quipped.

Sadie's lace gown curved down into a V at the front and cinched at the waist with a sash. Her arm linked around Oliver's and, instead of looking at the camera, they were smiling at each other, almost as if the photographer caught a candid look between the two lovers.

Clara ran a finger down the edge of the bag over the photo, the strange connection to this couple pressing in on her.

"They look like they love each other."

"Yes, they do," Mom agreed. She looked over at Clara and the awareness of how much her mother missed Dad rose into Clara's throat again.

"And Sadie's letters are here too." Max raised his bag. "Maggie trusted me with the originals with the distinct understanding that you'd return them after making copies."

"Of course." Clara pressed her palm against her smile. "I grew up hearing about Granny Sadie so much, but to read her letters? To see her photo here. It's like all those stories are finally connecting to this real person."

"She was such a joyful lady. So hopeful." Mom touched the edge of the photo. "And she seemed to carry this drive within her to try new things. Unafraid."

"I wonder if she was always that way?"

Mom shrugged. "I remember once she told your father and me that someone very special to her taught her how to be brave. I wonder if it was Oliver."

Clara held Max's stare. He'd introduced her to Maggie and traveled all the way to Asheville, North Carolina, for her. Could the same thing that fueled Max have been Sadie's too?

Love?

"Clara." Mom pulled Clara out of Max's hold. "Would you be kind enough to go to the nurses' desk and ask for some more ice chips?" Mom's attention moved from me to Max. "My throat is still dry from that early supper they gave me."

Clara stared at her mother, trying to sort out the mischievous look on her face, and then left the room. When she returned, Max and Mom were laughing, and the hint of reticence in Max's behavior had disappeared. Whatever had transpired over the five minutes Clara had been gone set Max at ease.

"Thank you, my dear." Mom smiled as Clara placed the cup with ice chips on the table by her bed. "Now, it's time for you to keep your promise and leave."

"What?"

"Max and I have already sorted it out, haven't we, Max?" She offered him a sneaky grin and he responded with a helpless one of his own. "You're going to take him to visit Biltmore so you can talk with Mrs. Carter about this letter she's found and then you're going to take him to a nice restaurant for dinner." Her finger raised to stop Clara's response. "And, since we have the extra guest room downstairs in the apartment, there's no reason he should have to stay in a hotel."

Max did very little to hide his amusement.

"It sounds like the rest of my day is already decided for me."

"It is." Mom gave a definitive nod. "But I don't think you'll complain too much for the company."

Her gaze found Max's again. "No, not one complaint."

Max kissed like a romantic—like a man who'd stored up a great deal of imagination just to unleash it, quite admirably, on the woman of his choice. Clara had always been a huge proponent of imagination, and she definitely wouldn't complain about Max's choice. In fact, his focused and expert skills certainly had to rub off and improve her own.

He'd gently coaxed her forward when they'd gotten inside her car, those umber eyes of his drawing her in before she even realized they'd both spanned the distance to greet each other in a rather knee-weakening way. She didn't flatter herself on being seductive, but the way Max responded to her generous attempts ensured she hadn't disappointed him.

Maybe the definition of romance wasn't some generic ideal dispersed among the romance-reading masses. Perhaps, in real life, romance corresponded to the intimate and individual needs of the two hearts. Unique. A handcrafted, heavenly match.

As she drove away from the hospital, her lips still humming with appreciation for his excellent care of them, she sent him a glance in her periphery.

"We don't have to go to the Biltmore if you don't want to." She turned her attention back to the road. "I mean, if you're uncomfortable with it or you want to rest? We can just pick up some dinner and take it back to the apartment."

He seemed to understand her reservation and touched her arm. "Your mother says I can't leave Asheville without seeing Biltmore at Christmas."

"It *is* beautiful, but I want you to enjoy the time you have here."

"I've enjoyed my time immensely already."

Heat crept up her neck at the very tangible memories of their mutual enjoyment. "Whew, so have I." She breathed out a sigh. "So I really don't want to ruin the momentum."

"If we engage in our previous activity a few more times, I don't think anything could ruin the rest of my year." He chuckled. "And as long as you don't mind that I wear my cap and turn up the collar of my jacket, then I'd like to go."

"I don't mind." She tossed him a grin. "It makes me feel like I'm walking around with a dashing Sherlock Holmes."

"Does it, now?" The hooded look he sent her tightened her throat and nearly had her running a red light.

She jerked her attention back to the road. "Stop it. You're distracting me with that look and your accent and the wonderful thought of kissing you."

When he didn't respond, she glanced back at him. He stared at her, the lines around his eyes and mouth, gentled, tender. "Clara, I want to be with you, and if that means taking a plane or touring a mansion or sitting in a restaurant, I want to experience them with you. I've given up enough of my life to fear. I don't want to lose any more."

Almost exactly what her mom had said to her. She and Max were more alike than she'd realized. Perhaps that was why they understood each other so well.

"And. . .when you're with someone who sees beyond the scars, then the scars don't seem as large anymore."

Neither does the fear.

They took their time walking hand in hand from the parking lot through the forest trail to the Biltmore. Clara always loved how it emerged through the trees like a great unveiling. Even Max, with his life among grand homes much larger than Biltmore, paused to appreciate the view and structure. Sunset glowed in burnt orange against the purple-hued mountains behind the house, casting the front of the magnificent chateau into gray-blue shadows. But the large pine in front of the house cheered the way with its white Christmas lights as well as the candles flickering in the many windows of the house.

As they waited for Mrs. Carter by the grand stairs, a stringed quartet played Christmas music from the lovely Winter Garden as festive Victorian decor displayed the gold and red of the season. She would bring Max back sometime so he could experience the beauties of her favorite room, the library.

Mrs. Carter greeted them with an enthusiastic welcome. "I was glad to hear your mother is recovering." She took Clara's hands into hers after introductions. "She's the dearest lady."

"She is and thank you."

"Come, I have a puzzle for you to sort out about Sadie Blackwell."

They followed her to the little office where Clara had joined her on the last visit. A letter housed in protective plastic waited on the desk and Mrs. Carter gestured toward it. "It's a letter from Sadie to Mrs. Vanderbilt. It's the only one I've found, but the note hints at perhaps one more. This one, as you can see from the date, was written in 1919, and it seems that Sadie was doing some sort of charitable work."

Clara raised the letter so that both she and Max could read the sentences reflecting Mrs. Carter's words.

Thank you for your generous contribution to me and my sister's efforts. You are one of the few people in the world who knows the truth of my specific situation and I appreciate your discretion and kindness. In answer to your previous questions, we have housed more than fifteen women in the past year and helped them to achieve independence either through their own employment or a happy marriage. Some came to us without any skills to recommend them or to help provide for themselves and their unborn children. I've employed a few in the bookshop, especially those who have had difficulty in finding suitors or positions, and some have been hired to help in your dairy, as you know. All have kept their children, except three, who found adoption to be the better choice for their children's futures. I am happy to say the children have been placed in loving homes.

Anna has proven indispensable in the navigation of so many people and has seemed to find her fit in our little "world across the pond," as she phrases it. We have paired Bible study and classic reading to provide the women with education for their souls, their minds, and their enjoyment. It also provides wonderful opportunities for them to increase their points of conversation when seeking husbands, should that be their hope.

Lark and I devised a special inauguration of each woman's exit from our care. On the day they leave, they carve their names on the largest wall of the upstairs room in the bookshop—the room they use as their quarters.

We have kept your support anonymous so that the actions of these women, or the perceived immorality, will not negatively reflect upon Biltmore in any way, but please know, your generosity has led to many women not only re-creating their lives, but some of them have even started their own businesses. Society often sees a "fallen woman" and nothing else, but each one of them has a story, and each deserves the opportunity for a new beginning.

During our last conversation, Oliver encouraged me that if the worst happened I should not waste my grief. Together, we dreamed of Blackwell's Books, and now, through knowing him, I have embraced another dream, one I am certain he would have encouraged with the same enthusiasm and magnanimity as he had for almost everything. It's remarkable how courage can be born from the love and confidence of another.

As to my beloved boy, John is happy and strong and so much like his father. Oliver would have adored him. When he laughs, I humor myself in imagining the sound bursting through the clouds of heaven just so Oliver will hear. He still fills my heart and memories. I have no wish for another. My life and dreams are contentedly wrapped up in loving my son, serving these women, and growing this bookshop.

It is strange how dreams can shift and change but the heart behind them beats with the same desire as when those dreams were forged. Books and imagination brought me love. Love inspired my hope, and hope led me to purpose. . .to serve others through generosity, kindness, and. . .books. Isn't it a wonder how God fashioned my desires into a greater story framed in by a beautiful binding —like the two covers of a book.

Please continue to pray for these women and their children. Hardship and injustice are heavy burdens, but hope and courage prevail.

Yours respectfully,
Sadie Blackwell Camden
P.S. Thank you for addressing me by my married name in our private letters. It is sweet to sign as the bride I once was.

"I'm sorry." Clara wiped at her eyes. "I just can't seem to help it when I read her letters, knowing how much she must have loved Oliver and then lost him."

She took Max's faithful handkerchief and smiled at him before returning her attention to the letter. "This tells us that Sadie not only came back to Asheville and opened Blackwell's, but she helped these broken women."

"That's what I surmised as well," Mrs. Carter said. "On the second floor of the bookshop, it seems."

"Have you ever found markings on the walls, Clara?"

She shook her head at Max's question. "We've never known to look for them. Dad replaced the bookshelves on one entire wall of the second floor about six years ago, with plans to replace the other ones at a later date, but. . ." Her eyes widened. "You don't think those names could still be there? After all this time?"

Max tilted his head, one brow raised like a question mark.

Clara stood. "Mrs. Carter, do you think I could get a copy of this—"

"I already made one for your records." She produced a page in hand. "But you must call me and let me know what you find."

"I will." Clara took Max's hand and they walked toward the door. Sadie's story had taken on its own rhythm, even apart from finding the deed. She needed to know what happened with her great-grandparents, and, hopefully, in the process, save Blackwell's.

Clara needed to know the rest of Sadie's story. More than Sadie's romance, or her bookshop, she needed to know about the possibility of another very special scene in a quietly remarkable life.

Chapter 23

Oliver's absence created an odd sort of loneliness. In all my life, I'd never truly experienced the emptiness of a vacant space, because I'd found great contentment in the imaginary worlds of so many stories. But, in truth, as remarkable as fiction painted the world and even lingered within my spirit, it couldn't replicate real life or the companionship of the man I'd grown to love.

Anna proved an excellent cook and companion. Once she overcame her overall mistrust of my acceptance of her, we readily engaged in book conversations and mutual dreaming. In fact, when I shared the plans Oliver and I had for a bookshop, she offered to go to the States with us, as an opportunity to continue working but also to escape the stigma of her past.

Having lived so many years as a servant or the daughter of a servant, I knew the interminable way in which society packaged people and the almost impossible feat of rising above one's station...or, in this case, reputation. Anna's story mirrored others within the community, some with less favorable futures than hers, and I wondered what could be done to change the course of these women's lives.

I'd seen it in Asheville, of course, and also in the opportunities the Vanderbilts created to help oppressed or disempowered people change their prospects. Biltmore School of Domestic Science offered training to young black women so they could find gainful employment and dictate their own futures. The Moonlight schools taught illiterate estate workers how to read and write, broadening not only their minds, but their opportunities.

Where would a woman like Anna fit if she wished to grow beyond her reputation?

I happily took over Anna's responsibilities at the bookshop, leaving her to clean and cook to her heart's content. She even enjoyed salvaging my attempts at a garden. Within the first week of Oliver's absence, I found myself wonderfully distracted by sore fingers from binding books as well as by delightful discoveries in the broken manuscripts Enoch recovered, pleasure in storybook reading to some of the children of the town, dinners with Helen. . .and, occasionally, Victoria, when she could get away.

Oliver's letters came almost as soon as his train left the station. He'd ceremoniously left one on our bed for me to discover when I came back from seeing him off. Anna found one the next morning, stored in my favorite teacup, and brought it to me straightaway.

Even as I cried, I smiled. I'd left letters in the pockets of his jacket, in a pair of socks, and one carefully tucked within his Bible. If he received half the pleasure I did at my little discoveries, then perhaps the distance and the uncertainty wouldn't feel so vast.

Victoria made the two-mile trek from Camden House to the gatehouse twice a week during her mother's shopping trips to Keswick, Durham, or Yorkshire. She happily joined in our book talk and gardening, and Anna took her into the kitchen and taught her how to make a few special treats.

The routine in my little world became enough to keep my mind busy during Oliver's absence, and the nights were punctuated by books and my bridegroom's letters. For he was as prolific in letter writing as he was in charm, and I harbored no complaints. If we couldn't be together in person, then at least I could have his words. He sprinkled a great deal of himself in those wonderful words.

We wrote of Anna and her situation and women similar to her, attempting to think of creative solutions. I even hired one of Anna's friends, Ellen, to help with the laundry once a week so she could earn extra money. Every day, after Ellen finished her duties, I helped Anna teach her to read.

Oliver encouraged me to write to Lark and make arrangements for her to travel to England. Having her safely away from Wolfe and sharing my castle with me until Oliver's return would ease the ache a little.

Two weeks into our separation, one of his letters gave me pause.

I cannot understand why the deed has not arrived to you as of yet, my darling. I received a letter from Mr. Long yesterday that confirmed he'd sent it at least two weeks ago. But do not be anxious, since the post during the war is inconsistent, at best. I feel certain it should arrive within a week or two, and then you can place it in our box. It will be safe there.

I wouldn't have been concerned, but the very next week one of Oliver's letters arrived with the seal broken. The postmaster apologized, his face growing redder the more he stuttered his regrets, but I just smiled and thanked him, thrilled to have words from my husband.

But the next week, another letter arrived, and something about the way the envelope seal hung loosely from the paper, as if it had never been closed at all, left an uneasy twist in my stomach. When I mentioned it to Anna, she suggested someone may have steamed the envelope open, but I dismissed the idea. Who would care to read my private letters from Oliver?

The third week, four letters arrived over two days. As soon as I finished at Enoch's, I rushed home to close myself away in our library to pour over Oliver's intimate messages. Though he mentioned a few elements of the war in passing, such as the tasteless rations or uncomfortable sleeping conditions, his letters kept his usual optimistic tone. Though once, he spent an entire page writing about a situation where one of his fellow soldiers died in his arms. He'd prayed with him at the last, offering some solace as they sat in the muddy ruins of a once beautiful French field. I prayed constantly for Oliver. For his heart as it stretched against the wounds and devastation of war.

He wrote mostly of books. Of his favorites, recalling my mind to certain scenes or characters. We shared ideas of our shop, and how we wanted to create a story world for anyone to enjoy, even those without the money to purchase new books. And he wrote of us. Special memories. Sweet scenes from our lives.

I dreamed of unpinning your hair last night. It is one of my favorite memories, the way it falls over my skin like silk and smells of spring. Perhaps our daughter will have hair like yours, and your magnificent eyes, and my dimple. No, perhaps not a dimple. I feel certain that a little girl who looked like her lovely mother and had a dimple would undo me.

Every letter ended the same way.

Until we meet again, my love.
Oliver

I often read parts of the letters to Victoria, for she craved information about her brother. A few times, I sent pictures she drew him or her own letters folded within mine, and he'd return in kind. Her little face would light up in sheer delight with letters from him.

It was a particularly long week, the fourth one after Oliver left. One of the children who came to the storybook readings at Enoch's became ill, so I visited her family and helped care for her mother, who was also sick with fever. Later in the week, Enoch traveled to visit his daughter, leaving the shop in my care. And two nights after that, a fire started in St. Peter's Church, destroying so much of the building that it could not be used. Once the medieval-era wall hangings caught fire, there was nothing to do to stop it from ravaging the wooden roof. Thankfully, no one was hurt, since the pastor had moved away two weeks before, quite unexpectedly, and the new pastor had not yet come to take up residence and keep watch on the place. No one was able to determine the source of the destruction, and the people of Fenwick felt the devastation of such an ancient place of worship, dimming the townsfolk's usual vibrancy.

As I swept the shop at the end of the week, grateful that Sunday meant a quiet day at the gatehouse and plenty of time to read Oliver's latest letter nestled in my apron pocket, the front door opened to alert me of a late afternoon visitor. I expected Enoch to arrive back from his visit at any moment, so when I turned to see a young man in uniform, the world suspended into motionlessness. The man had his back to me. Shoulders broad. Blond hair cut in a neat trim, though a little erratic.

My pulse stumbled and I nearly dropped the broom. Oliver? I blinked.

The man turned then, revealing a face very different from my husband's. Still young. Clean shaven, but instead of pale blue, a soft brown gaze rose to meet mine, a pair of eyes wreathed with weariness, aged with grief.

Thin and pale, he limped a step toward me, his lips pinched downward. "Mrs. Sadie Camden?"

My fingers tightened around the broomstick. . .and I knew. A gaping hollow branched through me with numbing fingers. Time slowed into a blur. Air thinned. His words droned into scattered syllables.

"I'm sorry. . .good man. . .saved my life."

My stomach heaved in protest, but I pressed my palm against it, forcing control. The agony wrinkling the poor man's face secured my attention.

"You look exactly like your photograph," the man whispered, pulling his cap from his head. "He spoke of you often, all the time actually. Of how you met and your imagination and excellent memory of stories." The man's voice broke, but he seemed to gather himself. His smile quivered, his eyes watery. "He talked of the bookshop the two of you would have and how you'd change the world through kindness and books." At this, a sob racked his body and he lowered his shaking head. "I'm so sorry."

A pinpoint pain pierced through the numbness, stabbing into my heart. This was real. I licked my dry lips and reached out my hand. "What is your name, sir?"

He looked up, tears lacing his long lashes. "Anthony Harlow, ma'am."

I looked away from him and smoothed my palms down my apron, searching the room. . .for what? I had no idea. "And you were injured?"

"Only my leg." He gestured toward his cane. "Your husband jumped in front of me and—" His words closed around another sob.

I pressed my eyes shut at the image of what must have happened next.

"He. . .he died in my arms, ma'am. He had me promise to find you."

My gaze came up to his. Oliver's words. Anything.

"To send you his love. To ask you to. . ." He swallowed so hard his Adam's apple bobbed beneath his collar. "To live for two until you meet again."

Until we meet again. I pressed my palm against the nearest wall, the tears no longer within my control.

"It should have been me, Mrs. Camden. Your husband is dead because of me." Mr. Harlow took a step closer, his expression pleading. "Forgive me. I've got no wife. Only my parents are waiting for me to come home. But he had you and dreams, and he gave them up for me. I should have been the one that died. Not him. Please, forgive me."

I saw the young man then, as Oliver must have seen him. Frail. Broken, yet a soul with a future. His heart rent with a guilt he shouldn't carry. Oliver did exactly as he would have done for anyone, on a battlefield or street or anywhere else.

"There is nothing to forgive, Mr. Harlow." I placed my palm against his arm and garnered what voice I could. "My Oliver did exactly one of things I love most about him. He cares. . ." I drew in a deep breath to correct myself. "He cared and lived with joyous courage. And though I would wish him back, I would never wish him to be anyone other than who he was."

The man's face crumbled into another sob but he nodded, fisting his cap in his hands. "He was the best of men." He blinked back up to look at me. "And if I might say so, ma'am, he was right proud to be your husband."

Air escaped me, half-sob, half-laugh. A sad sort of sound, and yet, it carried a hint of hope, of memory, of a sweet story which reverberated through the person I'd become since knowing Oliver. "Thank you, Mr. Harlow." I drew a handkerchief from my apron and wiped at my eyes. "When. . .when did he. . .?"

The man's brows came together, his eyes narrowed. "A bit over a week ago, but I would guess you knew that from the telegram."

"The telegram?"

He passed a hand over his face before meeting my gaze again. "The one sent from the war office. The one announcin' his death. It should have arrived before now."

A chill passed through me. Had the telegram gotten lost somewhere along the way or. . .The opened letters. The delayed notes. Had the mail been diverted to Camden House before it came to me at the gatehouse?

I shook my head as if the question had been spoken aloud. Surely not. Would Mrs. Camden resort to such deviousness? Reading my letters from Oliver and resealing them? And what other personal information had been redirected? The deed? My stomach dropped and I pressed my fingers into the wall to steady myself. *The marriage certificate.*

Mr. Harlow walked with me down the lane toward the postman's house as I, somewhat carefully, explained my concerns. Whether his presence, a wounded soldier in uniform, nudged Mr. Craven's guilt or not, the man blubbered through a confession, confirming all mail for the gatehouse had been directed to Camden House.

His appeal, so that I would not report him, was that the Camdens owned most of the buildings in Fenwick, or possessed the power to appoint or take away certain positions, which left Mrs. Camden with more power than I ever imagined. . .and perhaps more hatred than Oliver ever did.

The combination did not bode well for me as I bid Mr. Harlow a heartfelt goodbye and strode directly toward Camden House. What else had I to lose at this point?

Chapter 24

Clara unlocked the bookshop door and tugged Max through, nearly out of breath in her excitement.

"This is your shop?" He pulled free of her hold and glanced around, his eyes dancing in the white of the fairy lights glowing on all sides. "It's brilliant." He released a light laugh. "It's so much of you."

Clara paused in her mad dash to find Robbie and stared up at Max, then followed his gaze over the shelves and the stuffed animals and the decorative displays, even breathing in the scent of books and peppermint. Max's lips parted in a smile, his expression every bit as fascinated as a child with his first Christmas tree, and everything seemed to click into place like that moment when books fit onto a bookshelf perfectly aligned.

"I'm so glad you're here."

He looked down at her and squeezed her hand, the lights bringing out brighter hints of gold in his dusty blond hair. "So am I."

"Well, someone decided to take her mom's advice, I see." Robbie emerged from the back hallway, arms laden with a collection of books, biographies from the look of them. His gaze trailed from Clara to take in Max.

"And I'm guessing you're Max?"

Max shifted, almost imperceptibly to feature his right side. "Robbie?"

Robbie placed the books down and stepped forward, holding his chin a little higher as if it might increase his overall height. Clara smothered her grin with her palm. Robbie stepped forward, hand extended. "Says a lot that you'd come all this way."

Max's gaze sharpened almost imperceptibly, his smile flickering to life as he took Robbie's proffered hand. "Happy to meet you."

"Robbie, we need your help." Clara took his arm. "And your screwdriver."

Robbie's rust-colored brows skyrocketed. "A screwdriver, a bookshop owner, and a Brit." He squinted. "Why does that sound like the beginning of a bad joke?"

Clara rolled her eyes heavenward.

"Or a *Doctor Who* episode," Max offered as Robbie grabbed the toolbox he kept nestled in a storage closet near the shop office.

Robbie nearly dropped his toolbox, his smile taking a slow slide to full grin before he looked back at Clara. "Okay, you can keep him."

Clara tossed a look to Max. "I'm planning on it." She tugged Robbie toward the stairs. "Max and I found out another mystery about Granny Sadie's story. Mrs. Carter at Biltmore shared a letter." Clara handed the copy of the letter to Robbie, who skimmed over it as they mounted the stairs.

"It seems that Sadie did more than just open up a bookshop and raise a son when she came back to Asheville after Oliver's death."

"She helped women find jobs?" He looked up from the letter.

"Even more than that. It seems that she helped at least a dozen or so women who would have typically been outcasts in society. Unwed mothers. Those of ill repute."

"So the bookshop was used as a safe house of sorts?"

"And the women carved their names into the wall." Clara waved toward the back wall of the massive space lined with four large and old bookshelves.

"Women's fiction and history?" Max murmured as he came to Clara's side in front of the shelves. "Appropriate."

Robbie narrowed his eyes at Max, as if trying to figure him out, and then looked back at Clara. "So you think these names could be behind one of those bookshelves?"

"Maybe, if the wall hasn't been altered in a hundred years." Clara began removing books from the shelf closest to the windows. "And the only way we're going to find out is by using your brawn."

"My brawn?" Robbie puffed out his chest and tried to stand a little taller beside Max who clearly had at least six inches on him. "That's always the way to secure my help. Compliment my brawn."

Max's grin spread to a chuckle.

"Well, come on, Brawny." Clara waved him forward. "Let's get these books off and see what we can find out."

He released an exaggerated sigh and joined Max in helping Clara remove the books from the first bookshelf. "You know, these shelves have been here forever. We might find more than markings on the walls behind them."

Clara cringed and shot him a glare as she removed another stack of books and tossed a nod to Max. "That's okay. I brought a wizard with me, so he can take care of the other things."

"A wizard?" Robbie examined Max from head to toe, then shrugged. "For some reason the *Doctor Who* reference makes perfect sense now."

Robbie began unfastening the shelf from the wall. "Did Sadie ever mention anything about helping these women to your dad or mom?"

"Not that I know of." Clara smiled her thanks to Max, who took a stack of books from her arms and placed them with the others. "From what she said in the letter, Sadie seemed to want to keep it secret."

"Her marriage as well, it seems," Max added.

"But why?" Clara handed another armful of books to Max. "What happened in England that caused her to keep her marriage private? Did Oliver's mom say something? Do something?"

"Perhaps the other items Maggie has will shine light on the answer."

"So the second level of the bookshop was also a boardinghouse. The ladies lived here?" Robbie glanced around the upstairs again before continuing with the screws. "Like with rows of beds or something?"

"I don't know, but it sounds like it." Clara shrugged. "It seems to have been a transition place while Granny Sadie and her sister worked to find more permanent spots for these women, whether helping them become independent or get married. They'd keep them here until they were healed and healthy enough to leave."

"Okay, this one's done," Robbie announced. He handed the screwdriver to Clara. Without a word, Max moved to the opposite side of the shelf and, with a few slides back and forth, they succeeded in wiggling the shelf far enough away that the light slipped through, revealing an uneven, scarred-looking wall.

Clara peeked behind, her phone's flashlight shining a pale glow into the shadows. "Oh my goodness, they're still here, I think."

The two men framed her in on either side, peering into the shadows where faded markings covered the wall. "There are a whole lot more than a dozen, Clara."

"And the markings appear to disappear behind the next shelf as well."

Clara looked from Robbie to Max, and they immediately began taking books off the next three shelves, unscrewing them, and moving them with added speed, until all four shelves were emptied and pulled back to unveil the entire wall.

Name after name carved into the wall.

"Oh my. . ." Clara reached behind her to grip one of the reading benches in the center of the room, slowly lowering herself to sit.

"There have to be at least a hundred names," Robbie added, wiping his brow.

"If not more." Max joined Clara on the bench. "It's remarkable."

"She touched all those lives." Clara blinked against the tears. Is this how God turned Granny's heartbreak into something beautiful? Out of her pain she gave to others? Healed by healing? Received by giving?

She pushed up from the bench and walked forward, a name in the center drawing her attention. In crude, jagged slices, the name *Sadie Blackwell* marked an unassuming spot among the others. *Lark Wolfe* nearby.

Clara rubbed her fingers over Sadie's name, her vision blurring at the touch. How many people, like Sadie, lived a life that reverberated through many others and yet remained unknown and unnamed? How many of these women had felt unseen, discarded? Sadie's choice to have them carve their names into this wall must have given them a sense of permanence, of identity. Clara closed her eyes, a warm tear slipping down her cheek.

This was Sadie's legacy. . .and Clara's heritage. It shone as a reminder that being seen mattered—names mattered.

The verse from Sadie's Bible rushed into Clara's mind.

"I have redeemed you. . .I have called you by name. You are Mine."

Even if these carvings had been hidden behind bookshelves for decades, Sadie wouldn't let them be forgotten, even a hundred years later. Names like Eloise, Sarah, Ruby, Fannie, Clarrisa, some carved with a careful hand and others jaunty or almost illegible, but there.

But there.

Even if Sadie couldn't use her married name, Sadie still knew she was loved—knew who and whose she was. And that made all the difference in how she lived beyond the grief of losing the man she loved.

After they configured a new way to sort the shelves so that some of the wall remained visible, and Robbie went home by way of the hospital, Clara and Max sat on the couch in the apartment, eating some of Mom's leftover coffee cake and drinking hot tea. Cuddling up beside him, after Mom's hospitalization and discovering another of Sadie's secrets, felt like the perfect ending of a day filled with the gamut of emotions.

"I waited until we were alone to show you this." Max withdrew an envelope encased in plastic from his bag. "It seemed something that needed privacy to uncover."

She studied his face as he placed the envelope in her hand, then examined the paper. A simple envelope with the name *Sadie Blackwell Camden* was written across the front. The edges were creased and stained with. . .dirt? Sweat? Her breath stalled. Blood?

"Maggie said that it was the letter found on Oliver's body."

Air pushed from her lungs in a gust and she raised her gaze to Max. "His last letter."

Max nodded, his smile a gentle nudge of encouragement.

Clara turned it over, the seal apparently unbroken. "It's never been opened?"

"Maggie said her mother never opened it, but she wasn't certain about Mrs. Camden. It appears to have been delivered to Camden House instead of to Sadie, or that's what Maggie was told by her mother, Oliver's sister."

"So Sadie never saw this."

Max shook his head. "From what I understand, Oliver's mother intercepted this letter too, and never gave it to Sadie. Victoria found it years later."

"Should we even open it, then? It's not meant for us."

"Sadie will get no use from it, Clara." He slipped a hand over a strand of her hair as he seemed inclined to do in their private moments. "But perhaps *you* will. Another part of her story."

Clara slid her fingers over the envelope, hesitant to break the seal and yet, a need gnawed through her. What had been her great-grandfather's last words to his bride? With a steadying breath, she peeled back the seal, which came apart in ragged pieces, except on the stained parts. The paper inside had not been protected from the stains or the years. Faded, patched with the brownish hue of blood, the black ink stood untouched in some parts and faded to invisible in others.

Oliver's handwriting.

Clara cleared her throat and tilted the letter so that Max could see. " 'My darling Sadie. . .'" Her voice wobbled and then gained traction. " 'If you are reading this letter, then I have quit my earthly home for a heavenly one, though, to be honest, my time with you was as much a taste of heaven as I've ever known.'"

She looked up at Max, her eyes burning, her throat raw. "He sounds so sweet."

He brushed a kiss against her temple. "Do you want me to read it?"

She shifted the paper to him and leaned into his warmth as he draped his arm around her shoulder. " 'I don't regret serving my country in this way, my love. Know that I would do it again even had I been aware of the outcome. I fought to protect our future, now your future. But my greatest fulfilment in life has been being loved by you, dreaming with you. We did not have years of memories, nor decades to learn every intricate facet of each other's personalities, and many might say that love cannot bloom within the confines of our limited time and correspondence, but we would prove them wrong. Something within me came alive when I met you, and there was no going back to what I was before.'"

Max stopped reading, his brow bunched into mastiff intensity. "What?"

"That's how I felt when. . .when I met you."

A gasp slipped from Clara's lips. She lost all sense of time in those golden eyes and the gentleness of his gaze. Paired with the moment, the beautiful words still brewing in the air around them, she touched his cheek, the scarred side. Is this what Oliver felt with Sadie? This connection that couldn't be explained by time? This awareness that choosing him was exactly what her heart had craved before she'd ever met him?

He eased forward, the rich scents of cardamom and soap and something tangy enveloped her, and he claimed her lips with his own. His hand slipped across her cheek and into her hair. Her fingers curled from his face to slide down to his collar. Nothing but staccato breaths shook the darkness.

Except. . .

A scratching noise from just beyond the door between the apartment and the bookshop.

Clara almost didn't hear it, especially with Max's expert distraction on full tantalizing display against her mouth, but it scraped again. Metal on metal. And then a *click*.

She wouldn't have heard it a minute before with them reading the letter aloud or laughing over tea, but in the silence of the kiss, the noise annoyed enough to draw attention. A mismatched sound.

With a palm to Max's chest, she pulled back, holding his gaze. "Do you hear that?"

He blinked, his gaze coming back into focus, and she almost grinned at the pleasure of knowing she'd happily distracted him too. His brow quirked, and she raised her palm to hold his response.

A very quiet squeak, barely audible, slipped beneath the door. She knew that sound. It was the door to the bookshop office. Max's head jerked to the noise, watching her face. He'd heard it too.

Clara glanced at the clock over the mantel. Twelve thirty a.m.? "I don't think that's Robbie," she whispered, placing the letter on the coffee table.

Max rose at the same time she did. Who would break into the bookshop and then go directly to the office? She didn't have anything in the office except paperwork. Her gaze shot to Max. "The marriage certificate, Max. I put it in the office when we got back, along with some of Sadie's other papers."

"Why would someone want the marriage certificate?" His eyes widened. "Your uncle. Do you think he overheard us at the hospital?"

"I don't know, but that's the only thing that makes any sense. He's sent someone to take my documentation so he can get the bookshop, and he'd know I keep everything in there."

"Listen to me." Max took hold of her shoulders. "Do you have a weapon?"

She nodded. Her father had taken her to get one years ago when he'd traveled and Clara and her mom were left in the apartment alone.

"Get it. Call the police and stay here."

"Max." She grabbed his shirt. "You should stay here too."

"We don't have time, Clara. If he's in the office, he may already have it." He tugged free of her and took her mom's hardback copy of *Middlemarch* as he approached the door. His hand barely wrapped around the massive nine-hundred-page volume.

She stared, almost mesmerized, until he opened the adjoining door which led into a small hallway connecting the two buildings. A light flickered against the wall coming from the right—the direction of the office. Flickering?

Her throat closed around a scream. *Fire!*

She placed her phone to her ear and raced up the stairs to her room, retrieving the little pistol from the nightstand by her bed. Answering the dispatcher's questions as she descended the stairs, she ran through the doorway to the sounds of a crash. Then a groan. All the while the flickering lights grew brighter.

As she turned the corner toward the office, air lodged in her lungs at the sight.

Fire snaked up one office wall while Max struggled with an assailant in black. Max's size came as an advantage as he slammed the other man down against the desk. The man cried out, kicking back with enough force to knock free of Max's hold. With a push up from the desk, the assailant limped toward the doorway, his mask no longer covering his face. The papers Clara had left scattered around the floor during her research quickly caught the flames, igniting other parts of the room.

Clara raised the gun as the thief's gaze rose to meet hers. "Why, Uncle Julian? Is this property that important to you?"

"This place should have been mine all along, and if I can't get something from it, you won't either."

Her hand quivered holding the gun and he sneered, stepping forward, but Max caught him from behind and wrestled him to the floor, flames growing behind them through the office door. The dispatcher's voice rang in Clara's ear, asking a question she couldn't interpret.

"Fire," she managed to whisper. "Blackwell's is on fire."

Chapter 25

Taking a trail through the forest, the hour-long walk to Camden House afforded me alone time. Time to allow the ebb and flow of myriad emotions. Anger, loss, pain, denial—all swirled through me at random. Half my prayer erupted as cries, even screams, to God, and the other half dissolved into murmurs that only God could have understood. What was He doing in this? How was He working good from *this*? Why would He have brought me all the way to England to give my heart to Oliver only to take him away?

And now, as the lights of Camden House shone into the sunset shadows, my loss, my grief, twisted into a deeper sting. Betrayal.

The same butler answered the door, his brows barely flickering when he saw me standing in my day dress before him without invitation.

"Did you come for your telegram, miss?"

I refused to answer until he looked at me. "I came to speak to Mrs. Camden *and* retrieve any post that belongs to me."

His expression marked confusion, but with skill honed from years of cloaking his emotions, he gave little away—only enough for me to realize Mrs. Camden had not made the staff privy of her deception.

"Mrs. Camden is not seeing anyone at present. She is ill."

Oh no, she'd not get away with this. Grief or no. "Would you mind retrieving my mail for me, please, Mr. Drake."

He bent his head in assent. As soon as he turned the corner, I dashed down the hallway, moving past room after room, until I found her in some sort of sitting room, a maid at her side. Her pristine appearance boasted control, from sculpted hairstyle to the tip of her black velvet skirt. She sat in the shadows of the room, handkerchief in hand, waving it about as if she was having some sort of nervous fit.

Two months ago, I would never have dared confront someone of her station, but I was no longer the woman I'd once been. My shoes clipped the hardwood as I marched into the room.

The maid almost lost her hold on the teakettle in her hand. Mrs. Camden's head swiveled about like an owl's, her dark eyes widening before closing into serpentine slits. "What are *you* doing here?"

"How dare you." I came to a stop a few feet from her, my gaze holding hers with as much intensity. "All these weeks? You stole my mail."

Her expression didn't so much as quiver. "You stole my son."

I rocked back on my heels as if slapped. "I stole your son?"

"He would never have married you, had he been in his right mind." She pushed to a stand, facing me. "He knew his place. His station. Until you came along and bewitched him."

"Bewitched him?" A humorless laugh burst from me before I could stop it. "Your son chose to love me and give me his name."

"He would never have given up his situation had it not been for you." Her voice trembled with an almost palpable rage. "You took him from his rightful place. You forced him to give up his family for the likes of *you*."

"Clearly, you didn't know your son." I stood taller, refusing to break eye contact. "He never cared for the veneer of life that *you* forced upon him. He wanted freedom to live as he thought best for his own virtues. That is the reason he gave up his inheritance. His choice, as a grown man who is free to make such choices. And you. . ." I shifted a step closer, my eyes stinging with renewed tears. "You had no right to take my telegrams, to read the private letters from a husband to his wife."

"Wife?" Something flickered in her eyes, dangerous and wild. Her soft laugh pushed a chill through me. "You are only his wife if I say you are."

"I know who I am. I am Oliver's wife, and you can't change that."

"Can you prove it?" Her eyes took on a glossy look, her smile twitching, false and sinister.

And what I had feared when I'd first considered Mrs. Camden's villainy suddenly crystallized before me in her merciless sneer. She had possession of my marriage certificate.

"I have witnesses."

She chuckled again, a sound almost growl-like. "Lest you forget, Miss Blackwell, the former clergyman has been reassigned somewhere very far away. Quite suddenly, I believe, after this ill-conceived wedding of yours."

My face cooled, my pulse hammered. "Mr. Camden was there."

"You would hang your hope on Mr. Camden's testimony?" She shook her head and slowly returned to her seat. "Or Helen's? They have no real power here."

"And what control do you have over the Almighty? Who witnessed everything and knows what vows were spoken."

Her eyes flashed. "By all means, bring Him forward and let Him testify." She folded her hands together in her lap, the silence dealing a deafening blow. "Poor Sadie Blackwell. Who are you now, when everything is stripped away?"

"Why are you doing this?"

"You took him from me." She launched back to her feet. "You turned him against me, making me a laughingstock among my peers. *My* son! Marry a *maid*? I will not have you become a smudge on our family's name or history."

"If you loved your son at all, you would be more concerned with his wishes than your own."

"His name is what matters. Five years from now, if I have my way, you'll be forgotten from this place." She leveled those dark eyes on me, their coldness inciting a tremble over my skin. "By giving up his inheritance, he left little for your future, and with no legitimate documentation of the marriage in our little hamlet, I can ensure that it never happened."

No legitimate documentation? The church! The fire! Two days ago? I examined her, a sense of dread nearly weakening me to the floor. Could she have been the one? The wild look in her eyes, her erratic behavior, stalled my arguments. Had her grief and hatred plunged her into madness? Power, an unsound mind, and a bitter heart braided into a dangerous combination.

"He has no inheritance and you have no legitimate claim to anything of his."

"I have his heart and his dreams." I thrust the declaration through my burning throat. "That is enough."

"Yet he did not plan for your future." She edged a step closer, her long fingers fisting and unfisting like tentacles. "Which makes me wonder if he ever had any real intentions for you, other than a mere fling as so many young men are wont to do in these times."

My pulse thrummed behind the buttons of my shirtwaist, but I refused to give her the benefit of seeing the concern on my face. Doubt webbed through her words, but I closed my eyes, my hand brushing the pocket that held Oliver's most recent letter. I knew the truth. I'd felt the truth of his love.

"I'm not concerned for *my* future, Mrs. Camden. I'm not afraid of work."

"Of course. Return to your stock." Her sneer curled. "But you see, we have another problem. Should my son, Robert, fall prey to the same fate as his younger brother, there will be no male heirs for my husband's estate, unless. . ." Her gaze roamed down my body, splashing icicles in its wake. "By some horrible turn of events, you, even now, carry Oliver's child, a son, and can eventually prove his legitimacy, and therefore he would be the heir to *my* money?"

My palm flew instinctively to my stomach.

"I will ensure *my* grandson is raised as an Englishman under my care, not by some American servant. And *I*, unlike you, have the documents of proof to use as I will."

I had no idea if I carried a child, but even the thought of one in the clutches of such a woman gripped me from neck to knees. "You can't do that."

"Can't I?" Her unsettling laugh resounded again. "What power do you have in England, Sadie Blackwell? You're a penniless foreigner who used to be a servant. I hold all the money and all the influence. Even that little gatehouse that you call home reverts to this estate now that Oliver is gone."

"Mrs. Camden, ma'am." The butler emerged in the doorway, his usual pallor ruddied and breath erratic, likely from his search for me. "I didn't know she'd take to looking for you."

"Ah, perfect timing, Drake." Mrs. Camden strode to the butler and plucked a few envelopes and papers from the tray in his hands, sifting through them before holding them out to me. Her lips took a sinister turn. She recognized her status. She held all the cards. "As I understand it, your sister is not well."

I glanced from her to the papers in her hands, and grasped them when she held them out to me. The top one was a telegram. I read over the words, my knees weakening.

```
Lark in hospital. Wolfe dead. Come if you can.
```

"It seems to me it would be in your best interest to find your way back to your home, Miss Blackwell. You are certainly not welcome here."

I stepped back, and though my eyes stung and my heart pulsed a battered rhythm, I raised my chin and met her gaze. "Mrs. Camden, I would have cared for you with such generosity if you'd given me the chance. We could have helped one another grieve, but no matter what you say or do, I am not the one who lost Oliver. You are." I pressed my fist to my chest. "He is with me here and chose to be so. You can berate me, hate me, and cast me away, you can even steal my letters, but you can never take him away or the memories and love I have from him." I smiled even as tears blurred my vision. "In the end, your money and power and hatred can never give you back all you've truly lost."

I had made it halfway to Helen's house at a hard walk when someone called my name. When I turned, my heart broke all over again. Victoria, hair down and flying around her shoulders like a runaway angel, dashed toward me, her face red from crying, her eyes glossy and pleading. She raced into me, holding to my waist, burying her head into my stomach, sobs shaking through her little body.

"You can't leave too. You can't," she murmured into my shirtwaist.

Had she heard the argument? I sighed down to my knees and brushed away her hair from her damp cheeks. "Oh sweet girl." I pulled her back into a hug. "I would stay if I could."

"You cannot let Mother make you leave." She burrowed deep against me. "She makes everyone leave."

I squeezed my eyes closed against the new tears and begged God to protect Victoria's heart, her future. To hold her close, so that she would know love in all the right ways. "I want you to know that I love you." My voice rasped, and I cleared it. "That you are loved just as you are, Victoria." I pulled back and held her gaze. "You are every bit as intelligent and creative and joyful as your brother, you are all of those things. Don't forget it. Ever."

She sniffled, large tears pouring down her cheeks.

"And stay near your granny as much as you can. She will speak truth to you. You know that, don't you?"

The little girl nodded, her chin dimpled into a dozen creases.

My attention fell to the charm bracelet on my wrist, an idea forming. Something tangible. "I have something for you. Something to help you remember good things. True things." With a twist of my fingers, I plucked the book charm from my bracelet and pressed it into Victoria's little palm. "Don't forget that your story is special and important, and yours to write. You can be brave, even when it's difficult, and you're sad or frightened."

"I can't write stories," she murmured between sniffles.

"Yes, you can. Your best one. Your life." I kissed her fisted hand. "With your kindness and your compassion and joy, just like your brother. You can make your own story and touch others too."

"I miss him." Her whisper echoed to my soul.

"Yes, me too." My breath shuddered out. "Oliver may not be here with us anymore, but his love is. It always will be."

"Will we see him again?"

"Oh yes!" I smiled at the unexpected comfort lacing my declaration as I held to scripture's promise. "Your brother loved Christ, Vicky. He loved Him so well that it came out in almost everything he did without even using words sometimes. His story is even better than any fairy tale because he gets the best happy ending of all. And one day, we will too."

"I want to see Oliver now."

"So do I. Oh, so do I. But remember, he's only a page away. In all those fairy tales you read, about the brave knights or honorable princes. He's there, as he was when he lived, so kind and brave. And he's here." I pressed a hand to her chest. "In all our love for him, because God allows us the gift of memories to tide us over to eternity."

She covered her little palm over mine against her chest and nodded.

"Keep to your Bible and to your fairy tales, sweet girl. One is for your soul and the other is for your daydreams. Both will help you through this, and in both you'll find your story."

We walked hand in hand to Helen's, who gave me enough money for Anna and me to make the trip to America. Helen and I promised to correspond, and she'd find a way to get notes to Victoria, as she could.

Lark had been beaten rather badly, and during the altercation both she and Wolfe had fallen down the stairs of their home. Two of the maids bore witness to the event, which legally cleared Lark of any possible charges, but the shadow of her history and her husband's death still followed her.

And I discovered only a short while after arriving in Asheville, that I carried much more than a piece of Oliver in my heart. The knowledge brought with it a mixture of overwhelming joy and an awareness that I would become an outcast, of sorts, as Oliver and my story remained quietly tucked away in my heart to protect the future of our child.

But his story would not be forgotten and my grief would not be wasted, nor would our dreams. If I had to work three jobs and pursue every coin, Brick House would become more than just a bookshop and a sweet dream. It would become a place where hope lived between all the mortar and the pages.

Like an excellent story.

Chapter 26

The bookshop office gaped like a charred cave, walls burned to the cinder block on the apartment side and scorched through to the bookshop bathroom on the other. The stench permeated every part of the shop.

After Clara and Max had given their police report and Julian had been taken into custody, they got a few hours' sleep at Robbie's before returning to the bookshop.

The smoke damage alone cost thousands, not to mention the structural damage and the loss of inventory. At least insurance would take care of some of it, but not all. It wouldn't cover the loss of Christmas income. How could they recover from this? Would they end up having to sell Blackwell's anyway? After all she'd done to try and save it!

Max, with his usual calm, suggested Clara not "freak out" until after she'd talked to the insurance adjuster and Mr. Lawson.

"It may be a waste of good tears," he said as he wrapped her in one of his warm hugs. Then, with a small smile, he slipped his fingers through hers and they began evaluating the damage in the office.

The blackened remains of the marriage certificate lay singed in the corner of the office, along with many other unidentifiable pieces of paper. The oak desk stood blackened, but intact, so at least many of the things within the drawers remained intact as well. The bookkeeping. Important tax documents. Even some of the old papers of her dad's and the tiny key she'd discovered in the attic.

A family picture lay scorched beyond repair. The plastic pieces of the office chair were melted, and the nearby filing cabinet's corner curved inward from the heat. It could have been much worse.

She tried to reassure herself. Perhaps the books upstairs could be salvaged, and the main heart of the building was fine. The apartment too. Everything just needed a thorough cleaning or. . .she sighed against her tears. Replacement.

They'd moved ruined items out. Granny Sadie's massive chair that always stood in the corner of the room by the now-singed antique reading lamp, the two family photos that only had the frames remaining, a side table that had been reduced to a single leg.

Clara glanced around the nearly empty office at the remains. They'd have to replace the desk, but at least her laptop was still in her room. She'd not unpacked yet, so all of her digital files should be safe.

"Clara, come see this."

Max's voice drew her from her depressed examination of the withered peace lily she used to have by the door. He was crouched down near the corner of the office with the worst damage. She moved to his side and peered around the blackened remains of one wall where it met the now-nonexistent other wall, the spot where Granny Sadie's chair used to sit.

"What is it? A box?"

Clara followed his gesture to see some sort of metal container lodged within the exposed part of the wall. A box that would have remained hidden by the wall if not for the fire. "It. . .it looks like a. . .a lockbox, maybe? An old one."

Soot rolled from its cover as Max pulled it from its hiding spot, but otherwise it appeared undamaged. "How did it get there? In the wall?"

Max shrugged and placed the box on the desk. "How old is the office?"

Clara scanned the space again. "If I recall, Dad said Granny Sadie had this room and the indoor bathrooms built in the mid-1950s."

His gaze locked with mine. "Then someone placed the box there about 70 years ago."

The deed? Clara's breath caught, and she rushed around the desk to the drawers. "I have a few keys I found in the attic, but only one of them was small enough to fit a lock like that."

She produced the key and Max fitted it into the lock. After a few tries, the lid budged and Max forced it the rest of the way open. Clara wasn't certain what she'd expected to find, but nothing prepared her for the two simple items inside.

"It looks like a book of fairy tales." Max's words faltered as he withdrew the book from the box.

"And a ring box?" Clara took the small container into her hand and opened it. It housed a delicate pearl ring encased in simple white gold. "It's. . .it's beautiful. Do you think it was an engagement ring or something?"

"That would be a good guess, I'd say." He offered her the book. "I think this may be special as well."

As I took the book, I met his gaze, and he smiled. "Perhaps something good can come from this devastation too."

She cradled the book close and almost smiled. Like Sadie's life. Even in her heartbreak, she found hope. Clara looked down at the faded book cover, the intricate designs still visible around the title. *Finding Ever After.*

The first turn of the page brought its own surprise. A letter. She opened the page, carefully, and grinned up at Max. "A letter from Oliver." The pages fell open again, revealing another letter. She looked up at Max and his brow rose, as if nudging her internal question into action.

With a turn of her fingers, the pages flipped, revealing little notes interspersed throughout the entire book. They'd never found any of Oliver's letters, because Sadie had kept them all here, between the pages of a book of fairy tales. Clara slipped down to sit against the desk. What a beautiful sentiment to their love! His words of love, their story, pressed within a fairy tale.

As the final page turned over, an envelope pressed against the back cover of the book. Clara gently tugged it from its spot and slid her fingers behind the seal to draw out the paper. Her breath unlocked into a sob-like laugh. The deed, complete with the names Oliver Camden and Sadie Blackwell Camden.

Their names joined here on this official document. Together. She shook her head through another weak laugh. "Their story."

Max grinned. "Their dream."

She looked back down at the deed lying atop the book. Hope. Hope between the pages.

My father always told me to never outgrow my belief in faith and fairy tales, but fear has a way of darkening one's vision, and so I'd lost sight of the beauty God displayed through magical stories. Not so much the glass slippers or the poisoned apples, but the deeper truths. The light overcoming darkness. The rewards of perseverance. The beauty that can come through trials of thorns or battles or even sleeping death. I'd forgotten that imagination gives me so much more than the ability to fall into the world of a book. It motivates my dreams, inspires remarkable love, and helps me see beyond this world to a greater one.

On Christmas Eve, Max returned to England and Mom came home from the hospital to a limping bookshop, but a bookshop that belonged, through and through, to us. The same day, a package arrived from Maggie. Inside were the few letters Helen and Sadie had exchanged before Helen's untimely death, but another envelope hid beneath the faded photos and yellowed pages. Pristine. New. From Maggie's solicitor.

Inside was a check for twenty thousand dollars.

Due to the circumstances of Mrs. Helen Camden's death and unknown situation involving her estate, along with the behavior of her son and daughter-in-law, the inheritance Helen left for Sadie was never conferred to the recipient. Instead, after a year, it was placed, at the request of the deceased, in a special trust until such a time should arise that Sadie Blackwell Camden or one of her descendants should present him or herself to collect. I am pleased to award this money to Clara Blackwell, only descendent of Sadie Blackwell Camden.

The letter went on to discuss more particulars, and I smiled. Even beyond the years, Oliver and Sadie had found a way to rescue someone else. Me. The money paid for the repairs to Blackwell's that the insurance didn't cover, and by mid-January the doors had once again opened to the people of Asheville.

But life did not go on as before.

I had tasted the sweetness of dreams coming true and realized my heart belonged with Max *and* my love for books, but how to reconcile the two? The only way it could be done was with someone who loved Blackwell's as much as I.

I made Robbie co-owner of the shop, allowing me to work in the

United States but also giving me freedom to travel to a very special part of England. Mother came with me once, a grand tour of the Lake District, Fenwick, Camden House, the gatehouse, and Max's garden. She met Maggie, who regaled us both with many more stories of Victoria and their family memories.

Actually, it was Mom who finally spurred me into knowing exactly what I wanted. . .besides Max. One day as we walked from the gatehouse to Camden House, enjoying the spring blooms of the Lake District, she said, "Imagine what a bookshop or a library would do for Fenwick!"

Mother passed away in her sleep in June. I knew she was gone before I even opened her bedroom door. As far back as I could remember, she'd greeted me in the morning with a cup of tea and a kiss on the cheek, and that morning in June when I descended the stairs to a very quiet house, so still I could feel her absence, I wasn't surprised to open her door and know the truth. She looked like she'd fallen asleep reading, with the vintage copy of *The Pilgrim's Progress* I had bought in London lying across her chest and the bookmark Dad had brought back from Ireland for her which read, *"Never love anyone who treats you like you're ordinary. Oscar Wilde"* held in her fist. Dad had always seen her and treated her as extraordinary, as if there was no one in the world as lovely to him as her.

One of Mom's dreams came true during our visit to England.

She watched as Max proposed to me in his garden. I wonder if that's what helped her leave, because she knew I'd found someone to love me like Dad had loved her. A month after her death, I moved to England so Max and I could turn the gatehouse into a special, magical place of its own. One side of the archway became Fenwick Public Library, filled, at first, with books donated from Camden House. On the other side we opened The Castle Bookshop, a place which brought as much magic from its history as it did from the stories bound inside.

I could now spend time in England with my English family and also with Robbie at Blackwell's.

I'd never considered how some of our greatest losses lead us to choices that God uses for bigger things than we could have ever imagined. Sometimes brokenness and heartache force us into self-seclusion and fear, and sometimes they can propel us into something amazing, if we let them.

Love is powerful. It has the strength to change hearts, restore broken lives, bring healing from grief, and provide courage to push us beyond our self-defined limits. Love makes us brave.

And hope inspires our imaginations.

Pepper Basham is an award-winning author who writes romance peppered with grace and humor. A native of the Blue Ridge Mountains, her family has lived there for generations. She's the mom of five kids, speech-pathologist to about fifty more, lover of chocolate, jazz, and Jesus, and proud AlleyCat over at the award-winning Writer's Alley blog. Her debut historical romance novel, *The Thorn Bearer*, was released in April 2015, and the second in February 2016. Her first contemporary romance debuted in April 2016. You can connect with Pepper on her website at www.pepperdbasham.com, Facebook at https://www.facebook.com/pages/Pepper-D-Basham, or Twitter at https://twitter.com/pepperbasham.

ACKNOWLEDGMENTS

I am so pleased to have my third novel with Barbour. They've been very encouraging through the process of each novel and continued to allow me to "spread my writing wings" as I delved into writing my first dual timeline novel. Thank you so much, Becky Germany, Shalyn Sattler, Faith Nordine, Abbey Warschauer, and, last but not least, editor Ellen Tarver.

The Christian writing/reading community is a wonderful family of authors and readers who give such support to one another. Among those are the ladies who specifically encouraged me in this story, either by reading an early copy or reading for endorsement. Thank you SO much to Rachel McDaniel and Allison Pittman (fellow authors in the Doors to the Past series), Beth Erin, Joy Tiffany, Carrie Schmidt, and Gretchen Acheson (as early readers), and Kristy Cambron, Jaime Jo Wright, Rachel Hauck, Ashley Clark, and J'nell Ciesielski (as endorsers).

As ever, I am incredibly grateful for my Street Team. Some of the readers on this team have been with me from my first book six years ago. Since this book is number 15, it means they've lived through a lot of stories with me, and I can't express how thankful I am to them for the encouragement, kindness, and constant readiness to share in the joys and struggles of this journey with me.

For two years, I've had the honor of being represented by the amazing Rachel McMillan of the William K. Jensen Literary Agency. Besides being an avid reader and beautiful author in her own right, she is also one of the most encouraging cheerleaders. Thanks so much for believing in me, Rachel.

My best cheerleaders are the ones in my own family. Dad, Mom, and little bro, thanks for always encouraging me. Dwight, Ben, Aaron, Lydia, Samuel, and Phoebe, I'm so grateful that I get to spend every day being a part of the bigger story of our lives. Thank you for loving me and making this life-journey such a wonderful one.

And to the history-keeping, life-changing, loving Father who creates stories that weave from one life to another through generations. Thank You, Lord Jesus.

Next in the
DOORS TO THE PAST Series...

Bridge of Gold
(Coming June 2021)

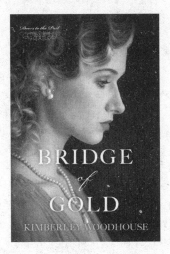

Underwater archaeologist Kayla Richardson is called to the Golden Gate Bridge where repairs to one of the towers uncovers two human remains from the late 1800s and the 1930s. The head of the bridge restoration is Mark Andrews, who dives with Kayla, and a friendship develops between them. But as the investigation heats up and gold is found that dates back to the gold rush, more complications come into play that threaten them both. Could clues leading to a Gold Rush era mystery that was first discovered during the building of the bridge still ignite an obsession worth killing for?

Paperback / 978-1-64352-957-8 / $12.99